D0909999

PRIDE OF THE MOOR

Books by Vian Smith

PRIDE OF THE MOOR

SONG OF THE UNSUNG

CANDLES TO THE DAWN

HUNGRY WATERS

HAND OF THE WIND

HOLIDAY FOR LAUGHTER

SO MANY WORLDS

STARS IN THE MORNING

PRIDE OF THE MOOR

Vian Smith

DOUBLEDAY & COMPANY, INC.
GARDEN CITY, NEW YORK
1962

Library of Congress Catalog Card Number 62–7683

Printed in the United States of America

To

MARK, MY SON

AUTHOR'S NOTE

This is a West Country novel and has West Country names. The names of Wonnacott, Maddicott, Buckpitt, and Jordan are good West Country names, belonging to their region as O'Casey belongs to Ireland and Macdonald to Scotland. Their use here has no purpose other than to establish their region with authenticity. All the people and events of this novel are wholly fictitious, and no reference to any person, living or dead, is intended.

PRIDE OF THE MOOR

Chapter One

The blackbird watched his game. It lifted its orange bill and listened with one eye; watching him jump a yellow burst of gorse, then come down the slope to the stream.

The stream was shallow and ran with light. It was the "water" and he poised to jump it; a fair-haired boy in a brown sweater, playing his race-horse game.

His jump left a footprint on one bank and made one on the other. He gathered his horse and galloped towards the evening sky, his game exalted because he was alone and could talk to himself, loving his horse aloud and refusing a million for it in the middle of the race.

He ran towards the hill where granite boulders were silent, full of shapes that would come out at night. He rode a brave finish, his horse responding to the drive-on of hands; but the climb was steep and only a gallant horse would have got there. There was a great flourish of hats and cheers, and the Queen was there to smile congratulations.

He plucked his forelock to the Queen and walked his horse through adoring crowds. His horse was blowing. Its nostrils were red and its ears were tired. Listen to its heart.

Congratulatory hands reached up, and he looked down at the big, round faces; as big and round as faces painted on balloons. He often won the Grand National in this way.

The granite boulders were high above him, cut by cracks as long and dark as alleys. At the end of the alleys were the dogs of darkness; for here superstition said that Satan kept the dogs of darkness kenneled.

He was not afraid, for now was daylight and he would be home by dark. He stood at the mouth of an alley, looking along it, being brave about it.

It ended in rock tall and narrow, like a door; and superstition said that behind this door the red-mouthed dogs were waiting, impatient of daylight and moaning for the dark. Then the rock would move and the black shapes would be out.

That's what superstition said, and although he answered "It isn't true," it might be true, and suddenly the kenneled dogs were watching; waiting for him to be deceived and be caught on the moor at night.

He ran down the hill, telling his fear that he was not running away but running home to supper. The hill was steep, and he ran on his heels, the pictures bouncing in his eyes. Then the steepness sloped out like a shoulder, and the joyful turf came back. This turf had a magic quality, and a merriment came into his running. Almost he played his game again; winning the Derby this time, for it would be nonsense to win the Grand National twice in one day.

Then he saw it.

He saw the movement of a tail. He saw the back of a horse; a brown horse, the color of old bracken, with a tatter of mane, black like witch's rags. His glance swept a half-circle, seeking other ponies and finding none. There were only boulders, fallen and nameless, like sleeping tramps; only trees with the holes of wind in them.

He moved down and down, watching the horse and waiting for it to lift its head. The horse lifted its head.

He made himself small like a conspirator, telling his excitement, "It's not a moorland pony, too big for a moorland pony. It's a horse, a beautiful horse, the most beautiful horse in the world."

The horse saw him and waited. It waited as he wriggled forward. It waited as he stood up, both hands held out in the age-old sign of peace.

Then the horse threw up its head, as though rejecting the age-old sign of peace; and when it ran, the boy ran, too, angry and cheated, running until his eyes wobbled with tears. He cuffed his eyes and watched the horse gallop. Oh glory, said his heart, a beautiful horse, what a beautiful horse. A quality horse, a thoroughbred even.

He waited for the horse to settle, to put down its head again. But the horse was all head and listen. The boy knew that pursuit was hopeless, and as he admitted this, he glanced to the hill where the dogs were kenneled and looked up to the sky and saw the homeward wings. On the opposite hill white chips of marble were moving up the slopes. He knew that they were sheep, going up the slopes for safety. Suddenly he felt day going out. Suddenly night was at his shoulder.

He ran. At first he ran from the creep of dark and the come-down of dogs from the hill; but as he saw the church and the first lights of his village, he ran towards his home and all that he had to tell.

Chapter Two

His mother said, "Where've you been? Out in the dark." She did not listen when he tried to tell her about the brown horse, not a moor pony, not likely, much bigger, as high as this, see, and galloping fast, fast as the wind, the fastest horse in the world most likely. She went to the hearth and the great black kettle. She tilted the kettle and splashed water into a basin. She put the basin on the table, with washcloth and soap beside it.

She said, "Where on earth have you been? No tea and now no time for supper."

He lifted his arms for the roll-up of his sweater. He was talking as his head went into the sweater, and he was talking as it came out. "Under Black Dog Tor," he said. "Never seen it before. The most wonderful horse in the world."

His gray flannel shirt came next, leaving him thin and white; like a peppermint stick when you have sucked off all the red.

His mother soaped the washcloth. "You and your games," she said.

He knew she was listening; listening not to him but for other sounds. He knew she was listening for the boots in the yard which would be his father.

"Hurry now. Your father's having trouble with a ewe."

She toweled his hands, then lifted him to the table, where he sat with legs dangling, like a ventriloquist's dummy. She peeled down a sock, leaving the red imprint of a garter. She said, "There's been so much rain. Rain always upsets the sheep."

He understood. He did not know what had happened or why or what it would cost in money or labor, but he understood that now the mood of the house was dark; tensed up with quarrels, each as long as a funeral and always about money.

He knew that in this mood his father would not want to hear about the most wonderful horse in the world; might even resent the story and forbid it, pointing a finger and saying, "That's enough, you got to stop these lies. Nobody can believe a word."

So he helped his mother hurry him to bed, feeling her alarm, her listening for the gate. He buttoned his striped pajamas and drank his milk and ate the potato cake which should have been his tea and had become his supper. It was warm and brown and he ate it quickly; although usually he played games with his supper, making it the last meal on a shipwreck island, making it important, making it last.

She lit the candle, taking the matches from the candlestick because once he had played flame games. He took the candlestick and went to the door. There he hesitated, thinking of the passage and the stairs and the landing; three dark countries which must be crossed. At the end of the journey there would be his room, with darkness behind the door and a cupboard big enough for a man.

He looked back at his mother, and she said, "Hurry up, you'll catch cold, don't spill the candle grease."

He lifted the latch and went out to the passage, showing his candle to the dark. On the first stair he said, "Mummy." His mother emptied the bowl of water. He heard the splash of it as she said, "I'll be up in a minute." Then he began to climb.

Bad nights were wind nights, when Satan laughed and blew the candle out. Good nights were when the quiet around the house had sleep in it, and the candle flame could be calm, like angel light.

Tonight the candle wagged once, as though from the far-off laugh of Satan. He stood, watching the flame and waiting for it to be his friend. Then he climbed past the long and sinister curtain; past the door of his parents' bedroom; past the empty room, as cold as a coffin, with only a text on a wall to show that it belonged. The sounds in this room were different from all others. When you walked in this room your footsteps were loud and the world shook; like God walking down the sky.

He reached his room, with the bed in a corner and the patchwork quilt all reds and yellows, like geography. He put the candlestick on the dressing table, and instantly the window had a yellow face looking in. He looked at the face and was frightened. Then he glanced to the cupboard where his Sunday suit hung on its hanger. He hated the suit because of the cupboard. A man could be in there. If the door was ajar, he was sure the man was listening. If the door was shut, he was sure the man was hiding. The man was tall, with long arms and a black handkerchief across his face.

He knelt on the bed, pressing his cold toes deep into the geography colors, ready for the prayers. His mother had taught him the Lord's Prayer and the twenty-third Psalm and he said them every night; with an informal prayer at the end, like a postscript.

He knew that every night God waited for these prayers. He imagined God listening and nodding, then sharing a smiling glance with Jesus Christ, whose Father he was. "The Lord Is My Shepherd" said the text on the wall; although the text in the spare room said, "Washed in the Blood of the Lamb," as though Jesus were a lamb, too, and how could He be lamb and shepherd? Once he had asked his father to explain this, and his father had said, "You, with your head all crammed, what you want is your seven times table."

His mother came in, her shadow all head and shoulders on the ceiling. She said, "Hands together," although he had them ready; his palms pressed, his fingers pointed upwards. He thought his thumbs were like an altar; that his fingers were climbing like a steeple.

"Our Father which art in heaven . . ." He knew that God had long, white hair, and that heaven was a kingdom of flowers and birds. It was always sunshine there, and the sunshine was gentle, like the smile of a priest on the head of the young.

"Hallowed be thy name . . ." He did not know what hallowed meant; but he liked the sound of the word in his head, the shape of it in his mouth. There were wonderful words in this prayer. "Power" and "glory" and "forgive." He tasted them like sweets.

His mother knelt beside the bed. She circled him with an arm, drawing him against her, into the deepest quiet of her day. He felt her tiredness without understanding it. He felt the warm tickle of her hair and opened his eyes, wanting to tell her about the horse.

But she said, "The Lord is my shepherd . . ." So he said, "I shall not want. He maketh me to lie down in green pastures . . ."

Like the brown horse of the moor. Perhaps now, with darkness all around, perhaps now the brown horse was stretched out. . . .

"He leadeth me beside the still waters . . ."

Or rolling; for horses love to roll. Rolling this way and that, its legs sketching silly patterns in the privacy of dark.

"He restoreth my soul, he leadeth me in the paths of righteousness . . ."

He did not know what "righteousness" meant, but he felt the importance of the word and dressed it for Sunday; black suit and hymn book and a sixpence buttoned up in mother's glove.

"Yea, though I walk through the valley of the shadow of death . . ."

This was his favorite. He said "Yea" loudly, aware that it was more important than yes. Then the shadow of death, reminding him of the valley beneath Black Dog Tor, with the hour of darkness struck and the dogs released. He thought Jesus was wise and kind to know about him and the dark valley.

He heard his father's boots. His mother heard them, too. He felt her stiffen, seem about to draw away. Then her arm tightened, protecting their quietness from the boot beats in the yard. He said, "And please God take care of Mummy and Daddy and help me to be an engineer for Mummy's sake and please God . . ."

His mother moved as though that were all he had to say. But he leaned into her and said in a hurry, "And please God let the brown horse be on the moor tomorrow."

A door slammed. They heard the boots in the kitchen. The passage door opened and the stubbled voice said, "You up there, Kate?"

She kissed him quickly and got up. She drew the blankets over him, tucking them beneath the mattress. She hesitated, then said gently, "Do you want the candle?"

He bit his lip, wishing he were old and brave, equal to the man in the cupboard. His head moved a little, asking her to know.

She left the candle and hurried down, and before the passage door was closed, he heard his father say, "What time did he come in?"

Then the door closed and he could not hear what they

said; only their voices, more important than voices were by day, more threatening than voices were when you could hear the words.

His father's voice was the louder. It was dark and lit by flashes of resentment, without a smile in it. Briefly he hated his father, telling the candle, "Poor Mummy." Then he wriggled down the bed, pulling the covers over him like an igloo, with a door through which he could watch the cupboard.

The warmth was private, cowling out the voices. He closed his eyes, then remembered the cupboard and opened one eye; keeping it open because you couldn't be sure. He said his prayer again: "Please God make sure it's there tomorrow."

He was afraid it might have been another of those things in his head.

Chapter Three

Howard Wonnacott lit his pipe. The pipe dragged down the right corner of his mouth, deepening the downward crease. He threw the match at the fire.

"Not as though I'm afraid of a day's work, Kate. Take Maddicott now and Jordan and Steer, always half-seas over on market days. Even Buckpitt, even he never misses a race meetin'. But not me. I'm not like that. I work all the hours God sends."

Kate had heard it before. She dealt the plates for supper.

"There's got to be a change of luck some time, Kate. It can't go on forever."

He was begging for her to help and reassure; to tell him what he needed most to hear, that he was a good farmer, as good as his brothers and almost as good as his father. He needed only luck.

She said, "How did it happen?"

His pipe whistled as he puffed. "Ewe was all right when I went down midday. Nice lamb, too, no sign of nothin'. Then five o'clock, there she was, over on her back in the gulley and her neck gone."

She brought out the cold meat, the cheese, and the bread. "Are you sure you didn't miss her midday?"

"Sure? Course I'm sure." He said it fiercely because he was not. "I counted them and the dog was there. I sent the dog down along to make sure."

"But you didn't go down."

He knew he should have gone; that perhaps the ewe had been in the gulley at midday; that perhaps he could have saved her. The guilt was behind his need to find excuses, to call in "bad luck" to save him.

She knew about the guilt and let him have his luck. Her tiredness said, what does it matter, too late now, last week it was a lamb, now it's a ewe, next week it will be something else. Always something.

"You think it's my fault." Howard threw another match at the fire. "You think I should've done something. But how could I? Me, with a hundred and one jobs to do, and no man to help." He struck a third match and held it to the tobacco. A moment he puffed. Then he said, "No boy neither."

Her glance was sharp, warning him not to bring their son into it. He wanted Mark to help on the small holding; to learn farming and nothing else, to become a farmer as he had become a farmer, because the Wonnacotts were always farmers. There were five of them on the moor and two in Canada and Willie in Australia. Especially Willie in Australia.

But she didn't want their son to be a farmer. She wanted him to get away from the village; forever shut up in its weather, forever governed by its weather. She saw him in Birmingham where wages were high and opportunities many. Mark would be something important. Mark would be somebody. An engineer perhaps.

Howard said, "Ten years old. Other men have their sons working for them at ten. Maddicott got three boys, all working so good's men. Me meself and me brothers, too. We was all working for our father before we was ten."

Kate cut the bread. Her silence derided those farmers who considered their sons to be investments; the more sons the more free labor.

"So why can't he do something? For not only now but for the years to come. What's so special about him?"

She put the bread beside his plate. Carefully she said nothing.

"Him and engineering," Howard said. "Birmingham and a car and two thousand a year. When are you going to realize? You need exams for that."

Almost she answered. Almost she said, "There's the eleven-plus examination, and after the eleven-plus there's grammar school and college. It will all be open to him."

"He won't even work at school. Ask Fairweather." His voice pursued her to the larder, where she stayed a long time; unnecessarily long. "Fairweather was only saying the other day. He can't add up and you can't read what he writes. He tries to write too fast and it's all scribble. None of it makes sense. In my day they'd have broke the cane over him."

She came out of the larder. "You'd like that."

It wasn't true and he flinched. He fumbled with his pipe, fingering more tobacco from his pouch. Quietly he said, "A boy can't be an engineer without exams, and you can't have exams without sums, without writing what people can read. So what's the use of pretending?"

She shook her head; telling her alarm that there was plenty of time, he was only ten.

"What's there so wrong about being a farmer?" Howard's voice followed her again. "All my family's been farmers. Generations. Five generations. Then there's Willie in Australia. Look at Willie in Australia. Went out there in 1931 and well off now. Thousands of sheep, and doubling his money with wool the price it is. Went out there with nothing except what Father learned him, and now look at him."

Willie's name was important in the Wonnacott family. He was the success. His money made him the success.

"It could have been me, Kate. I could have done it, given

the luck. But I was too young, being the youngest, and Willie was old enough, being the oldest. That's the way it was."

He glowered at the fire; thinking of Willie, who could afford college education for his sons, a swank wedding for his daughter.

"What more can a man do, Kate? Fifteen hours a day, seven days a week. What more must a man do to make a living?"

She thought, that's what I mean. Fifteen hours a day, seven days a week, and nothing to show for it. That's why I want something different for Mark. That's why he must work hard at school and pass examinations. That's why he must get away.

"Supper's ready," she said.

He put down his pipe and came to the table. He sat and she sat. He saw that she had bread and cheese only; that he had all the meat. He was not hungry then. He reached out a hand for hers and she gave it.

It was always like this. First the mistake, the luckless mistake; then the excuses, the self-pity, the talking to find a way out; then the flare of spirit, and at the end the weariness. Weary of thin shillings. Weary of pretending that tomorrow it would be different. Weary of being hurt and hurting.

His grasp tightened on her hand. He remembered fourteen years ago, before they were married. They had held hands like this and he had boasted; of his family and of Willie, most of all of himself. Twenty-five acres now, he had said, with free grazing for sheep on the moor, free bracken and free peat, too. But soon, Kate, soon there will be a big farm, one hundred acres, two hundred acres; soon like the Buckpitts, soon with two cars and tractors and ponies and subscriptions to the hunt.

It had seemed possible then, with his arm around this pretty girl from the town. It had seemed that marriage to her would transform him; that she would touch him with some magic and make him what he wished to be.

He remembered her head on his shoulder; the matching of their strides; their wonderful unity. He remembered their belief in themselves, their vision in the stars. He remembered how they had seemed bigger than life; like the hero and heroine of a book.

Kate had been pretty then. She was not pretty now. She was more than pretty now.

The years between had been hard and cold; and in a moment of deep tenderness, he loved her thinness and pallor and tiredness as he had never loved her town-dressed prettiness.

"Kate," he said.

She looked at his plate. "Aren't you hungry?"

"Don't let's quarrel, Kate. Everything's all right as long as there's you. . . ."

"And the boy."

His gentleness admitted that he might be wrong about the boy. She was grateful for this admission and pressed his hand, confirming their unity in a moment as still as a photograph. The clock, long as a coffin, the "long-sleeve" clock, his father had called it, the clock dropped its sound like the summer tock of rain. The dog felt the stillness and came from its place beneath the settle. It looked at the woman first, at the man longer; because its fear of him was stronger than its love of her. It nudged at them, and the woman's hand came down to its head, fingering the ragged ears. The dog gulped and stammered its feet, and there was goodness in the kitchen.

She said, "When he came in, he was full of a horse he'd seen on the moor. Couldn't talk about anything else. The fastest horse in the world. The most wonderful horse in the world. A thoroughbred."

They laughed; kind laughter, astonished by the imagination of this boy who played strange games and believed them, who invented impossible stories and believed them. The laughter was good to hear, and the dog danced with pleasure and made the man aware of it.

He growled a wordless sound which the dog understood. It went back to its place beneath the settle, lying with chin on forepaws and its eyebrows up. Lamplight was reflected in its eyes, and each was bright like the evening star.

"He's a good boy," she said. "He doesn't mean it to be lies."

Upstairs the good boy peeled back the covers and strained to hear. He heard the laughter in the kitchen. He felt the goodness in the house, and when he was sure of it, he called up his courage and leaned from his bed and blew the candle out.

The smell crept up from the wick. He knew that the smell must be gone before his father came; for his father would say that candles cost money and were dangerous and was his son a coward?

He ducked beneath the covers, peering at the bulging dark. Nothing became shapes and the shapes gibbered, crowding in on him. Then suddenly his father laughed, not a small laugh from the throat but a big laugh from the chest; the best sound in the world. It frightened the shapes. It sent them back. You see, he thought at them, my father's down there and he's big and strong, the biggest and strongest, my father's laughing, he's not afraid, and all I need do is call.

The shapes were listening to the sounds downstairs. They heard the man's voice; his step in the passage, his step on the stairs; and suddenly they were routed, flying nowhere like bats, one black brush of wings and they were gone.

He turned his face to the wall and pretended to be asleep; for it was late and he ought to be asleep. He felt the sounds approaching. A hand touched his shoulder. He knew by the indecision, the inability to say anything, that it was his father's hand.

The hand pressed him, remaining a moment as though hoping for response. "Night, Mark," the dark voice said, while a lighter step told him that his mother was on the landing. She came into the room and bent over him, retucking the covers beneath the mattress. She always fussed about the covers. She didn't realize that he had to drag them free to make his igloo.

A moment they stood there, looking down at him; and the goodness which had been in the house was now in this room, standing over him in gentleness. The gentleness called to him so that almost he threw off pretense and opened his eyes and said, "There's a brown horse on the moor, I seen him, the best horse in the world."

But the gentleness moved away and the old boards creaked. The latch of their bedroom door went up with a small explosive sound. The door whined as it opened; a melancholy sound like the whine of a dog left home on market day, and when the door closed, the sound was definite, like the full stop at the end of an essay at school. It marked the end of the day.

He was not afraid now. He opened his eyes to the darkness and said, almost aloud, "Tomorrow I'll go back and see that horse again. The brown horse with the long black tail. The wonderful horse. My horse."

He fell asleep saying "My horse" to his dreams.

Chapter Four

He told Mr. Fairweather, and the schoolteacher looked down from his exalted status and thought, your head all stuffed with dreams, boy, you'll never pass the exam.

He told Fred Warrener, who wheeled cement to the mason. Fred said, "All right, I heard you, now hop it."

He told Ezekiel, who had been the village wheelwright and was now the village barber. Ezekiel snapped his scissors derisively and said to his customer, "Howard Wonnacott's boy. Maze as a sheep."

Then Mark ran to the street and along the street to a wooden seat. It had "Jubilee of King George V and Queen Mary, erected by public subscription" on the back. Around the carved panel were amateur scratches; the initials of boys with Sunday-afternoon knives and nothing else to do.

Nathan sat there, his stick between his knees, his ginger hands clasped upon the handle. Those hands were huge. Tufts of ginger whiskers grew out of them.

Nathan had been the village horsebreaker, known in three counties for the strength in those hands and the persuasion. Old men said that in his day Nathan could mouth a three-year-old like velvet, so that you could hold it on cotton afterwards.

Nathan had had stable and yard near the White Hart inn; where eighty years ago the post horses had been stabled and the coach horn had told the street to come and see the swank.

His boxes had made three sides of the yard, and men who had been boys still told of how they had crouched at the gates, watching Nathan Shillabeer break wild horses to bridle and saddle and harness.

Now Nathan's yard was a garage, with "Taxi Service" and a telephone number above the door. Now Nathan was old and stiff, doomed to sit in the sun and watch the cars go by.

Mark said, "I seen a wonderful horse on the moor. That high."

Nathan said, "Well, now," looking at the boy and thinking, Howard Wonnacott's boy, how they do grow to be sure.

Mark told all about his horse, and Nathan watched the cars and half smiled to himself. Now there's a funny thing. Forty years ago there wasn't no boy interested in horses. They was all for gathering round the doctor's car, asking could they clean the head lamps or polish the beautiful paint. The doctor had the first car hereabouts, and a mortal terror it was. Went up hills backwards, and sometimes come down likewise.

I can see that doctor now, done up with goggles and gauntlets and a great leather coat, shoutin' for the hosses to be kept aside, bossin' as though he owned the road. Outside that car Dr. Wainwright was as nice a man as you could wish. But put him on that seat and take the wooden chock away, and suddenly there he was, a terror. Mad for speed and twenty miles an hour.

That was the beginning. Soon all the gentry had cars, and soon even the women were riding beside the men, their faces hidden by veils because of the dust, one hand clapped to their hats and ready to jump at the first sign of trouble.

Then traders got little vans with solid tires. Bill Wakeham, the baker, Bill was the first. He had delivered his bread by pony and four-wheeler, the pony a fast-stepping bay, with the harness shining like mother's brasses and the four-wheeler as new as paint. "William Wakeham and Sons" the letters had said; gold letters with fancy curls, like a circus. Then the pony had got old and slow, too slow for the moorland hills, and the village had waited for Bill to buy another.

Nathan had waited, too; waiting for Bill to say, "Take him in hand, Nathan." But Bill had kept silent, and once when they had met in the Sunday street, Nathan on his way to a Brethren meeting and Bill on his way to the parish church, both formal in Sunday clothes and their wives accompanying, this time the Wakehams had not paused for the exchange of courtesies. This time the women had spoken, inclining their heads and nodding their hats; but Bill Wakeham had looked at nothing, not meeting the old man's eyes.

Nathan had said, "Fancy that now," wondering what he had done for the Wakehams to be like that. The next day he had known. The next day the van had come and the secret was out. The youngest of the Wakeham sons had learned to drive. There would be no more ponies for them. Ponies were out of date.

Nathan remembered the old men, suddenly out of work because they could not learn machines; bewildered and angry, with humiliation in their idleness and mourning in their silences. He remembered the young men, jubilant behind driving wheels, boasting of their speeds and of how out of date the horsemen were.

Nathan put a hand on the boy's knee, talking not to the boy but to all that he remembered.

"Forget about hosses, boy. You want to learn about machines and make your fortune. Nobody wants you these days, nobody wants a man when all you know is hosses."

Mark told the children of his class, and they gathered round to listen, then looked at the tall, dark girl to see what reception they should give it. The girl was Laura Buckpitt, and the children recognized the authority implicit in her aloofness.

Laura smiled the shadow of a smile, and the children recognized her derision and howled in glee.

"True, true," Mark cried. "I seen it more than once."

But that was a lie; for when he went back to the moor, he could not find the horse. There were sheep on Black Dog Tor. There were wind-rough ponies and fat mares followed by their foals. But there was no horse; no brown horse with drums in its gallop and the wind in its tail.

He searched Fox Tor and Bridle Tor, stumbling across heather, plunging through bracken, running miles on a fading hope. So he kept the truth alive with lies; telling Nathan how tame the horse was, wild of spirit and fierce with pride, but tamed by him because they were friends and he had the gift. He said his horse liked sugar, but a slice of carrot best.

He told Mr. Fairweather he had ridden the horse. He told the children of his class that they had galloped like the wind. The bigger the lie, the louder he told it.

He told his father, and Howard said, "Now look, that's enough. You got to stop." His mother said, "It's his imagination," and his father said, "It's lies. He's told everybody and nobody believes a word."

"True," Mark said, clinging to the little that he remembered.

Howard covered one side of his face, the way he did when he was exasperated and tired and ready to let ill-temper out.

"Now look, once and for all, there's no horse on the moor. There are ponies, plenty of ponies, some bigger than others, but all ponies. They belong on the moor, each of them belonging to somebody with a brand to prove it. So there's nothing wonderful about it." He saw the boy's white, stricken face and held up a hand to prevent more lies. "That's enough. Take the dog around the sheep. That'll do more good than running the moor, looking for a horse that isn't there."

But the horse was there one evening when the moor stood

quietly like a church, the sun in its colors like stained glass. He came towards it slowly, and the horse knew he was coming and let him come until he was near; ten yards near and he with a hand out, crooning a lullaby sound, over and over so that the wonderful horse would know.

The horse lifted its head. He came nearer, a stride a minute; waiting with his weight on one leg, waiting so long that little pains prickled up the calf. The horse flinched its head higher, and suddenly he saw them. Holes in its throat. Two holes in its throat. Round like bullet holes.

The holes were ragged and the edges were moving. He saw that the edges were flies. He gave a little cry, and the horse tossed its head and turned with a murmur of hooves. The boy watched, bewildered by the holes and the gluttony of flies.

He ran to tell his father, "My horse has been shot, here and here," and his father looked up from the shearing, a sheep sitting stupidly in the crook of his arm, its expressionless face saying nothing, its legs expressing the fret.

The sheep struggled its thin, white legs, startled by the running. His father shouted, "Stand still, don't you know better than running?"

Mark stood on the brown threshold, looking into the linhay where his father crouched on a tarpaulin, the shears in his right hand, his weight and strength controlling the sheep. The wool came away, leaving the skin as white as moonlight. The sheep's face seemed bigger of a sudden; a long face, like a harridan, with white powdered on black, like an ugly woman who powders to cover dirt.

The sheep got up and ran out, its nostrils trembling in its bleat, its ears too big and flopping.

"Shot twice," the boy said. "Bullet holes as big as this."

His father kicked the wool into a brown heap, then moved to a corner of the linhay where other sheep were penned. He threw a leg over a hurdle and grabbed a fat back, his fingers digging deep into the wool, his weight leaning into the sheep, forcing it towards a corner where a hurdle could be moved.

"Move it," his father said, and Mark moved the hurdle; the gap wide enough for the sheep to bounce through, bucking from the fingers in its wool. Meanwhile the dog watched, ready to block the sheep if its bouncing proved stronger than the grasp.

"Shut it," his father said, and Mark lifted the hurdle so that two walls and two hurdles made a box. The sheep still heavy with wool gathered in the darkest corner. They panted. Their backsides were heavy with filth.

His father threw the sheep, pinning it with a leg across its shoulder, the boot under its chin, forcing its head flat. He began to snip, thinking about the stabbing pains in his back and how many sheep were left. He had been taught to shear by his father. He was an expert. He could shear four sheep an hour for eight hours.

"Twice," Mark said and waited. But his father gave no sign.

So he ran to his mother, and his mother said, "Oh, Mark, are you sure?" When he said quite sure, she said, "But nobody would shoot a horse."

He ran then to Fairweather, to Ezekiel, and to Nathan.

Nathan listened as he told of the two holes; one here, one there, one above the other and the flies in them. Then Nathan took a tin from his waistcoat pocket, and from the tin he took a peppermint. He sucked the peppermint and hesitated, then held out the tin to Mark.

"You believe it? You believe it, Mr. Shillabeer?"

Nathan smiled as he savored the peppermint. He allowed himself six peppermints a day. It was cheaper than smoking.

"Not bullet holes, son."

"But round," Mark said. "Round like bullet holes."

"Tube holes, son."

Mark looked his bewilderment, and Nathan's smile deepened. Fancy, his thoughts said, after all this time, that poor old mare after all this time.

The old horsebreaker put a hand on the boy's knee. "That horse you've found is Pride of the Moor. She was tubed twice, here in the throat because of her wind. She was gone in the wind when she was about seven, and tubing helped. Then she was tubed again so that Charnley could get another race out of her. Charnley of Captain Court, that was."

"Race?" Mark said. "You mean she's a race horse?"

"Pride of the Moor was a race hoss all right. Years ago, before the war. She won several point-to-points round about, and ran under National Hunt rules, too. All the West Country meetings and once at Cheltenham even. In those days she was owned by Major Lorrimer, of White Gables, but the Major went out to South Africa to join his son, so the mare was sold cheap to this chap Charnley who had come to Captain Court. Not long before the war that was. Can't you remember, son?"

Mark did the sum in his head. "I wasn't born then."

"No, no more you wasn't. Never did think much of this Charnley chap, all swank and blow. He run the mare two–three seasons, but then the war come and soon that was the end of racin' and soon it was the end of Charnley, too. He disappeared, nobody never knew where. Nobody never knew much except that he left his poor wife and family to fend for themselves. They couldn't stay at Captain Court, no money, you see, so they went back to wherever they'd come from, and turned the mare out on the moor. There was nothing else they could do. Nobody wanted a mare so old, not when you couldn't get fodder for love nor money, all the grass being plowed up for food. It was all part of the war hereabouts. 'Dig for Victory' they called it."

Mark said, "But a race horse."

"For a while the mare stayed around these parts, and now and again you'd hear of somebody seein' her round Fox Tor or Bridle Tor. But after a time she disappeared, runnin' no doubt with the ponies, and nobody never heard much nor cared much. Not till you come telling of the fastest hoss in the world." Nathan laughed his silent laugh, and took his red handkerchief to his eyes. "Poor old Pride of the Moor, the fastest hoss in the world."

"But a race horse," Mark said. It was more than he had dared pretend.

"Not all race hosses is good hosses, son, though the standard now is better than it used to be. There was some pretty poor cattle racin' round these parts one time. Never a hope of winnin' and their legs all jarred to pieces. Pride of the Moor for one. Hurdlin' when she was three, and jumpin' fences when she was five. Her legs was gone before she was seven, before she was rightly in her prime. Poor Pride of the Moor never had no chance."

Nathan remembered her legs; fired once, then fired again in the hope of burning them to a travesty of youth.

"A hoss is as old as its legs, never mind what the calendar says. By the time that mare was eight, her legs was old enough for a pension. Only Pride of the Moor was unlucky. She didn't never get no pension. If the Major had stayed, then it might've been different. But the Major went off to South Africa and Charnley got hold of her. Charnley didn't care. He wasn't the kind. By the time he'd had her a season, the poor soul hadn't a sound leg to stand on, with pretty white bandages to cover it up."

He remembered the last time he had seen Pride of the Moor run. He remembered how she had limped to the paddock, head down and nostrils blazing, pitying her legs as an old cow pities its feet. He remembered saying to someone, perhaps to no one, if that mare is ever brought out again, it will be a cryin' shame. But Charnley had brought her out again.

"And do you know what it was all for, boy? Not to win races. Even Charnley knew she was gone past that. But having her entered, having her name on the card, that gave him the badge he wanted, lettin' him in among the few, where he could hobnob with his betters and pretend to be one of them. Field glasses and shooting stick and officer's coat. Charnley had the lot."

Nathan looked at nothing; remembering how Charnley had mocked his mare as a dead beat, calling her "the crab," making a joke of it. The old man's anger came back, becoming a taste in his mouth. He wanted to spit. It would have been his comment on owners like Charnley.

"He brought her out for the Whitsun meeting of 1939. That was just before the war, although nobody knew there was going to be a war. But the Whitsun meeting there she was, bottom of the handicap and any price you wanted. Everyone knew it would be a miracle for her to get round, and there wasn't no miracle, son. The old mare kept them in sight for a mile, gallopin' as though the ground was red hot, so sore her legs was, wincin' like bad teeth in your head. Then after a mile her legs wouldn' have no more, and the jockey larruped her twice, showin' off in front of the stands. But the stands weren't havin' that. There were people in the stands, ordinary people who'd knowed that mare for years, and they wouldn' let no jockey larrup the life out of her."

Nathan remembered that sound from the stands; a wordless sound, beginning small, then rising in anger, the instinctive protest of people who were suddenly aware that one horse could be more important than the race. It had been a threatening, faceless sound. Nathan was proud of it.

"So the jockey gave it up, knowin' what was good for him, and the old mare turned round, lookin' for the paddock, knowin' the way, knowin' more about the game than the lad on her back ever would. They tell me Charnley was in a fair wax, talkin' about a run for his money and blaming the jockey, but Charnley never said much in this village, for this village knew more about his mare than he did and thought more of her likewise. So she was turned out in the field behind Captain Court, where the allotments grow now, and then came the war and 'Dig for Victory' and that was the end for the poor old mare. Out she goes to the moor."

Mark waited, his heart swollen with love for the stricken horse.

"No use to nobody now, of course." Nathan stood up, his knuckles reaching for the pain in his back. He winced. He tried to straighten. He prepared his legs for the short walk home.

In the street a brown door opened and a voice cried, "Father." Mark knew that it was Nathan's daughter, calling him home to dinner.

"All right," Nathan said, "I'm coming." Over his shoulder he said to Mark, "Must be twenty-five years old now, more most likely. But she always was a tough one. I was wondering if Pride of the Moor would ever turn up again."

Chapter Five

He told his mother. "Not bullet holes, tube holes. Nathan knows and Nathan said."

She went through the evening ceremony of warm water, soap, and washcloth.

"Turned out on the moor because it was wartime and no hay nor grass and no money neither."

"Either," Kate said.

"And no money either. So now she doesn't belong to anyone. Just wandering there all day, all night. Nobody wants her. No good to nobody, that's what Nathan said."

"Other knee." Kate soaped the washcloth and folded it, then held the warm cloth to the scratches on his knee. "How do you get so many scratches on your knees?"

"A race horse, turned out there, no good to nobody. So why can't I have her, Mummy? . . ."

Kate didn't think about it. Her rejection was instinctive. "Don't be so silly. I'm surprised at Nathan. Filling your head with rubbish."

"It's not." He looked past her as the door opened and Howard came in. "Pride of the Moor was a race horse, wasn't she, Dad?"

Howard Wonnacott dropped to a chair which had been his father's. Its back was tall and straight, as his father had been.

He leaned forward to pluck a boot lace. "What's this about Pride of the Moor?"

"That horse," Mark said, ducking as his mother fussed him with the towel. "My horse, my horse on the moor . . ."

Howard made a short sound, almost a laugh. "You mean all this fuss has been about Pride of the Moor? Good heavens, son, that mare was broke down years ago."

He put his boots beside the fire. His woollen socks steamed. He stretched his legs so that he could see them steaming. It deepened his sense of comfort to know that his boots were off for the day.

"She must be twenty-five years old," he said, reaching for his pipe. "More perhaps. Yes, must be more." He pointed the stem at his wife, bringing her into the scene which he remembered. "She was racing years ago, Kate, before we was married. Remember that time at Market Town races? You met me at the station when I came down on the branch line. Then we went to the races. Remember? You had a funny hat."

She smiled. What he called a funny hat had been smart then; the latest.

"Pride of the Moor was running that day. I remember who rode her. J. Hamey rode her, and the colors was black and gold with a red cap. Major Lorrimer's colors. Half the village was there, and the Major was supposed to have told someone who told someone that the mare had a chance. So everybody knew about it and had their money on. Some had ten shillin' on. Remember, Kate?"

Mark glanced from his father to his mother and back again. "Did she win?"

"Win?" Howard made a laughing sound down the stem of his pipe. "From here to the linhay behind the winner. She wasn't never a good horse, son. But it was a good day, Kate. Remember? We went to the pictures afterwards."

She remembered the film; Greta Garbo in *The Painted Veil*. It was the first talkie he had seen.

Mark glanced from mother to father; feeling that they shared a memory which shut him out. It gave him a silence in which to say: "So can I have her, Dad?"

His father started, and suddenly his mother lifted him from the table and began to hustle him to bed.

"Well, nobody wants her, Nathan said so, and if nobody wants her . . ."

Howard lit his pipe. "Bag of bones last time I seen her. Nobody would give her stable room."

Mark began to speak, but his father said: "Only one thing left for her, boy. The hunt kennels for hound meat. Best thing that could happen, too. Poor old soul. Can't be no picnic for her, winterin' on the moor with two holes like that in her."

He leaned back in his chair, and when he closed his eyes, the dark circles were as black as coal dust. He was haggard suddenly.

"Shush," Kate said, buttoning the pajama coat. "We can't afford it. A horse means hay in winter and grass in summer, and a horse so old, it's not worth anything."

But how do you explain to a boy that a store for turnips is more important than a stable for a horse? How do you explain that turnips are roots, and that roots are fed to cattle and sheep; that roots make beef and mutton and wool, while an old horse makes . . . Well, what does an old horse make?

His father spoke. With his head tilted back, and his eyes closed, Howard said, "An old horse eats as much as a young horse. The grass is poor now. There's never enough. We need all we can get with these young bullocks comin' on."

Mark tried to say something, but no words would come. He glanced to his mother and she shook her head. Then he went up the stairs while his father said, "Some day, son, you'll have a pony. Like the Buckpitts, they've got ponies.

Some day, son, you'll have the best pony money can buy. But not now, not yet. Not till there's a change of luck."

Kate stood in the doorway, looking up the stairs to the slow pajama legs, then back to the man beside the fire. She knew he was right; that an old horse would eat too much, that an old horse would be a luxury which they could not afford. But beneath this acknowledgment, there was resentment; resentment of him because he worked so hard and achieved so little, making them the poorest farmers in the neighborhood. Almost she thought, if only you were like Buckpitt. Buckpitt's well off. One horse more or less, what would that mean to Buckpitt? Then she brushed the thought away, knowing that his failure wasn't his fault. He was doomed to it.

She went up the stairs to the boy's room and sat in the window seat while he prayed. She looked out to the eight o'clock, feeling the heal of evening come around. It was the best hour of the day; as quiet as Hallowed Be Thy Name.

She heard her son say, "And thank you God for making the mare be there and please God keep the flies away." She knew what he would add, and after a pause to find the words, he said it: "And please God let me have the mare and look after her and let her be my own. Through Jesus Christ's sake, amen."

She got up from the window seat and hurried him into bed. He put an arm around her, and she could feel the pleading. She tried to remember that an old horse meant hay in winter and grass in summer and that there was never enough; but the argument which had seemed strong in the kitchen was not so strong in this moment of silence beside the bed.

She stayed a long minute beside his bed. Her head was averted, so that he could not see her face; but in the silence that resentment was swelling again. Why shouldn't my son have a horse of his own? Other boys have ponies of their own. The Maddicott boys and the Jordan boys; while Laura Buckpitt, she has ponies, Laura Buckpitt has three, the best ponies on the moor.

She straightened from his arm and tucked in the covers. "Good night," she said, firmly, briskly, knowing what she must do.

She went down the stairs to the kitchen and Howard felt her silence. It disturbed him on the edge of sleep.

Without opening his eyes, he said, "What's the matter?"

She did not answer.

He opened his eyes. "Look, I asked you. What's the matter?"

She emptied the bowl and folded the towel. She reached for her darning box and brought it to the kitchen table. It was always full. She said, "Why can't the boy have the horse? Other farmers have ponies for their sons."

He was shocked. "You know. You know about the hay and grass. You know what happens when there's snow."

"Nobody else wants it. It wouldn't cost much. Surely we can afford a little hay and grass. . . ."

She took a sock and pushed a hand within, making it a fist as it reached the hole. Her needle went in and out, making a pattern across her skin. She watched the needle, knowing that she mustn't look up; that she was not being fair; that Howard was right about the hay and grass.

"Two winters ago," Howard said. "You know what happened then. You saw me go on bended knees for hay, borrowing it from Maddicott and Buckpitt, begging for it with the snow that deep and freezing every wind. This winter it might be the same all over again."

She began to say, "The Maddicott boys . . ." But Howard said: "The Maddicotts don't bring their ponies in. Neither do the other farmers with ponies runnin' the moor. None of them bring their ponies in for the winter. They let'm take their chance. They know there's nothing to spare."

She knew it was true, but she knew also that somehow she must achieve the impossible. Mark deserved it, needed it. She felt again the pleading in his arm.

"Besides," Howard said, "the mare might be branded. All the stock carry brand or markings."

She looked up. "And if it isn't?"

He smeared the back of his hand across his mouth; tired of talking about it, tired of his resistance. His stubble made a scraping sound.

"Look, Kate, I don't want to deny the boy. If I could . . ."

He waited, hoping that she would understand and help him. But she did not speak. She made him say, "Look, Kate, tell you what. If the mare's still there after the next roundup . . ."

Happiness leaped in her, as suddenly as a flame.

"If the mare's still there after roundup. Can't be fairer than that."

It seemed that she had won, but in a little moment of fright she realized that she had won too easily; that perhaps she had not won at all.

"Don't tell the boy," Howard said. "Year after year the mare's been left there, the roundup missing her all the time. But you can never be sure, not certain sure. So don't tell the boy till we're sure."

She turned in her chair and looked at him, but he would not meet her eyes. He leaned from the chair and picked up a burning brand. There was a sudden sharp smell of wood flame. Then he returned it to the fire, placing it carefully as though the placing were important. His hand was too hard and tough to flinch from the heat.

She said, "You mean it?"

"That's right, Kate. I mean it. If the mare's still there after roundup."

It was reassurance, yet that leap of happiness would not come again. She knew that he had thought of something; perhaps remembered something. She knew that he was sure of one thing.

The mare would not be there after roundup.

The village rested in the evening light. The tower of the church was quiet, and the slow drift of rooks freckled the sky, as black and frail as paper ash. Waistcoats stooped in cottage gardens, ministering to the dark, reluctant earth, and old men leaned on gates to smoke their pipes. The breath of their pipes was in the twilight.

"Evenin'," the old men said.

"Evenin'," Howard answered. "Nice day."

"Proper," the old men agreed. Then they raised a glance to the sky. "Though it can't never last."

There was always this exchange about the weather; for the weather on the moor was like the weather at sea. You lived with it.

Howard came to the green, where two great yews threw early darkness, their branches twisted like arthritis. There were pens on the green. The pens were ready for the roundup, when the ponies would be "drifted" from the moor.

Some would become breeding stock and would be branded and returned to the moor. Most would come up for sale. Skewbalds and piebalds always fetched good prices; for children thought them pretty. Riding stables would bid for them. So would weekend farmers from the valleys, and country gentlemen with city incomes. A pretty skewbald with white mane and tail; a really pretty one might make as much as forty guineas.

There would be about two hundred for sale, of which perhaps fifty would become first ponies for children. The rest would be sold to dealers, and the village wasn't sure what would happen to them then. Perhaps the best were trucked to other markets. Probably most became cats' food in tins.

The mines no longer needed them, and at one time farmers had said, you know what that'll mean, prices down, prices down so low it won't be worth the drive hardly. But prices had been maintained by more country gentlemen with city money to spend; by more pony clubs; by more daughters saying, "I want a pony for my birthday." Ponies were still important to most moorland farmers.

But not to me, Howard thought. Nor my father nor grandfather. Ponies were never important to the Wonnacotts. The Wonnacotts have been sheep men always. I remember Father speaking out against the ponies. The moor's overstocked, that's what he always said. It was true then and it's true now. The moor's overstocked, and when there's so many ponies, the sheep have got to suffer.

He went into the public bar of the White Hart inn. Young men were playing darts. Others sat in a corner, smoking thin cigarettes and drinking dark pints and playing euchre. They nodded to him and one of them said, "Evening, Mr. Wonnacott," while another said, "Your deal, Charlie."

Howard moved to the counter, where Jacob said, "What's it going to be?" His silence added, first time you've been in for years. Thought you Brethren didn't hold with strong drink.

"Business," Howard said to Jacob's silence. To the spoken question, he answered, "Bitter."

Jacob reached for a pint glass. He always assumed you wanted a pint; convinced that the half-pint was effeminate, like crooking your little finger when you drank tea.

Howard groped with forefinger and thumb in his breeches pocket. He brought up half a crown. He realized it was all he had, and the chime of money at the card table made his coin seem a joke. He looked towards the table. Where do they get the money? Fred Rickaby's boy and young Jordan. They're laborers. And that boy Charlie with the hair oil; he's a garage mechanic. All better off than me, and me a farmer.

Howard laughed as he remembered a line from a song: "Yeomen of England," as though to be a yeoman was to be somebody, the backbone of a fundamental industry, according to the newspapers. The truth was that the yeomen, honored in song and in editorials, worked seven days a week with nothing to show for it, while youths in overalls gambled and drank and passed the cigarettes around.

"Should be a good drift," Jacob said, resting his forearms on the counter. "They say Buckpitt's got eight spotted ones to bring in."

And you, Jacob, Howard thought, turning towards him; you used to strike for Baskerville at the forge. You used to do a man's job in a man's way. Now look at you; potman at the White Hart, serving behind the bar in the early hours of the evening, filling out your time with odd jobs, touching your forelock to visitors when you carry in their bags and they tip you silver, yet earning more than you ever earned at the forge. What's happening to the world when a blacksmith's striker is better paid as a potman? When garage hands are better off than farmers? When a working man can be suddenly rich because he's got the results right on a football coupon?

"Eight spotted ones," Jacob said, thinking about it.

Howard thought about it, too. Eight spotted ponies selling, say, for twenty-five pounds each. That's two hundred pounds. Just like that. All profit. Not even a bale of hay when the snow is deep. The Royal Society for the Prevention of Cruelty to Animals takes care of that.

Howard put down his glass. He could taste anger with the beer. He was angry because if he had those ponies, if he had that two hundred pounds, then he would be able to afford what was impossible now. Then he could buy hay for the winter; enough hay for an old mare. Then he could say to his son, "Come and see," and there the old mare would be. There would be no need for deception then.

He said, "I wanted to see Buckpitt."

Jacob glanced at the clock. "Pretty sure to be in. But no tellin' what time."

The door lunged open and other farmers came in, their cheeks red, their voices loud. Maddicott and Steer and Jordan. They spoke to Howard and he moved from the counter; letting them crowd there, letting them argue, "It's your turn, Herbert, time you paid."

Herbert Steer said, "Let's toss. Odd man out, he pays."

They tossed coins, each covering it with thick, strong fingers and waiting, their mouths laughing, their eyes as narrow as slits. "Tails," said Maddicott, uncovering. "Tails," said Steer jubilantly. Jordan moved his hand slowly. "Heads," cried Maddicott and Steer. "Jordan pays. Three whiskies, Jacob."

Their game shut Howard out, as though he were among the laborers. He looked at his beer and wished he could have said, "Maddicott, Steer, Jordan, have this with me." Then he would have been among them. He would have bought his place.

Tomorrow, they were saying, got a hard drive tomorrow. Dr. Andrews is coming, he always likes a good day, and the butcher and baker and Colonel Llewellyn, we ought to make an early start. But they did not decide how early. They were waiting for Buckpitt to come and make the decision for them.

Buckpitt came in with Colonel Llewellyn. Howard moved to a corner, feeling Buckpitt's bold glance, aware that Buckpitt had seen the pool at the bottom of his glass and had guessed about the eight-pence in his pocket. He wished he had not come.

Buckpitt stood in the middle. The others were half turned towards him, acknowledging his leadership. The youths put away their darts. The game of euchre petered out. All were aware that Buckpitt commanded the room. All were relieved that Buckpitt was in good humor.

Howard thought, how can I interrupt? But I must. That's why I'm here. It's what I've been waiting for ever since that night I agreed about the mare.

Buckpitt shared a joke with the Colonel, and his laugh struck sparks from the room. The youths smiled nervously, although they had not heard the joke. Jacob said, "Very good, very good," although Howard doubted that he had heard it either.

They waited for Buckpitt to give them their instructions, their willing deference such that Howard rebelled against it.

I remember, his thoughts said. I remember Kirk Buckpitt years ago, when he was no better than anyone else. He took over Narrastun from his father and did well, moderately well, until the war. The war made Buckpitt. The war meant the black market, and Buckpitt sold in it. He was clever enough to beat the regulations, selling for cash, with trucks from the towns and cities to take it away at midnight. Then, when the war was over, Buckpitt made Narrastun. It had always been a good farm. He made it the best farm, and the village looked up to him. Looked up to him as clever; clever enough to beat the city men who made the regulations, clever enough to buy right and sell right, clever enough to drive a hard bargain, then clever enough to give generously to charities.

Howard thought the war was the flaw in Buckpitt. He tried to sneer at money made in this way; trying to remember town lines waiting for scraps of meat while Buckpitt sold their pork and beef and mutton to those who could pay fancy prices. He tried to remember how the newspapers had made "black market" a sinister phrase, but the war was years away. It did not matter now.

They were talking of the "drift." Howard knew that they would find almost all the ponies in four valleys, for the ponies seldom wandered far from the valleys where they were born. A few might be scattered on high ground. The rest would run the valleys, and the greater the number, the easier they would be to drive; all in a distress of tails and manes and upflung heads, with the drum of their hooves deep in the ground.

"We'll all of us make for Black Dog Tor," Buckpitt said. "Coming in from four directions and meeting on the other side of Black Dog."

The name of the tor was a cue. Howard thought, now's my opportunity, I must speak now. He heard himself say, "There's one thing."

The bar went silent, turning towards him.

"One thing surprises me," Howard said, smiling to show that he meant no offense. He tried to look at Buckpitt, but his eyes flicked to Maddicott, to Jordan, and to Steer. "Year after year, you drive the moor. Yet you've never brought in the old mare."

Maddicott frowned. "What mare?"

Then Jordan laughed. "He means that old race mare." And Steer said, "It's years since she's been this way."

Buckpitt's gaze was level, looking into Howard for the secret. "But she's this way now. She's been in Black Dog valley all summer."

Howard tried to smile, but his face muscles were stiff and cold. He heard himself say, "You ought to bring her in," while at the back of his mind another voice said, "It is not Mark's father who's doing this. It's a farmer who knows that it's the best thing to do, the businesslike thing to do."

The whisky flush was in Maddicott. He was ready to be truculent. "Why? What's it to you?"

"Well, the grass." Howard touched his lips with the tip of his tongue, feeling the need for caution. "The more that old mare has, the less there is for sheep."

Maddicott nodded, admitting that.

"Besides," Howard said, knowing that all were members of the hunt, "the hunt needs kennel meat."

He looked down and saw that his words were crawling in the silence, ugly and gray, like wood lice. The father heard the cry out of his son; but the farmer answered, it's the best thing to do, the wisest, the most businesslike.

Buckpitt considered him. "Isn't this the mare your boy's been telling about?"

Steer and Maddicott laughed, but Buckpitt flicked them a glance. The laughing stopped. They waited for Howard, and finally he said, "What use is a mare as old as that?"

Buckpitt hesitated, then nodded. "All right, we'll pick her up on the way in." He turned his back and it was over.

Howard emptied his glass, surprised by the palsy in his hand. His throat trembled so that he could scarcely swallow. Some of it dribbled from the corners of his mouth. God forgive me, the father said; and this time the farmer was ashamed and silent.

He moved to the door while his thoughts said, some day it will be different, some day it will be all right. You'll have a pony, son, a show pony, good enough to win rosettes, red rosettes and blue rosettes and trophies for the parlor. Some day, son, just as though I was Buckpitt.

He reached the door. "Good night," he said. Only Jacob answered.

Chapter Six

The class was restless. Boys knew that their fathers and uncles and brothers were on the moor, driving the ponies in. They watched the windows, where the world had blue in it. They wished that they were old enough.

Jonathan Fairweather threw down his chalk. You can't teach when boys are restless; especially you can't teach decimals. His hostility for decimals was complementary to his regard for fractions. He welcomed the mathematical problem which was an excuse for fractions. He spoke of them as a gardener speaks of roses or a woman of her cats. But decimals. He swept the chalked figures from the board, and his contempt was in the gesture.

Of course the boys were restless. The pony drift was part of their year; like May Day and Midsummer and the harvest festival. Of course the drift was more important than moving the decimal point.

He glanced around the class. You could feel the excitement. Only one boy sat small and tense, watching the board, his eyes round, his mouth opened a little. Only Mark Wonnacott turned his back upon the world with blue in it.

Fairweather said, "You realize that most of them are mongrels."

The girls tittered in surprise. The boys jerked their eyes from the windows, discovered in their longing.

"The original moorland breed, you don't find that on the

moor these days. It's preserved by some breeders in the valley and exhibited at shows. But almost all the ponies on the moor are mongrels. Does anyone know why?"

Willie Steer put up a hand. "Please, sir, because breeding ponies for shows costs money and nobody on the moor got the money." He hesitated and added, "My father said."

"Breeding pedigree stock always costs money, but it's not always those who can afford it best who take most pride in it. It's always easier to breed mongrels."

The boys' faces went cold. They suspected an implied criticism of their fathers. They remembered that Fairweather was a town man and that town people never understood.

"The reason for the mongrels on the moor begins in the last century, when ponies became a good investment. They were wanted for work in coal mines, taking the place of children. At one time children worked in the mines. Children like you."

He let them think about it. He saw the girls' distress. Then Benjamin Jordan said, "You mean in Wales, sir?"

"The mines in Wales and other places."

The breath of the class came out in a sigh. It was a sigh which said, Wales is far away, it couldn't happen here.

Fairweather's smile was tight; for everything is always all right as long as it couldn't happen here.

"They pushed the trucks," he said. "Twelve hours a day with the water running and the darkness all around. They were afraid of the dark. They were prisoners underground."

He watched their faces. He knew that Laura Buckpitt understood; that she could see the children underground, thin as ghosts, with eyes as deep and round as burn holes.

"They thought they were forgotten, that none knew about them or cared about them. But some men and women cared. Cranks, the mine owners called them. And these men and women told others until the rise-up of indignation was such that Parliament had to approve a bill forbidding any mine owner to send children underground."

The class moved, as at the turning of a page.

"Many of the parents were angry, for those children had earned money and a man with eight children often had all those children working underground and bringing home their pennies. But now the children didn't work underground and there wasn't enough money to buy them food and shelter, so how could they be better off? That's what the parents said, and a great grumble went up from them, as there are always grumbles at reform. But coal had still to be trucked out, so the mine owners wanted ponies. Strong ponies. Cheap ponies. Small ponies. They came to the moor to find them, and the commoners, your grandfathers, they were quick to see that the demand meant money. So they brought in ponies from other parts of the country. Different breeds, and soon the different breeds were running together, producing a mongrel type which was still strong and small and cheap. Cheap because they cost nothing to feed."

He told them how the ponies, sold on the green, had been driven off in herds; down that brown road to the nearest rail head.

"That was before the branch line," Fairweather said. "One of the reasons for building the branch line was this traffic in ponies, and some of the farmers were among the shareholders in the first railway company. But none of the ponies had ever been shod, so the hard roads split their feet and the dust got into them and by the time they reached the railway junction, by that time many were lame and some were so crippled that they would never be able to work."

He let them think about that, and Benjamin Jordan said, "It's different now."

"They were sold, like cattle are sold, to be slaughtered for meat. Poor people bought horse meat. There were horse-meat shops in big towns, although country people would never think of eating horse, no matter how poor they were."

Fairweather told them about the ponies in mines; stabled underground so that their eyes grew faint and would have been blinded by the cruelty of sun.

"Sometimes these ponies worked underground for twenty years, and everyone supposed that they were as indispensable as the children had seemed. But progress brought in other methods, and not long ago fewer and fewer ponies were needed for the mines. That brought its protests, too, for the boys who had driven the ponies said, what about us, we've still got to make a living? And the farmers who had bred the ponies said, what about us, we've ponies running the moor and if we lose the pit trade, we'll lose the money? They blamed the sentimentalists, the cranks. They blamed the reformers who said that working ponies underground was cruel."

He looked at their faces and thought, it's your fathers I'm talking about.

"They were afraid the price would go down to nothing, but a curious thing happened. More and more machines were on the roads. Traders had vans and boys had bicycles and farmers had cars, and everyone said that the pony was finished, except for hunting or riding round the sheep. But then more and more young people grew tired of machines. Their machines weren't wonderful any more. They wanted ponies. So their parents bought them ponies and they formed pony clubs and went on pony treks, so that now, despite jet aircraft and motorcycles touching one hundred and ten miles per hour, the pony fair is as important as it ever was. Quite a few of the ponies tomorrow will go to riding schools and good homes."

Fairweather wondered if all the homes were "good." He had observed that many children who rode ponies rode them for the wrong reasons; nagging them with heel and whip, bossing them as though the child's pony is the child's plaything.

Gymkhanas encourage it, Fairweather thought. Gymkhanas encourage the yanking about, the desperation to win silly games.

A boy put up his hand. "Please, sir, there are holidays for Whitsun. Why can't there be a holiday for the pony drift?"

Excitement rustled in the room like a warm, brown body in the bracken. That's right, the excitement said, then we could all join in.

Joe Maddicott put up a hand. "Please, sir, those mongrels, sir. There's a mongrel in Black Dog valley and my father said . . ."

The girls knew. Their bright eyes leaped to the boy in the corner, then switched to Laura Buckpitt to see what she would do. She half laughed, and Fairweather remembered that nonsense about the fastest horse in the world.

Joe Maddicott said, "My father said they're going to bring it in. About time, too, no use to no one. That's what my father said."

Fairweather thought, that's right, Maddicott, be cruel, like your father. Two years ago your father told the R.S.P.C.A. that he couldn't afford hay for his ponies. So they were fed by helicopter while your father laughed, because it's not every farmer who is smart enough to have his stock fed for nothing.

Joe Maddicott remained standing, looking towards the white boy in the corner. He made the mistake of enjoying his cruelty and showing it.

Sharply Fairweather said, "What's a quarter in decimal terms?"

Maddicott's grin vanished. He began to sit.

"Stand up when you're spoken to."

Maddicott stood up, his stupidity on its feet for all to see. Fairweather harassed him with questions, and none of the children realized that the teacher did this to cover the distress of the boy in the corner.

Mark looked out to the sky where God was. His lip trembled and he pulled it in. He fought the terrible tears while Fairweather nagged, "Seven point five multiplied by seven point zero five. Come now, Maddicott, where does the decimal point go?" He made Maddicott pay for that moment of glory; while at the back of his mind a thought said, but what does that make me? Doesn't that make me cruel, too?

A bell rang and morning school was over. There was a sound like the clap of wings as other children were released, but Fairweather delayed his class a minute, wondering what to do with Wonnacott in the corner. The boy was white. The boy was ill.

Fairweather said, "All right, put your books away. And file out quietly. Girls first."

It was an old-fashioned courtesy which the boys resented. They sat on the edge of their seats until the last girl had gone. Then they got up, wary of the teacher and retaining a prim civility until they reached the door. Then they ran.

They climbed the granite walls of the playground, looking out to the moor. Their voices were rough with excitement because perhaps they would see the ponies coming in before school shut them up again.

Fairweather beckoned Mark. "Not you," he said. The boy came to him. They regarded each other.

Fairweather said, "What's it all about?" But Mark could not explain. It was big now; too big now; too big for words.

"You're afraid they're bringing her in? That old mare you told me about?"

Mark nodded and the nodding moved a tear. It was hot. He was ashamed of it. He knew that tears were a betrayal of the big pain which all morning had been his secret. Only girls cried.

Fairweather said, "An old horse, too old to stand another winter, it will be the best thing. . . ."

But Mark did not hear. He tasted the tears. They would leave his eyes red and swollen for everyone to see.

The teacher let him go, considering him a weak boy in a community as tough as hawthorn. You can't protect the weak forever. At some time they must go out to the playground where boys turn from the wall and jump down and come around, making yahing noises, while girls point to his eyes and the noises of derision become as harsh as rooks.

Fairweather looked down from a window. He knew that the boy would run; running in torment like the hunted.

Mark ran.

He ran down the street; past groups of women who said, "Can't bide chinnerin', there's dinner in the oven"; past the forge, where blackness was in the rafters, folded thick like bats; past the wheelwright's store and bright paint daubs on the door. Chip that paint and the colors would be there; smooth like quartz. Once he had chipped with a stone, and Ezekiel, who was the barber now, looked up from his snip-snipping and said, "Here, what're you doin'? You leave my door."

He passed the post office and the garage. He passed the vicarage where the firs were scarecrow-ragged. He ran out of the village and up towards the moor.

He heard Nathan's daughter say, "That's Howard Wonnacott's boy." Then he heard her scream "Father" towards the jubilee seat. It was Nathan's call to dinner.

He thought, I can be there before anyone knows.

The hill hurt. He pressed hands on thighs, forcing his legs faster. He imagined that he could hear the shouts of riders. He ran faster until his heart was in his ears.

From the crest of the hill he looked along Black Dog valley. No sign. Not here. But she must be here. He ran again, a hand to his side because of a searing pain which he called the stitch. He talked at it, telling it to go away. He told his legs to go on and on, the pain will be gone in a minute.

He ran along the stream. It counted its stones like an old man counting gold. It counted them aloud, like an old man counting in a room; not loud enough for anyone to hear.

He looked up to the rim of the world. The brown wilderness looked back at him, pretending that it had nothing to hide. He listened. For a while he heard only his own sounds. Then he heard the sounds that made the silence. The water and the bracken. The bracken made prickling sounds, like wood ash in a draft.

Then he ran again, sure that he would find the mare beside the steppingstones. The grass was green there. It had a special lilt there, and legend made it a midsummer circle where little folk danced their magic. He had found the mare there often.

The mare was there. He jumped the steppingstones towards her, slipping once and startling her. She ran and he called. She turned in a half-circle, her head up in alarm. He realized that it was not alarm of him only. She felt the tremor of hooves in the ground. She felt the fright on the moor.

He held out his hands and she bobbed her head, trusting his age-old sign of peace. She made her neck long, her lips moving, making little popping noises like fish in the evening stream. She touched his hand, and he put up the other hand and took the lock that flopped between her ears.

He pressed the old hard cheek against his shoulder, explaining that this was no ordinary day. Today meant they're coming. Today meant escape; somewhere, anywhere. He didn't know where.

He looked up to Black Dog Tor.

Howard Wonnacott built a long shape in the field. It was humped up like a grave. Inside it were potatoes, protected by bracken and earth from winter frost. He called it a "cave."

The dog sat on his coat. The dog was guarding it. He knew they were coming when the dog got up; not moving from the coat but straddling it, pointing towards the road down which the ponies came.

Howard straightened as the muddle of heads approached. Their manes were as wild as battle flags. Fat mares trudged, their foals hugged in. They made an anonymous rabble of browns and bays, with the few spotted ones among them seeming as bright as clowns by contrast. Howard thought, the spotted are Buckpitt's, he'll have a good sale again. Then he turned his back and stooped to his work. He did not want to see the mare among them.

Guilt was dark in him and he attacked it with his shovel; heaping up the earth, then smacking it tight. He heard the shout of riders and hoped they would not call out. He did not want to hear them say, "We picked up the mare all right."

There was no alarm until Kate called, "Have you seen Mark?"

Mark told his cowardice, it isn't true. But darkness came around, and the darkness said, it is true. The dogs are moaning to get out.

He thought, I will think of God, for God is light and Satan is afraid of light. I will say, "Yea, though I walk through the valley of the shadow of death . . ." He said, "Yea, though I walk," but the thought would not go on. He watched the darkness move.

Fear fluttered in him like a pigeon in his hands. He thought, I will think of the chapel, and he saw the austere chapel where the Brethren met. The seats were brown and the hassocks had limp ears. He felt the militant conviction of big, broad-shouldered hymns. He felt the bearded strength of Baskerville, preaching while the wind howled.

He felt his mother near. She stood on one side; his Sunday

mother, black hat, black coat, thin gloves, singing so quietly that sometimes it seemed she was moving her lips only. On the other side he felt his father; his Sunday father, black coat, black boots, with a watch chain across his waistcoat and his stubble shaved.

They were members of the Brethren; a sect which renounced all emblems. No cross, no surplices, no organ, no minister. The word of God was enough. The word of God was Holy Scripture, and Holy Scripture said, "In this place is one greater than the temple." So the table with the red cloth was enough.

The mare's foot slipped from a stone and the sound snatched his heart. It was a sinister sound, like the slipback of bars. There were bars to keep the dogs in. Dogs with yellow eyes and red mouths. The pant of their breaths scorched white skin. That's what the legend said.

Elsie dashed water from the kettle to the brown teapot. She held a hand under the spout, feeling it warm like the breast of the brown hen. She said, "Well, I don't like it."

Nathan wasn't listening. Blimmin' woman, always on. Yesterday it was the cat next door.

"Think I'll go up Yarnator and tell the Wonnacotts. Not that I want to interfere. But that boy was runnin' very queer."

Nathan thought, poor Howard Wonnacott, he got it comin'. "Pour the tea first," he said.

His daughter poured the tea. Then she reproached, "Tea's never good for you, goin' to bed. You ought to have cocoa and sleep better."

"He's on the moor," Kate said. "He's hiding on the moor."

Howard went to the window, looking out at nothing. "He wouldn't go there. You know what he is, afraid of the dark."

"But he's out there. . . ."

The dog heard the footsteps. They turned to the door. Kate

ran to the door, ready to say, "Where on earth have you been, frightening us like that?" But the footsteps were not Mark.

"Hope you won't think I'm interferin'," Elsie said.

Kate drew back as Elsie came in. She said, "It's Nathan's daughter."

"It isn't that I want to interfere, but I just think you ought to know."

"Where?" Kate said. "Where is he?"

"I seen him dinnertime," Elsie said. "I went out to call Father in, you know what he is for the jubilee seat, and there was your boy, runnin' along the pavement, white's a ghost, runnin' up the hill to the moor."

Kate threw a glance at Howard.

"Didn't think much of it at the time, but during the afternoon I thought, that's funny, that boy's michin' from school."

"He's not here," Kate said. "He's not come home."

Elsie put a hand to her mouth. Her eyes were alight with excitement.

"Baskerville," Kate said. "Baskerville will help."

Howard moved forward slowly. He thought, but what can Baskerville do? You can't search the moor. He might be anywhere in the dark.

"He's gone to Black Dog valley. That's where he found the mare." Kate was suddenly sure that he had not run away; that he had gone to protect the mare. "He's been going there every day."

Elsie said, "I'll do anything."

A moment Kate shook her head. Then she caught Elsie's arm, turning her towards the door. "Knock on doors and tell the Brethren. Say Howard will meet them outside the chapel in . . ." She glanced at the clock. "In half an hour."

Elsie stepped to the porch. "Father would go if it wasn't for his legs."

"Yes, yes," Kate said and closed the door. She leaned her

back against it, watching her husband. She said, "Did the drive bring the mare in?"

Howard lifted the lantern, squinting at the wicks, shaking it for paraffin. "I don't know, how should I know? I saw them go by but I didn't look to see if the mare was there."

Kate thought, somebody told Mark. Somebody said, they're going to bring the mare in, this time for sure they're going to bring the mare in. "So he ran to be there first. To catch the mare and hide with her. He's hiding somewhere with the mare."

Howard struck a match. The stick broke. He struck another and lit the lantern. He was trembling.

"You did it. That's why you agreed. And now he's out there. . . ."

Howard dragged on his cap and reached for the latch. He thought, the dog; the dog knows the boy, the dog will find him. He growled to the dog and it came forward, feeling the urgency. He looked back at Kate, seeing her fright and sharing it. He thought, it's me. I've done this to him, and Kate knows it's me.

He said, "I'll find him."

Their lanterns hovered like goblin light. They moved along the side of the stream; moving like children, keeping close like children, for the moor made children of them.

"Could be anywhere," a voice said, watching the night wind move the bracken.

They gathered near the steppingstones. Baskerville held up his lantern, and they saw the imprint of unshod hooves. He had no need to say, it doesn't mean nothing, could be old prints, could be yesterday's.

"Once more," Baskerville said. "Spread out both sides of the stream. Some this side, the rest over there. If we don't find him this time . . ."

They knew they wouldn't. They reached the end of the valley and grouped again, muttering about not enough paraffin, they had to be up early tomorrow.

"Only one place left," Baskerville said. He looked up to the black outline of the tor.

Howard thought, he won't be there, he can't be there. He's afraid to go to bed without a candle.

"He might be," Baskerville said. His tone said that they could not go back without being sure.

They looked up to the tor again. They felt superstition come around. All their lives they had heard of the black dogs on the tor.

Nobody spoke. Nobody said, I'll go. They were waiting for Baskerville to lead them, but Baskerville said nothing, looked at nothing. They realized that his silence was filled with meaning and turned to Howard to see if he understood.

Howard gripped his lantern, his fingers digging the palm. He thought, it'll be all right, I'll have the dog. I'll send the dog up round. He heard himself say, "I'll go."

They looked at him. Their eyes darted to the tor and back to him. He said, "You try the valley again. I'll go up to the tor."

Baskerville nodded. "Once more then, friends."

Howard watched their lanterns go down the valley. They were taking the world away. Then he growled to the dog and turned towards the tor.

There were two men; the man at work in the field or at ease beside his fire, and the man alone on the moor. The man at ease beside his fire did not believe the legends which his grandfather had told; but the man on the moor was not so sure. He clung to his daylight and called it truth, but the moor belonged to the powers of darkness.

He felt this power all around. The darkness bulged with

shapes. He stopped. He was afraid. His mouth was dry with fear. He thought, I'll send the dog around.

He growled to the dog and the dog came near. He made a sweeping motion with his arm; a gesture which every sheep dog understood. The dog stepped forward as though to obey. Then it stopped. It looked back at him. It made its back low, looking up to the black outline of the tor. He knew that it had seen something, sensed something. He knew what the dog knew; that something was there.

He threw a glance for the lanterns, searching the darkness for the comfort which pinpoints of light would be. The lanterns were gone; lost in a fold of the valley. He thought, they've gone, they've left me. He thought, I can't go on. But he knew that he must go on.

He climbed again, sure that the dog would follow. The dog did not follow. He turned for it, he held the lantern up, but the dog was gone. A shout of rage swelled in his throat, but he could not make a sound. He tasted salt on his top lip and knew that it was sweat.

Peter was a fisherman, only a fisherman, yet he walked on the sea because he had faith. I am a farmer and I will have faith. I will go up to Black Dog Tor, up and up, although I know about the black dogs, everyone knows about the black dogs. Nathan's father saw the black dogs.

He climbed up and up, seeing the black granite grow above him.

Kate saw the lanterns coming down the hill. She ran towards them, looking for Howard, looking for her son.

"We took the valley," a voice said. "Howard went up to the tor."

Then other voices mumbled, couldn't search no longer, not enough paraffin, not enough time, got to be up early in the morning. But reasons which had been good enough on the moor became excuses now. They shuffled their embarrassment, feeling the woman's scorn.

You mean you left him. You were afraid of Black Dog Tor, so you left him to search alone. She moved to pass them, but Baskerville put out an arm. He shook his head and the movement said, there's nothing you can do. Then other voices said if the boy's on the tor, Howard will find him. Bound to. Sure to. They said this several times because they were not sure.

Kate wanted to say, but he's afraid, like the rest of you, more than the rest of you. All of you are afraid on the moor at night. She wanted to say, Howard won't do it, won't go through with it, he'll need someone to help.

Baskerville's hand was big and gentle on her arm; persuading her towards Yarnator and the forgotten fire, reminding her that they would need food and drink when they came in.

"He's a good man," Baskerville said. Then in a voice so low that the others did not hear, he added, "There comes a time for every man. When he got to face the test."

Mark heard the sounds coming nearer; panting sounds and now and again a blink of light. He crouched beside the mare, afraid of every sound, afraid of his own sounds. One hand was tight in the tattered old mane. The other was cupped to the soft muzzle. He thought he was whispering, it's all right, they won't get you, I'll look after you. But he had no voice for the words. His eyes burned the darkness, hearing the climbing sounds.

They were near now. A stone slipped down with a great sound; like a blasphemous sound in church. The mare lifted her head, straining his arm. She blew in fright and the darkness listened to that sound.

Then a black shape rose up, blacker than the sky, shutting out the sky. The black shape spoke and the mare bobbed her head, tearing her mane from the boy's fingers. She turned in the alley between the rocks, slithering recklessly, trying to get away. But the black shape changed shape. It held out its arms, keeping the mare in, and the lantern in one hand wagged and blinked, worse than no light.

"Mark," the voice said, and the boy scarcely recognized it. He tried to answer but no sound would come. He moved towards the lantern, pressing against the granite to avoid the mare. He put a hand on her wither and felt her tremble and thought, it's all right, it's not them, it's my father. He reached up for the tatter of mane, trying to say, Joe Maddicott told me, they were going to bring the mare in; trying to explain because he thought his father would be angry.

His father's arm was hard, his cheek scraped with stubble. His father's breath made a rasping sound, as though he had been running a long way and was very tired. His father did not say, you ran away from school, you'll be in trouble. His father did not say, you frightened your mother, no tea, no supper, you'll catch your death of cold.

His father held the mare with one hand and put the lantern down. He lifted the boy in one strong arm and sat him on the mare. Then down the hill they went; the man leading the mare by the forelock, and the boy with both hands in her mane.

The moor did not belong to the powers of darkness now. Howard was not afraid of it now.

He wanted to laugh, to sing; to boast aloud that the boy had won. He had beaten the Maddicotts and Steers and Buckpitts. A ten-year-old boy had shown what could be done if you wanted it enough.

His stride lengthened, longer than the mare's poor potter. He was hurrying towards the light of Yarnator; hurrying towards Kate, so that she could see their son riding the most wonderful horse in the world.

She was waiting for them at the gate, holding up her lantern and peering, then calling the boy's name and running. She fell into step beside them, she on one side of the mare, Howard on the other; while their son swayed with the rhythm of the ride, almost asleep but smiling, as the young smile in their dreams.

At the gate of Yarnator the dog came back. It moved like a shadow. It hung its head. It knew what it had done.

Chapter Seven

The auctioneer's voice cawed above the noises of the morning. As black as a crow it cawed its selling language, while ponies blew white-eyed and the village gathered round; the men with sticks, the women with arms folded, gossiping in groups.

At one time the fair had been notorious for violence. Respectable mothers had banished their daughters to upper rooms and had shuttered lower windows against stones and the drunken lurch. Only defiant daughters had looked down from the windows, attracting the red cries of men and the hold-up of tankards.

There had been booths around the green; selling nougat and gingerbread and ale. Boys had gone from booth to booth with hot pennies in their fists. Youths had bought ale by the quart, swaggering to show that they were as good as their fathers. Meanwhile their fathers had said that ale was not what it had been; a tame cat compared with the tiger of their young days.

There had always been the hope that a pony would escape the ring of sticks and would charge among the booths in a wonderful blunder of hooves. Every year some had made their gestures of outlawry. All had been overwhelmed by strong arms and dragged back to the ring; but the overwhelming had been fun, the best fun of the year. One pony had got as far as the churchyard despite the hanging-on of six great arms.

In recent years the fair had changed. Sucking foals were no longer taken from mares. Ponies were no longer fisted between the ears; a downward blow which could bring them to their knees, stunned silly and for a moment tamed. Neither were they overloaded in a truck, because you paid as much for six as you did for twenty.

The village had become aware of public opinion, as it was expressed in newspapers; long, hot letters, signed by "Animal Lover" and "Fair Play." The village was also aware of the R.S.P.C.A. uniform; standing quietly in the background with the threat of prosecution implicit in its presence. The village was not afraid of a fine, but individuals were afraid of standing alone in court and especially afraid of seeing the case reported in the county newspaper. They knew that relatives in other towns and villages would see the names and say, "Jack's been caught then." The offense was the folly of being caught. The shame was in yielding victory to the uniform.

The village did not speak to this uniform, resenting the intrusion, the implication of supervision. "Meddling" was the word; denying you the freedom of doing as you liked with your own property. Not like it used to be. Long memories recalled the time Danny Morgan, as strong as three policemen, was dragged down the street by a stallion; his fingers in its mane but the stallion bucking and kicking, dragging Danny as far as the White Hart before he got hold of it and threw it, sitting on its head and lighting his pipe while the crowd gathered round admiringly. The White Hart had sent out a free quart to show appreciation.

Then there was Rendle, the gypsy. He was bitten by a stallion, and his brothers penned that stallion with pitchforks while Rendle took a whip; lacing that stallion to a frenzy and beyond, whipping until the stallion went to its knees, its spirit gone forever in a sobbing sound. Men still talked of that. They had not known that a horse can cry.

Ponies were sold and loaded into trucks; pulled and shoved up the tailboard, their toes stumbling, their eyes swollen white like billiard balls. The men struggled, aware of the R.S.P.C.A.; sweating out their patience, saying in their thoughts, do you think we like having to shove and push, do you think we like them to be so stupid?

Tailboards slammed up quickly. Bolts struggled across. Drivers hurried to their cabs, climbing in with a sense of escape. A mile down the road they could stop for a smoke; where the R.S.P.C.A. could not see. But not here; not when any moment might bring a command to reload because you had one too many. The drivers clashed their gears and the trucks lurched from the green.

The village did not ask where the ponies were going or how soon they would get there. The village did not ask about water or what would happen if one pony went down and could not get up. The village knew better than to ask questions.

The talk was of prices. Glances switched to Buckpitt as bidding for a spotted mare touched forty guineas. Buckpitt talked with Colonel Llewellyn, pretending not to notice; but the village knew that he was listening. The auctioneer's hammer came down at forty-two, and when Buckpitt laughed with Colonel Llewellyn those with nothing to sell knew that he was satisfied. They were pleased, almost relieved; as though they could see the money going into his pocket, a wad of wealth which gave them a vicarious sense of sharing, like reading about the fantastic wealth of film stars.

Women nodded and lifted their folded arms, hugging the good news. There would be drinks all round in the White Hart soon. A good sale always meant free drinks. "You can rely on Mr. Buckpitt for that," Elsie said. "His father was the same."

They were talking about the free drinks of the past when a pony broke from the grasp which held it. Someone aimed a blow and the pony threw up its head and lunged. Arms grasped its neck. The pony put down its head, down between its forelegs. Its quarters came up in a lash of legs. A man reeled, staggering back with a clamor of boots. He fell and the crowd let out a sound. There was anger in it and excitement. The man put up an arm to protect his face. He made little sobbing sounds.

Young men jumped into the ring. They grappled with the pony. They put arm locks on its head. They pulled its tail up to its withers. They threw their weight until it went down. They were panting and laughing, showing off their strength.

The pony went down with a thud, and its breath came shrill; torn in a shriek from blown-out nostrils. The women cheered. One woman said, "That's my boy done it." Their faces were alight, compelling the young men to show their strength against what was now the enemy.

It was a good pony. It did not know when it was beaten. It fought the men away and lurched to its feet. Men swiped at its legs, knocking its legs away.

Colonel Llewellyn glanced at Buckpitt, but neither moved. They knew that this incident had become a sort of contest; a sort of sport. They knew better than to interfere.

They heard the crack, a sharp little white sound. The pony tried to find its feet and as it swayed up, they all saw it. A foreleg was as grotesque as a black stocking with coal in it. A moan came from the crowd, and the men drew back.

Buckpitt's voice was sudden with authority. "Keep him down."

The men pushed at the pony's neck, pushing it down and on to a side.

"Sit on his head," Buckpitt said, and one of them sat on its head. They could see the eyes staring. It seemed that the pony was as surprised as they were.

Buckpitt nodded to a workman, and the workman ran to a car, bringing a shotgun from the back seat. Buckpitt loaded it. He came to the pony in a silence like a church.

The R.S.P.C.A. inspector crouched to the broken leg. He straightened as Buckpitt came up, then stood back. All the men stood back. Their heads were bowed, like mourners at a grave.

Buckpitt fired and the pony lurched, its three legs scratching as though it were not dead. Buckpitt fired the other barrel. The sounds rolled along the village. None spoke. There was only the smell of shot, and a half-smile in the teeth of the dead pony.

Buckpitt passed the gun to his workman. "Take it away," he said. Out of sight; hide it; don't let it spoil the morning. He glanced at the auctioneer, and the black voice cawed again; taking up the morning where it had been interrupted. But now the crowd was silent. Their faces were dead. They were shocked by the accident; by the memory of that black stocking with coal in it.

The auctioneer sold the last pony. The last truck slammed its tailboard. The crowd moved away, still silent with shock. Then a voice cried, "Mr. Buckpitt says drinks all round in the White Hart," and the crowd shook off the shock and turned towards the White Hart. Their voices came back again.

A woman said, "It was an accident," and others said, yes, of course it was an accident. Nobody could help it. Nobody wanted that to happen. Let's forget it, let's pretend it didn't happen. Let's hope Jacob has got in plenty of beer.

They crowded the bars of the White Hart, and soon men and women were laughing again; celebrating the good prices.

Only the children were left in the street. They climbed to the windows of the White Hart, peering in at their mothers and fathers, wishing they could share the red laughter. Then they wandered along the street towards Yarnator; the little girls following the boys and the boys following Joe Maddicott, who had heard about Mark and the mare which nobody wanted.

They came to the wall of Yarnator and climbed to it, watching the field where the boy was.

Mark felt them watching and came forward, holding the mare by the forelock. She followed slowly, her feet big, her coat rougher than it had seemed on the moor. She hung her head, as though to hide the holes in her throat.

Mark patted her, finger-combing the tatter of mane. He said, "She's going to have a foal." None answered, so he said, "My father told me. About February. The year will be up by then."

They kept their taut silence. They could hear the old mare wheezing. Then Joe Maddicott said, "Can't run, can't gallop, can't hardly stand up even." Then they all said, "What's the use of a mare that can't hardly stand up even?"

"She's a race horse," Mark said.

They laughed.

"The foal will be a race horse."

The boys laughed again. Then Joe Maddicott ran and they all ran. Their laughter came back on the wind, and in the new stillness the old mare wheezed as she leaned against the boy.

Chapter Eight

The match spluttered and from the candle wick a flower of flame grew up. Howard Wonnacott looked at the silver watch beside the bed, and got out coughing his early morning cough. His fingers bumbled the buttons as he dressed; shirt and breeches and socks, with his waistcoat left unfastened.

He dug nails into his hair and yawned, looking back to the bed and the imprint which his head had left. Kate turned towards the imprint. Her face was swollen with sleep. She made a sound but did not open her eyes. She knew what the sounds he made meant, and that she had another quarter of an hour.

He carried the candle down to the kitchen, where the grave of yesterday's fire was white and the face of the clock was moon yellow. He lit a lantern and carried it to the porch, where his boots stood like forgotten feet. Their leather was frozen into creases which only his feet could understand. He dragged at the laces and half tied them. Then he reached for the top bolt and stooped to the lower. They exploded from their night holes, and the door whined like coarse green grass when you blow through it. He took the lantern into a darkness which chilled the heart, so hostile was it, without moon or stars.

The dog was there. It came forward with a tremor of tail, and Howard growled a sound which meant get-out-the-way. The dog got, following but going nowhere; aware that there was nothing for it to do.

His boots broke the thin glass of ice as he crossed the yard to the barn. He heard a wheezing and knew it was the mare, dozing near the gate. The mare was heavy with foal, and Howard thought, "More trouble, there's sure to be trouble."

His lantern disturbed the shadows of the barn, driving them to the rafters where they waited. The cows turned to look at him.

He brought his stool to the first cow and nudged the flank. The nudge said, come on, shift over, and the cow shifted over. He drew in the stool and rested his forehead against her. He yawned again, a great yawn that left tears of strain in his eyes. He waited for the tears to go away. Then he stroked down the rain.

The first sounds in the bucket were like the tune-up of violins in an orchestra pit. Then the flow began, hitting the side of the bucket in a rhythm that lulled. He yawned again, more than half asleep.

The barn cat crept in, the lamplight in her eyes. She stayed near the door, ready to run if he saw her. She smelled the warm smell of new milk and showed the tip of her red tongue.

Howard got up to tip the bucket over a churn. The milk swept in with a rich smooth sound. He spilled enough to form a puddle and the cat watched the puddle; waiting for him to move away. Then she came to it and crouched, her tongue making little ticking sounds, her eyes on the man and his boots.

Howard moved to the second cow and scuffed in the stool. He leaned against the warm side, awaking slowly from his early morning stupor. He thought, there's going to be snow, it's the month for snow, Kate said yesterday there's going to be snow. He was afraid of snow. He knew what it could do.

He tilted the bucket over the churn, spilling another puddle. The cat came forward to it, lapping and watching. She lapped the pool dry, then turned towards the door. She passed out of the barn to the iron light of morning. There she paused, tense with watchfulness. She watched the dog, and the dog knew she was watching and looked the other way. The cat knew it was a coward.

She flicked her tail once, a contemptuous movement, threatening its cowardice; then she moved across the yard and around a litter of logs and upward to the loft. The steps were broken and full of weeds. At the top was a door, crusted on its irons. No one used this door. Two of its boards were broken, and the hole was her way in.

She passed into the new darkness, hurrying towards her secret, hurrying because now she was alone and could show her fear. She was afraid for her young.

She stood a long moment, looking back and listening; listening to the darkness. Then she came to them and licked them. She lay down and stretched and soon the darkness had a new sound; the pant of her body, giving of its goodness.

Howard followed the cows out of the barn. They moved slowly, smelling the cold and puffing smoke at it. Their feet felt for the soft places in the yard. They ignored the dog. They knew the way.

He moved around them to the gate. The gate slumped, rutting back the mud. He lifted as he pulled, opening it outward, against the nose of the first cow. They hesitated, waiting for the mare to move away.

Howard stepped into the field, and the mare moved away, bobbing her head. Then he called the cows, and they came through with a slip-slop of hooves in mud. He replaced the gate, thinking about the hasp. The hasp wouldn't fit. It reached for its staple and missed. He knew that he would have to fix it. "Fake it," his father had always said. Any repair was a "fake" in the Wonnacott family.

The door of the house opened, splashing light as bright as a garden. Footsteps came through it and the dog moved towards them. Howard knew the footsteps were the boy. Every morning the boy came early, bringing sugar to the mare.

The boy was shivering, still fumbling his buttons. He spoke to Howard on a breath and climbed two bars of the gate, leaning out to the dark shape of the mare. The mare came forward a pace, then tossed her head; rejecting the boy's hand. She was petulant with foal.

"It's what having a foal does," Howard said. "Some mares go all sentimental. Others get bad-tempered." He looked at the boy and added, "It doesn't mean anything."

The boy went up another bar so that he could reach out further. "When do you think it will be?"

"Soon," Howard said.

"As long as it's not during the snow. Mummy says it's sure to snow."

Howard looked up to the sky, feeling the weight of it. The dawn was late. The sky was bulging and the air was as dead as bone. He knew what the day would bring.

"Your mother's right. It's going to snow, all right."

Mark felt his father's fear. He turned his face to the sky and thought, I can smell the snow. He said, "Will there be room in the barn?" and Howard knew he was thinking of the mare.

"Have to bring the sheep in." Howard turned, his fear sharpened by the boy's fear. He shouted for the dog. "Tell your mother, son. Say be sure about candles and paraffin. Say it's sure to snow."

It came in a graveyard silence. It made the world new, so that when you walked you left footprints; like the first man of the world. The animals were afraid. They knew it was a foreign thing.

Around the house the wind wound its sheet of white; worrying the snow into shapes, deep shapes that leaned against walls, deep enough to lose a man. After a day and a night the wind hardened and had ice in it. The snow froze. It became as hard as stone and streams dripped icicles like spears.

The village was shut up in white. Sheep crowded the lee, their teeth tearing the yellow flesh of mangolds. Cattle stood in committees, as black as smudges of soot, their mouths dribbling hay like whiskers. Hens pecked ice in search of water. The barn cat went thin to her kittens, consoling them with warmth.

The school was closed. No bread. No paraffin. No candles. Telegraph wires collapsed. Birds died on the window sills, as empty as paper ash. In every house the fire was the altar. You worked for it like missionaries.

Mark worked for it, carrying the logs which his father sawed. The sawdust fell like the blood of dolls.

He helped with the pigs, the sheep, the cattle; and although Kate protested, "You ought to be doing homework. No school all the week and you with exams," she knew what Howard would say. Howard would say, "Animals come first, Kate, this weather," and although she knew that this was right, she felt also that her control of Mark's future was slipping away.

Once it had been coherent; work hard at school, pass the eleven-plus, then to grammar school and college, and after that to Birmingham and a good job and two thousand a year. Once it had added up like a sum. Now the first link was being strained. He was working harder on the farm than at school. Now he was becoming a farmer, imitating his father, even wearing sacks like his father; and there was nothing she could do about it.

Howard wore sacks against the snow. There were four sacks. The first was fastened by binder cord across his coat to keep his shoulders dry. The second was fastened around his middle, and the third around his waist where it hung down like an apron. Over that he drew an old overcoat, once much too large but now shrunken and smelling of wet. This overcoat had no buttons. The fourth sack went across its shoulders, smothering him in a warmth which soon steamed with melted snow.

From the window she saw Howard coming through the snow; a comic figure in his many sacks. She saw his face, burned red with cold, his nose looking bigger because of the cold. He sniffed, then wristed his nose. He spoke over his shoulder to Mark, and Mark appeared, leaning forward and plodding because of the snow. The boy wore his sacks like a man; had dragged on his cap like a man. The boy was trying to be a man, and suddenly her resentment melted.

Examinations did not matter. Birmingham and two thousand a year did not matter. In this moment nothing mattered except this picture of father and son, being men together. Her hands in the water, she watched them; quietly as you would watch a bird. She was warm with affection for the comic figures in their many sacks.

Then she thought, they'll be in soon, they'll need something hot. She dried her hands on the towel behind the door. She put another log on the fire, stirring the kettle out of its snore. She cut bread and cheese, and waited for them.

At the back of her mind she heard her mother say, "You ought to be firm, Kate. You ought to make sure he does his homework." At the back of her mind she heard her own voice say, "Everything depends on the examinations. He isn't meant to be a farmer, trudging the snow like all the other boys."

But it wasn't as easy as it seemed. Snow meant more work; the struggle for survival; and more work meant that Howard needed help. It was right that a boy should help his father.

Kate paused a moment, seeing her mother in the small,

precise kitchen in Market Town. She saw the furniture shining, the linoleum, too, the doors varnished to reflect the window light. She felt the sensible comfort of that kitchen; a terrace house, kept warm by houses on either side. She saw the fire flames and heard the singing kettle, and suddenly she ached to be home. Home in a small kitchen, shut off from the weather; with the snow something you saw from the window, as polite as icing on a wedding cake. Almost she said aloud, that's where I ought to be. Not here, forever struggling to keep things tidy and warm and dry. Forever drying sacks.

Then she looked to the window, where the comic figures were moving away. She knew they were going towards the pen, where two pigs grunted in brown gloom. The top of the door was open, and she saw their cruel, ugly snouts. The snouts strained up, hoping that the boots meant food. They nudged each other and the bully won. She heard the squeal as the other went back.

She saw Howard reach over the door and drag the bolt back. She said aloud, "I ought to be firm, I ought to insist about the homework. But I can't. There are compensations."

Mark followed his father towards the barn. The cows were restless, and their restlessness pointed towards the mare in the darkest corner. Mark saw his father's quick glance and a hole of panic opened in his stomach. He thought, something is going to happen, the mare is going to die.

Howard moved towards the mare. She stamped, swishing her tail in a fret of pain. He thought, I must be able to do something, the boy is watching, expecting me to do something.

He heard the boy say, "Will it be now? Shall I get the vet?"

He shook his head. There could be no vet. A vet cost money. Besides, there was the snow.

He moved slowly towards the mare, reaching back in memory, dragging up all his father had told him; years ago, when there had been horses on the farm.

He knew that the uterus would be painful from distention. He made noises to the mare, reaching for the udder. He brought milk from the two teats and glanced at his fingers; looking for that sticky substance which comes around the teats about ten hours before foaling. His fingers were blunt with cold, but he felt the stickiness. There would be more soon.

He touched the teats again, wishing the mare would let him milk her to ease the pressure. But she flattened her ears and whisked her tail. He leaned aside as she kicked.

He turned and remembered the boy. "Tell your mother, say it won't be long now. And bring the lantern."

He leaned against the wall, watching the mare and bringing into his mind the image of his father. The image of his father said, make sure the hind legs are well apart so the bladder can swell out. Give the mare something to bite and watch the nostrils for pneumonia. Years ago we lost a good mare with pneumonia.

Mark appeared at the door. He had no lantern. "She won't give it. She said you got to come."

"Didn't you tell her?"

"I told her," Mark said. "But she kept on saying."

Howard moved towards the door, still watching the mare. She was still now, her head hanging in weariness. He crossed the yard to the porch, listening to what his father had said. Make sure the foal takes the first milk. Remember all I used to say about the first milk.

He opened the door and Kate said, "You're not going to let that boy watch." He stepped into the kitchen and Kate said, "Oh, Howard, why do you do it?"

He took a lantern from its place behind the settle, shaking it slightly to hear the slop of paraffin. He held it up to be sure of the wicks.

"You don't realize, he's sensitive, he's not like all the others."

He lit the lamp. "He's a farmer's son. He's got to learn sometime."

She knew that her plans for the boy's future were being challenged. "But you know he'll never be a farmer." Her voice rose as he stepped to the porch. "There's no need for him to see."

Why shouldn't he see? What's so secret about birth? Wasn't it wonderful, something to sing about? Wasn't it a miracle, this bringing out of life? He thought suddenly of Bethlehem, then let the thought go; not finding words for it.

His stride lengthened as he heard the mare. She was moving in a rhythm of pain, bobbing her head and lifting her tail.

"She keeps lifting her tail," Mark said.

Howard put down the lantern. "Let the cows out. Let them stand in the yard. They'll be all right."

Mark released the cows and they hesitated, their heads lowered towards the mare. They did not want to go. Habit told them not to go.

"Get them out," Howard said.

Mark stamped his boots and waved his arms. One went out to the mildewed twilight and the others followed. Then he came towards his father.

"Do you want to stay?" Howard said.

Mark did not answer.

"Take the lantern then. Hold it up when I say. Hold it high so I can see."

Mark took the lantern. Howard heard him shivering.

"The heaving's good, don't worry about that. There's got to be heaving, see."

The mare set her hind legs wide apart and the sounds of her breathing swelled; filling the brain like the roar of a train in a tunnel. The membranes came out like a bladder.

"She'll be all right," Howard said. "She's foaled on the moor with nobody to help. She knows what it's all about."

The bladder broke and Mark almost ran. His father's face was lit with fury. "Stand still," his father said. Neither realized that it was the face which spoke; that there was no voice in it.

The foal began to come. The mare shook with the final spasms. The foal came. So did the afterbirth. Howard crouched over the foal. Its lungs began to breathe and he helped it to stand. It took the first milk; the purgative milk which clears the alimentary canal of meconium. Howard said, "There's plenty of milk, but she won't be in full till the fourth day."

He wiped the mare's eyes with a cloth, then squeezed the cloth in a bucket and wiped her nostrils. He thought, the water's too cold, watching her nostrils for the blue tinge of pneumonia. He squeezed the cloth again, giving it to her to bite. His hands moved over her ears and legs, feeling for cold. He heard his voice say, "It's nature, see. It looks worse than it is because it's nature, see."

Mark made himself small against the wall, shaken by the grotesque miracle. He watched the foal, and the mare looked back to watch it, too.

"A colt foal," his father said. "You'd better go and tell your mother."

Mark moved sideways, still pressed against the wall.

"Leave the lantern," Howard said.

He hooked the lantern on a nail. Then he sidled away. It seemed that moving stretched the strings of horror. They snapped and suddenly he was free. He ran. The yard was clumsy with darkness and the cows were darker. He startled them with his boots. He slipped and fell and cut a knee, then ran on without knowing. He burst into the kitchen, calling his mother, calling her to come and see. "A colt foal, Mummy, and I saw it all."

She put on a coat and turned up its collar. She came out shivering, nervous of the ice.

"A beautiful colt foal, Mummy, and the mare was as good as gold."

He followed her into the barn, seeing the scene in sharper detail than before. He saw the mare making a long neck towards her foal. All distress was gone. Now she was mellow with pride. He saw the foal, curled up in straw, the color of wine in the lamplight. Then he saw his father, an absurd figure with sacks around his waist, but his coat off and his shirt sleeves rolled.

His mother looked down at the foal. She made a muff of the sleeves of her coat; her right hand up the left sleeve, her left hand up the other. The sleeves met so that she seemed to have no hands. "Lovely," she said.

She felt the boy's wonder and excitement and thought, I'm glad it's all right, but what use will it be? A foal from a broken-down mare like that.

"Nobody knows what the old mare's pedigree is." Howard reached for his coat. "And nobody knows who the stallion was." He darted a glance to Kate, asking her to think of a good idea. "So what shall we call him?"

Mark shuffled the names which he had invented in anticipation; Sonny Boy and Valley Stream and Son of Pride. He thought Valley Stream was best because of Black Dog valley and those summer hours with the mare beside the stepping-stones. But as he began to say it, Kate's lips moved in that little, secretive smile; as though she were tasting her thoughts before giving them away.

"He's a question mark," she said. "We ought to call him that."

Chapter Nine

Howard opened his eyes to the darkness, wondering what had awakened him. He listened and heard nothing. Almost he turned over. Then he heard it again; a drip from the eaves, a sinister, dungeon sound. He sat up, waiting for it to come again.

He put a hand on Kate's shoulder. She awakened slowly, clinging to the shreds of sleep as the shivering cling to the rags of warmth.

Urgently he said, "Listen." He knew that her eyes were open by the change of breathing. He knew that her silence was listening. "It's the thaw," he said.

By morning the moor was moving. Snow slipped down to the valley, swelling streams to the conceit of rivers, rampaging down to nowhere. Water became the new menace. It dragged down a litter of torn trees. It swept away the legs of a sheep and let the white head fight for life a long time. It left a slobber of mud.

Then spring came like a new beginning. You could feel the grass coming back. The air had the sing of wine, and the spirit of the village opened like a morning flower.

You knew why moorland people of the nineteenth century had paid homage to spring; as though spring were a prince of the fairytale, releasing you from a prison of cold. You knew why they had dances for it, and why those dances were symbolic of escape. The spirit was of happiness. You could hear the village laughing; talking louder than it had talked in winter, calling to friends with each call a salute to the new. You could feel the village young.

Howard turned out mare and foal to the home field, where the foal tasted movement with an air of surprise; like the nursery toy which suddenly finds itself alive. Its long yellow legs were full of experiment. It raced in a comedy of endeavor, while the mare watched in a boredom of toleration.

Mark watched, too. He flattered the mare with congratulations about the foal; assuring her that the foal made no difference, she was still his favorite. It was not true, for the young promise of the one was more exciting than the old dullness of the other; but he wanted it to be true.

He looked towards the wall, his eye caught by a red movement. A girl put both hands on the granite and vaulted to the wall. She stood erect, with the wind in her hair. She wore a red sweater and jodhpurs. He recognized Laura Buckpitt.

He waited for her to go, but she did not. He waited for her to speak, but she did not. There was an arrogance about her that called him. He wanted her to see the foal in the hope that she would respect him the more for it; so he moved towards the wall, taking the mare by the forelock, sure that the foal would follow. The foal hugged the mare's side, then darted away; less in fright than in a boredom with slow movement. It did not understand the sense of rest.

They came to the wall and Mark looked up. Laura Buckpitt seemed tall against the sky.

"Ten weeks old," he said.

"A nice foal," she admitted, and his heart swelled with pride and gratitude. "Although you can never tell with foals." She waited a minute, then asked, "Is it yours?"

It was not a polite question. It was a challenge. Mark felt the thrust in it and answered in a flurry, "Yes, of course it's mine, everyone knows it's mine. Born during the snow."

Laura Buckpitt said, "Is the mare yours?"

She did not smile, but he sensed the smile in her. He felt it to be a smile of triumph and pity; as though she knew what he did not know.

"The mare came off the moor," she said. "The Wonnacotts have never had ponies on the moor."

He wanted to say, nobody wanted her, she'd been there years. He said, "She'd have died in the snow."

Calmly the girl said, "If the mare isn't yours, I don't see how the foal can be."

The logic of it was frightening. His heart went frog cold, and his hand on the mare tightened.

She saw the hand tighten. "Nobody minds the mare. You can have the mare." She looked beyond him to the foal, and silence spoke the rest.

"Not yours," Mark said, his voice a tremble. "Neither of them yours."

She said, "My father . . ." And simultaneously he said, "My father . . ."

For a moment they imagined the two men facing each other. On one side Buckpitt, tall and dark, alight with an authority that intimidated; leader of the commoners, chairman of the parish council, people's warden and school manager; he was as important as his two hundred acres. On the other side was Howard Wonnacott, known to be the least successful of the Wonnacotts; a bad-luck farmer, dressed up in sacks, farming without electricity or tractor or pedigree stock; he was as small as his twenty-five acres.

The girl laughed, jumping from the wall. Her laugh dismissed his father as a joke.

"You wait," Mark said. "You'll see. You Buckpitts can't have everything you want."

Day after day Mark watched the wall, waiting for the men to come. They came.

Buckpitt came with Maddicott and Jordan. Maddicott pointed towards the foal, and Jordan leaned towards Buckpitt, talking urgently. Then they turned and ducked into the car. Doors slammed and as they drove away, Mark sent his hot hatred after them. I'll kill you. I'll get a knife and kill you. I'll sharpen it on the whetstone, making it thin like a dagger, like a dagger in books.

He knew the men would come again. They came one Sunday evening.

Mark returned from chapel with his parents, then went to bed with his mother saying, "School tomorrow." He tried to sleep, but behind closed eyes his fears were alive with faces. Maddicott's was the sneering face, but Buckpitt's was the darkest. Buckpitt was his Satan.

He heard the gate and knew that they had come. Evensong at the parish church was over. They had opened their books to hymns; had leaned forward in pretense of prayer; had lifted their faces to the sermon in the civility of indifference. Then they had come from their pews and met in the porch and turned towards Yarnator. He waited for the knocking; a short, authoritative knuckling of the front door. Buckpitt wouldn't go round the back.

He heard his mother come to the door. He heard her exclamation of surprise and the growl of voices coming in. The door closed. He heard them waiting in the passage. Then she opened the door of the parlor; the parlor because it was Sunday and as a tribute to their importance. He heard her say, "I'll tell him you're here." He listened; listening until his ears sang.

The door of the kitchen opened. He heard his father's step. There was diffidence in it, an indecision expressed in the shuffle. He heard his father say, "Evening, Mr. Buckpitt. Jordan, Maddicott. What can I do for you?"

There was surprise in the house, and he could not understand why his parents were surprised. Surely they had known that Laura Buckpitt, who had everything, surely they had guessed that she would want the foal.

They moved into the parlor, while his mother said, "Would you gentlemen care for a cup of tea?"

Jordan said no, while Maddicott murmured, "No time for that." But Buckpitt said, "Thank you, Mrs. Wonnacott. That would be very nice."

Then the door closed, and Mark came to the landing. He could hear only a growl that began quietly, then rose in confusion as several spoke at once. He heard his father saying, "But wait a minute." Then a quiet voice took over. Mark knew that it was Buckpitt.

Buckpitt said, "It's not a matter of opinion. It's a matter of fact. The mare ran the moor for years. You admit that. You took her in, although you have no ponies on the moor. You admit that."

He glanced at Howard, waiting for him to admit it. Howard thought, I must admit it, everyone knows it's true.

"Personally there was no objection to that. If you wanted the mare, we were willing to make an exception."

He paused and Jordan and Maddicott leaned into the pause. Their leaning said, that's right, we didn't want to quibble, we know how you are for money.

"At the time," Buckpitt said, "we thought you wanted the mare for your boy. Nobody objected to that. Now we know why you wanted the mare." He paused again. "You wanted her because she was in foal."

It sounded ugly and clever. Buckpitt let the silence come around like guilt.

Then he said, "The mare had been covered by a stallion on the moor. My stallion on the moor. The foal has the markings of my bay stallion, and the mare was seen running with the bay last spring."

Howard said, "Who says that?"

Buckpitt straightened. His glance had a glint in it. He said, "I say that," and Jordan and Maddicott said, "We all say that." Then Maddicott added, "Seen her often. No mistaking those tube holes."

Howard turned to Buckpitt. "You can't be sure, it could be any stallion." Then he wagged his head in distress, thinking one at a time, you're confusing me, give me time to think.

"That evening in the White Hart," Maddicott said. "When you asked us to drive the mare in special. I thought that was funny at the time."

"You did that to make your story good," Jordan said. "You knew the mare wouldn't be there next day."

Howard shook his head and Maddicott leaned forward again.

"We drove Black Dog valley special, but couldn't see head nor tail of her. At the time it didn't seem to matter and we already had our hands full. But now . . ."

"Now we see," Jordan put in. "Now it matters. We got the foal to consider."

Howard's head wagged in distress. He turned to Buckpitt, his hands saying, you know better than that, you know it isn't true. But Buckpitt's expression was hard. Only his eyes had a gleam of amusement, and Howard knew that in the amusement there was contempt.

He said, "You know it isn't true. You know I didn't know about the foal." He watched a framed engraving of the *Relief of Ladysmith*. It leaned out from the opposite wall, brave with silent shouts and brandished swords and cries of Queen and Empire. Its glass caught the evening light. He said in a tremble, "I kept that mare all winter. My grass, my hay."

Maddicott brushed it aside. "We're not talking about the mare."

"But if the mare had died, there could have been no foal. She'd never have foaled if we'd left her out."

Buckpitt's eyes were sharp. "So you knew about the foal. You're admitting it."

"I'm not, I don't admit nothing. My boy . . ."

Maddicott said, "You can't blame your boy, Wonnacott." And Jordan added, "You can't get out of it like that."

Howard felt trapped; trapped by what he had not said. He heard Buckpitt say, "You admit you have a foal which doesn't belong to you. We can't allow that sort of thing. Our ponies run the moor, year in, year out, with no protection except the law, understood by all of us, that no man tries to take what doesn't belong to him."

Howard was not listening. Behind the creases of bewilderment he was thinking, perhaps they're right about the foal, there're so many of them, all saying the same thing, accusing me, they'll turn the village against me. Perhaps it will be enough to keep the mare. It was the mare the boy wanted.

He turned to Buckpitt. "What I can't understand is—you got all the ponies any man could want. What's so important about one more?"

Almost Jordan answered, but Maddicott's brown boot moved to touch his. They were silent as the door opened and Kate came in with a tray. Buckpitt moved quickly to the door, holding it away from the tray. Howard recognized the best teapot, the best cups and saucers.

She put the tray on the table and began to pour. "Sugar for you, Mr. Jordan? And for you, Mr. Maddicott?"

They fidgeted their replies. They did not want tea or the social courtesies which it implied.

"Sugar for you, Mr. Buckpitt?" There was a subtle difference in her tone. It had admiration and deference.

"Thank you. One lump, please."

They accepted the cups and sipped. Maddicott's sip was a shooshing sound. He emptied the cup and placed it between his feet. He rested forearms on knees, clasping his hands in the gulf between his knees. He said, "Well, look here, no sense beating about the bush."

Kate glanced at Howard, and Howard said, "It's the foal. They've come about the foal."

Kate's surprise said, well, what about the foal?

"It's Mr. Buckpitt's foal," Maddicott said, and Jordan added, "It's his by right."

Kate turned to Buckpitt, waiting for him to deny what they said. He sipped, his eyes up, watching her. The silence stretched.

"Never your mare in the first place," Jordan said. "Everyone knows that."

Howard found the words on his tongue. "The mare never belonged to no one. Not since years ago and never no brand. Nobody thought her worth the while."

Buckpitt put down his cup. "I thought I'd made that clear. There's no objection to the mare." He brought his head up and his eyes were cold. "But I want the foal, Wonnacott."

Howard was astonished by the coldness. He tried to say, it's ours, that evening in the barn, that makes it ours. Then he realized how hopeless it was, and glanced his helplessness to Kate.

She said, "Just like that."

Maddicott and Jordan looked at each other, as though to say, just like what?

Kate said, "You come in here on a Sunday evening, and in five minutes you've got it all decided. Mr. Buckpitt, the great Mr. Buckpitt of Narrastun, he must have the foal."

"It's his," Jordan said; and Maddicott added, "It's not only us. It's the commoners. We all met last night and everyone decided what ought to be done. Everyone agreed that we should come here today and tell your husband, man to man, straight up and proper, though he shouldn't need no telling. The Wonnacotts have known the law for generations."

Kate's eyes flicked up to Buckpitt. "Your daughter, who has everything, she's seen the foal and wants the foal. That makes it law, does it?"

Buckpitt did not answer, matching her gaze; but Maddicott said, "His stallion," and Jordan said, "All the village knows. Wonnacott never had no stallion, so how can it be yours?"

Kate looked at Buckpitt. "You can't prove it."

Jordan stood up. "We can prove it isn't yours."

"But we have possession." Kate watched Buckpitt, compelling him to answer. "You'll have to go to court to get possession."

"That'll cost money," Maddicott said. "You haven't got the money to fight in court."

"There's no need to go to court," Buckpitt said, speaking to her eyes. "There are other ways."

"Meaning what?"

"The commoners are jealous of their rights, Mrs. Wonnacott. They've defended them for generations against all kinds of encroachment. Your husband's father, he always fought to defend those rights. So ask your husband. He ought to know how powerful the commoners can be."

Howard thought, that's right, the commoners will back Buckpitt, all the village will be against us.

They waited for Kate to speak, but Kate did not.

"You realize what you're doing." Buckpitt picked up his hat, looking down at it. "Your husband will be outside the organization. A man apart. And you realize what that means, Mrs. Wonnacott. When he needs hay to tide him over. Credit to tide him over. When he needs help, he'll find no one to give it."

Kate said, "We need no help."

"You're always needing help." Maddicott made a sound of disgust. "Hay, roots, you're always borrowing."

"We pay back." Kate flicked a glance of contempt. "We don't owe you anything."

"Hay when you need it. That's worth more than you can ever pay back."

Buckpitt made a little gesture with his hat. "You need to be big to stand alone. You aren't big enough." He took a step to the door. "Ask yourself what the foal is worth, then wonder if it's worth all you'll have to pay. Think it over, Mrs. Wonnacott."

He had his fingers on the latch as Kate said, "We don't have to think it over."

Maddicott said, "That's all right then"; and Jordan said, "It don't never do to go against the law."

Kate brought the tips of her fingers together, then lifted her hands to her mouth. She was thinking, shaping the words. They could hear her breath in the hollow her hands made.

"You're a fair man, Mr. Buckpitt. I don't think you cared twopence about this foal until one day your daughter saw it and wanted it."

Howard saw that this was true. Buckpitt's eyes said that it was true.

"You want the foal for your daughter." Kate held up her head, proud and tense. "I want it for my son. I'm not ashamed of that. Because of it I'm prepared to face whatever you may do."

Buckpitt thought about it. Then he glanced at Howard.

"My husband, too," Kate said.

Buckpitt nodded, while Jordan said, "You'll rue the day,"

and Maddicott said, "The foal's never worth all the trouble it will bring."

"The foal stays. The mare stays. They've wintered here and they'll summer here. You didn't attempt to claim ownership until the grass was back."

Buckpitt gave a slight, sardonic inclination of his head. He went out to the passage. A boy crouched on the stairs, his face white with hatred. A moment Buckpitt looked up at him, amused by the hatred. Then Maddicott and Jordan came into the passage. They weren't worth the hatred, so the boy disappeared; taking his hatred to the privacy of his room, there to find words for it. Fine words like murder and torture and I'll do it when I'm big enough.

Buckpitt smiled to Kate, knowing that she had seen the boy's face.

"Thank you for the tea." He stepped down to the path which led to the front gate. The path was green with weeds. "Good night to you." He put on his hat, but did not speak to Howard. He moved down the path with Maddicott and Jordan. They seemed angrier than he.

Howard closed the door and turned to his wife. You did it, Kate. Even Buckpitt, even Buckpitt knew you meant every word. He looked up to the face on the stairs.

"It's all right. They won't take the foal. Your mother told them." Howard laughed a trembling laugh, feeling that it had been a victory. "Your mother was too clever for anything they had to say."

Mark came down the stairs and hid his face against his mother. They stood in the passage a moment, celebrating their little victory.

But later that night, when the warm darkness was all around, any sense of victory seemed premature and foolish. Kate said, "It's done now, we're on our own now." After a while she said, "We'll have to make more grass."

Howard felt her alarm and reached for her hand. A moment her fingers remained passive. Then she answered his pressure as he said, "We'll make it, Kate. We'll start at once. We'll drive the bracken back."

Chapter Ten

There was a corner of the twenty-five acres which for years had been thick with bracken. You cut it and turned your back, and the bracken was there again; tenacious and malicious, refusing to yield ground which it had owned for longer than the longest memory.

Howard had fought this corner for five years, scything the green stuff in a vicious silence of sweat. He had taken the mattock to it, driving deep for the roots, tearing the earth into new shapes, scabbling with his hands in a personal battle; as though the roots were alive and fighting back. Once he thought he had won. He had told Kate in a glory of exhaustion, "I've got the bracken out."

Then he had been ill, with a cough that tore red lights in his chest, and for a while, not long, but long enough, he had not been able to pursue the fight. So the bracken had come back, drowning the earth in darkness, starving it of light; laughing at him and his mattock as the sea had laughed at the woman and her broom.

He had let the bracken win then. The lonely battle had no longer seemed important. He had ceased to believe that there ever could be grass. It was easier to borrow hay and roots, then repay in months of plenty.

"Now we can't," he said, taking the whetstone to the scythe. "Buckpitt and Maddicott and Jordan, they're waiting for us to try to borrow. Then they will have won. They're sure they'll win. They're sure we'll never beat the bracken and get those acres back."

"I'm coming, too," Mark said.

It began as a campaign against a resourceful and cunning enemy. Soon it was slavery.

Howard taught the boy to scythe and hook and dig, and the boy felt wetness dribbling from the blisters. Sweat itched his head like fleas. He was afraid to straighten, for when he straightened, his back screamed, opening his mouth with the pain.

They spoke seldom. They had nothing to say when their strength was high; and when it was low, so that they came to the work with the trudge of slaves, they knew that whatever they said would be dark with defeat. Their sweat would be in it and their weariness. They would lose patience with the task and with each other. Every evening they were on the edge of defeat; almost ready to compromise, almost ready to say that the bracken had a use, it could be used for bedding.

But when at last the evening stint was done and they could come to supper, their mood moved out of despair to an elation that made their weariness itself an achievement, like a wound of battle. They came down the hill in a unity of spirit, the evening wind in their shirts, the day's sun still panting in their bodies.

Mark no longer went early to bed. His mother glanced at the clock, making a schoolboy of him, but his father did not support the glance.

Howard stretched his legs on one side of the white-dust fire, his boots off and his socks steaming. Mark stretched on the other, his boots off and his socks, too, his feet paddling the cool as children paddle the sea. He looked at his father, and in their silence they shared the day again; thinking about it, the monotony of it, the achievement, telling each other in their silence that there could be no thought of compromise now. Tomorrow they must go back and keep on going back until at least the bracken understood that it was beaten.

Mark never knew when the drowzing, as contented as a sunflower in the sun, fell over the edge to sleep. He felt his head heavying until it was ready to fall. Then he put up his hands to catch his head.

"Open the door," his father said. "I'll carry him up."

His mother whispered, "Look at his feet. His boots were full of earth," but his father made a sound as though dirty feet did not matter; as though dirt were an emblem of manliness.

"Worn out," Kate said, as she opened the door. "Look at his poor hands."

The acres were torn bare, as new as the earth of the third day in Genesis. They called Kate to come and see, and she praised the new brown earth, knowing what it had cost them. She did not say, it seems small for all the struggle. She said, "When are you going to put in the grass?"

"Potatoes first," Howard said. "To clean the ground, there's nothing like potatoes to clean the ground. Then in ten weeks they'll be ready, and digging up will turn the earth again. Then the grass, the Italian rye grass."

In his excitement Howard shouted, feeling big like a conqueror. He turned towards Narrastun and shouted, "Do you see this, Buckpitt? The bracken beat. Ready for the grass."

"Don't shout," Kate said, putting a hand on his arm, feeling the sweat drying in his shirt. "You've done very well and I'm proud of you both. Now come in to supper."

She put out a hand for Mark and walked between them down the hill. As they reached the gate she said, "Early to bed tonight, ready for school tomorrow." She moved through the gate, saying over her shoulder, "You ought to hear the results of the eleven-plus soon."

Howard glanced at Mark and felt the shadow come upon

him. The boy was afraid, the boy knew he had failed. Fairweather knew, the other children knew. Everyone knew. Only Kate pretended.

"Make a bet he's cleverer than me," Howard said. "I was a duffer going to school."

Chapter Eleven

A fly ticked at the glass. It waited, then whirred its sounds again. It was a fat fly, given a green sheen by the sun. All afternoon it fussed at the window, seeking a way to sunshine as heavy as honey.

Mark watched the fly and bit his pen. He thought, if you rub the pen and hold it out, it will pick up paper. A crumb of paper, not too big. You've got to do it fair.

He took the pen from his mouth and pushed it into the short hairs above one ear; scratching it to and fro in a sound like grasshoppers. Then he held it above the paper on his desk, and a corner of the paper stirred towards the pen. Electricity. Wonderful. All life had this magic called electricity, but no one had known until whoever it was, whenever it was; thousands of years but no one had known. Not even Moses in the Old Testament, wonderfully wise; not even Moses had known.

Fairweather looked around the room. Mark caught his eye and they shared a glance. Then Fairweather looked down. Mark thought, he knows about me, he knows I haven't done one yet.

He focused the questions, calling his mind to stop mucking about and come and look. This is a test and I'm supposed to know the answers. Others know the answers. Laura Buckpitt, she knows the answers, trust her, she's a girl and girls always know the answers, making life difficult for boys who have other things to know.

He tried to concentrate: "If twenty-five pounds of soap costs twelve shillings sixpence, what will be the cost of one hundredweight?"

A moment he thought soap, who's interested in soap? If they had any sense, they would make it hay; hay for horses. Then a finger of his mind pointed; divide twelve shillings sixpence by twenty-five and you'll find the cost of a pound. Twenty-five sixpences in twelve shillings sixpence, so each pound costs sixpence. He wrote the figures hurriedly, as though catching minnows that almost got away.

But how many pounds in a hundredweight? He stared at nothing; imagining the back of his exercise book where all the tables were printed by clever men who never made a mistake. A hundred and twelve pounds in a hundredweight; but is that right? How can that be right? If there's a hundred and twelve, why call it a hundredweight? Nobody in their senses would call it a hundredweight.

So it must be a hundred, that's common sense. That's one hundred sixpences, and one hundred sixpences are fifty shillings and fifty shillings make two pounds ten shillings, which would be enough for a second-hand bicycle if I wanted a second-hand bicycle. He wrote "two pounds ten shillings" in large figures, underlining them so that Fairweather would see and perhaps put "V.G." for "very good" beside them.

Then he called his thoughts to the next. "A troop of six hundred soldiers in a fortress have provisions for thirty days. How long will the food last if the garrison is increased to nine hundred men?"

His imagination jumped awake, photographing these men in their besieged fortress while the relief force of three hundred came riding down the hill. He remembered the *Relief of Ladysmith* in the parlor. Years ago he had been fascinated by the mustaches.

But what soldiers was the textbook talking about; what

uniforms did they wear? Were they Foreign Legion, which was good; or British, which was better? If they were British he had no doubts at all; the food would last long enough, long enough for the enemy to be outwitted, out-couraged, out-fought. Everyone knew that for everyone's good the British must win in the end.

But you couldn't be sure. The question didn't say. He fidgeted, impatient of adults who, having provoked your interest, abandon you with insufficient details. He watched the fly and decided. They were the Foreign Legion like in *Beau Geste*, half crazy with sunshine and thirst.

Then he looked at the question again. "How long will the food last?" Now there's a thing. Food isn't important. You'd think the expert who wrote the book and was clever enough to know all the answers, you'd think he'd know that food isn't important compared with water. How long will the water last? That would have been good sense. You could be concerned about a sum like that. You could take an interest.

A bell rang and the breath of the room came out in a sigh; like the end of episode five in the Saturday picture house. A girl said, "Oh, sir, I nearly finished," while another whispered, "What did you put for number five?" Laura Buckpitt did not speak. She had completed the test, and the whole room knew that her paper would be the best.

"Before you go," Fairweather said, "I have here the results you've been waiting for."

A girl said, "The eleven-plus," her voice a hiss of excitement.

Mark looked down, his finger tracing the outline of initials in the desk: "F.W." Everyone said that they were Fred Warrener's initials and that Fred had had three years to perfect the carving; passing the time like a prisoner in his cell, waiting for his fourteenth birthday and an end to penal servitude.

"Only one has passed," Fairweather said.

The breath hissed in. The room looked to Laura.

Mark thought, it could be me, there could be a miracle.

"Laura Buckpitt has passed." Fairweather gave her a slight, secret smile. "Well done, Laura."

Mark's finger went up and down the "W." He heard his mother say, it could have been you, it would have been you if only you would concentrate.

"The rest of you mustn't be disappointed. You'll go to the secondary modern school in Market Town. It's a good school, with up-to-date equipment and big playing fields and a boxing team. You'll enjoy it there."

Joe Maddicott put up a hand. "Please, sir, why can't we stay, sir? We don't want to go to no new school."

Fairweather smiled. "That's very flattering, Maddicott. I had no idea you wished to prolong the acquaintance. But you must go on. This school is too small now."

"It was big enough years ago, sir. We don't want to change, and our fathers don't want it neither."

Almost Fairweather said, your fathers want you home at four so that you'll become free labor on the farm. Only the enlightened parent knows how important this can be to you. He said, "This new secondary modern school has been provided at great expense to the community. There's more money spent on education now than ever there used to be. You must take advantage of it."

Mark remembered his mother saying, it's so important, you're too young to realize. When I was your age, I didn't realize, so I never went to the grammar school. But my sister, she was clever and she realized, and look at Auntie Barbara now. She's in South Africa.

All right, Mark thought, what's so wonderful about South Africa?

Then he remembered his grandmother in Market Town. She had promised him the half-sovereign in the glass cupboard; Grandfather's half-sovereign, wonderful because it was old and rare and because it had rested for years in Grandfather's skittles cup. "Real gold," she had said, "and it will be yours the day you pass for the grammar school." As though all the world is yours if you pass for the grammar school.

He knew that his grandparents would be hurt, disappointed, as though he had let them down and had not been clever like Auntie Barbara. He knew that when they thought he was not listening, his mother would make excuses: "He's a very clever boy, but he just won't concentrate."

"All right," Fairweather said. "You can go now."

The girls went first, surrounding Laura like maids-in-waiting to a queen; but as the boys followed, Fairweather put out a hand.

"Not you, Wonnacott. Come here a minute."

Fairweather tidied the books on his desk, wondering what he could say and how saying anything could help to explain the inevitable. I told the mother. I told her repeatedly that he hadn't a chance. But she insisted, making him take the eleven-plus, clever enough to see the possibilities on the other side of it but not wise enough to know that you can't realize your ambition through your son. Now that the inevitable has happened, she still won't believe it. She'll blame the system, she'll blame the boy, she'll blame me. Heaven protect teachers from ambitious parents who resent seeing their own failures repeated in their children.

He said, "Tell your mother only one passed out of nineteen. That's how difficult it was."

He waited, but the boy had nothing to say.

"Tell your mother you did very well." He looked at the lie, then adorned it. "She should be proud of you."

Mark thought, how can you do well if you don't know the answers? I didn't know the answers. I was thinking about other things; like why should two and two make four, who decided that two and two must always equal four? Why not five for a change?

Fairweather watched him; strange boy, you never know what's going on in his head. Then he said, "All right, run on now. But remember, tell your mother, tell her it might be best in the long run. Best that you didn't pass."

But how can you tell your mother? You know what her eyes will do; fill with hurt, as though you had blown to pieces the plans in her head, making you feel ashamed and how dreadful it was and how well you could have done if you'd tried.

He wished he were Laura Buckpitt. If I were Laura Buckpitt, I'd run to her and say I passed, the only one who passed. But she wouldn't believe the bit about the only one because it sounds too good to be true. So I'd say ask Mr. Fairweather, he'll tell you. And when she was sure, she would take the train to Market Town and tell grannie and grandfather, and the next letter she wrote to Auntie Barbara would be very long indeed.

But now she won't want to tell grannie and grandfather, and there won't be anything important to tell Auntie Barbara. And all because I didn't know about subject and predicate or how long the bath took to fill. I wish we had a bath. Not just a tin bath in front of the fire on Saturday night, but a real bath with two taps. I could work it out then, turning both taps and watching it fill and timing it to see if the experts who wrote the textbook, to see if they were right.

He climbed to the middle bar of the gate, watching the mare and foal. I'll have to tell her. She's sure to ask, she's been asking every day for a week, and it's no use pretending. She always knows when it's lies.

Howard found him there and Mark moved sideways a little, so that his father could lean on the gate. After a while Howard said, "Had a good day at school?"

Mark made a long sound which meant nothing. I'll tell him in a minute. I don't mind telling him.

"I wasn't never no good at school," Howard said. "Teacher Griffiths, he was master in those days, a Welshman with a temper like fire and all the brains in the world. Music, Wordsworth, algebra, the tribes of Israel, all came alike to him and he loved it all. Poor old Griffiths tried to larrup it into me, but I dunno, what went in one day was gone the next."

Howard took the pipe from his mouth and looked at the crusted bowl and put it back again. There was no tobacco in it. He was thinking around it, as Mark at school had sucked his pen.

"Poetry now. Griffiths was a master hand for poetry and wanted us to like it, too. But I couldn't never remember two lines together. Walter de la Mare, he was the poet when I went to school. Don't reckon there was anybody ever hated more."

The foal pretended sudden fright, galloping stiff-legged, then stopping abruptly and listening and looking, then galloping again. It was showing off for them.

"As for sums," Howard said. "You any good at sums?"

Mark thought, well, I got one right today and underlined it for Fairweather to see. Then he shook his head, admitting that one right wasn't enough.

"Whenever it was sums," Howard said, "then all the maidens would turn and look at me and laugh, knowin' that I was going to be caned for certain. Decimals and fractions, add up and take away. I couldn't fathom it at all. Not like your mother. Your mother's clever. It makes sense to her."

Mark watched the foal. "But why the cane? If you didn't know . . ."

Howard smiled around the pipe. "It was always the cane for boys who didn't know. Girls got the ruler, across their palms most times, but across their knuckles if it was serious or the end of the day and Griffiths had had enough. You expected it."

"What did your father say?"

"If I'd told your grandfather Wonnacott, he'd have leathered me for tellin'. You were never supposed to tell. As for old Griffiths, he never held it against us, and when the boys grew up, nobody held it against him. In fact he had one of the biggest carrying funerals ever."

Howard saw the coffin, carried by men who had been boys. It had been a mile from Griffiths' house of retirement to the church, but there had been no hearse. The hearse was for ordinary men. Griffiths had been carried by the men who had been boys; carrying in teams, two hundred paces each, with the undertaker walking in front, counting the paces so that no team had the honor of carrying longer than others.

"Wreaths from everyone," Howard said. "Especially the Warrener family because it was always said that he'd leathered Fred the hardest. Two columns of names in the paper."

"Did you carry, Dad?"

Howard hesitated, remembering that when the names of the teams had been chosen, his had been left out. The hurt was still there.

"Everyone couldn't carry, son. Not when so many offered."

"Yes, but why you, why did they leave you out?"

Howard thought, I dunno, I've always been left out. He said, "Well, bein' a Brethren, son."

They watched the foal a long time; and the foal, knowing they were watching, performed for them in an extravagance of delight. Then suddenly its light went out. It came quietly to the mare, taking short steps like a girl in long skirts. It nuzzled the mare, but she bumped it away, petulant with droop-down. The foal was chastened. It hung around in a conciliatory way, proving that her mood was its mood. Then it came into her shadow and lay down, stretching its legs out of shadow to the sun.

Howard flicked a hand, and a fly rose from his forehead. "You and Mr. Fairweather, you get on all right?"

"All right," Mark said.

"He don't cane you, does he?"

"He got a cane in the cupboard."

"But he don't cane you, does he?"

Mark shook his head.

"Because if he ever touched you, son . . ." Howard felt the rise of rage and laughed at it. "A funny thing. When I went to school I expected it and thought no worse of the master for it. But if it was you now. If the teacher touched you now."

Mark slipped from the gate. Fairweather didn't hit you. Fairweather glanced a reproach and that hit you. He smiled at Laura Buckpitt and that hit you. You knew he was proud of Laura.

Mark said, "Mr. Fairweather told us. This afternoon he told us."

Howard's glance was alarmed. He knew what Mr. Fairweather had told; he had been waiting for it for a week. Carefully he took out his pipe and looked at it and put it back again.

"Only one passed," Mark said. "Only Laura passed."

Howard straightened and turned, leaning his shoulders against the gate. He looked towards the yard, where hens shuffled their feathers in the dust holes. They waddled deep into their holes and scuffled the dust and turned on a side with deep contentment. Then one got up to scuffle deeper, and they all got up to scuffle deeper. They had the jealous restlessness of women.

"You haven't told your mother yet?"

Mark shook his head.

"She wants the best for you, son. That's why she takes it hard." He sucked his pipe, making a mournful sound. "Not as though you're the only one. Must have been a terrible exam if only Laura passed."

"I'm like you," Mark said. "I'm no good at sums."

Howard nodded, remembering how bewildered he had been. That decimal point had tormented him like a flea in your shirt. "Still you got one right today."

Mark thought, well, I think I got one right today. He asked, "How many pounds in a hundredweight?"

Howard considered the question. He wanted to be sure. "Hundred and twelve," he said.

Mark made a little death sound. I thought it was, but then I thought it couldn't be. After a while he said, "But why a hundred and twelve? That's what I don't see."

"Well, it is. You got to learn it, like two and two make four. No sense arguin'."

"Yes, but why?"

They watched the hens, each bewildered by the apparent absurdity of calling one hundred and twelve pounds a hundredweight.

Howard said, "Your mother, she'll know why." He sent the mournful sound down his pipe again. "Do you want me to tell her?"

Mark watched the speckledy hen lift a wing to the sun. "Mr. Fairweather said I done very well."

"And I reckon you did. Not like me now. If you'd showed those questions to me, I'd have stopped runnin' somewhere near Okehampton."

Mark's smile was pale.

"They used to call me cloth-head." Howard watched for the smile to come back. "You're as clever as Parliament compared to me."

The smile did not come back. The boy looked towards the house, thinking of his mother.

"I'll tell her, son. Tonight when you've gone bed. She'll know you done your best. She'll know you can't do more."

"It's Fairweather," Kate said. "He's got favorites. Laura Buckpitt's a favorite. That's why she passed." She thought of her parents, saying everything in silence. She thought of Barbara in South Africa, being nice about it. "You don't care. You don't want him to get on and be an engineer."

Howard didn't answer. He thought, that future was never real, Kate. All those plans for the eleven-plus and grammar school and college, then to Birmingham and two thousand a year. They were never real, Kate. They were only in your head.

"You never believed it possible. You never believed the importance of education, what it can do to you, do for you, what it can mean when you get away. Out of this hole on the moor."

Howard said, "I don't want him to go away."

"Do you think I want him to go away? But he must if he's to be anything, anybody. What's there for him here? A garage mechanic. A farm hand, six pounds a week and poverty all his life. While in other parts of the country, see what's in the other parts of the country. The wages people earn. The opportunities."

Howard took out his pipe and looked at the bowl. It's like this, Kate. If he was clever and passed exams, he'd go away, away to school, then away to work, and although for a time he'd write every week and come home for holidays, soon there'd be other people to write to, other places to go for holidays. He'd make friends we don't know, marry a girl we don't know, make a home so far away it would be another world almost. Then there'd be children, our grandchildren, and we'd hardly ever see our grandchildren, we'd be just names to them, and soon there would be just one or two letters a year with a long letter at Christmas and perhaps some photographs. And that would be all, Kate. You'd be able to tell your parents, our Mark's doing very well. You'd be able to tell your sister in South Africa, Mark's promoted, he's got a new car and buying his own house, as soon as somebody retires he'll be the manager. But that would be all, Kate, and that isn't much. Being able to boast, that isn't much.

"You don't want him to be more than you are, better than you are. You want him to be a hill farmer, seven days a week, all the hours God sends, and what's there to show for it? Paraffin lamps and candles, buckets for the water, not even a decent bath. Don't you know there's money, big money, enough for comfort, for all the nice things? Don't you want your son to have the nice things?"

He didn't answer. He let her aim her dismay at him; realizing how deeply she had believed those plans in her head.

She looked around the big kitchen, her eyes hating it. "He'll be in this village all his life. He'll marry some village girl, because who else is there? And they'll scrimp to make a home and there'll be children and the poverty will begin all over again. For him like it's been for us. For him like it's been for me."

He watched the fire. The embers panted like the tongue of a harvest dog. He thought, we got land, hundreds of men would like their own land. Never mind their cars and television, their travel by air. Just give them the chance of land.

"And you just sit there." She threw it at him, infuriated by the doleful sound which his pipe made. "You don't care."

She knew that argument could not help; that the fact was established and she must become resigned to it. Yet she shook her head, still trying to resist it, her face crumbling in distress as she said, "You've got what you wanted. He'll be a farmer now like all the Wonnacotts."

She put scorn into her voice, as though to be a farmer were small achievement, much less than an engineer in Birmingham; but later, when the lamp had been blown and the fire made ready for the night, when the candles had climbed the stairs and the stars were at the windows, then she knelt beside the sleeping boy, holding him with an arm, her breath on his cheek.

Then the anger, the disappointment, the sense of being cheated, then all were gone, leaving only a tenderness that said, it's all right, it doesn't matter, perhaps it will work out for the best.

She didn't believe it, so she said it again, slowly and firmly and with conviction. You'll see, it will work out for the best.

Chapter Twelve

Nathan came to the gate, and that was a tribute to the foal, for the old horsebreaker had not walked so far for years. He leaned on his stick, listening to the clamor of his heart and telling his legs to be quiet. He could scarcely speak. His gesture explained that soon he would say something. Just give his heart a chance.

Mark asked, "Are you all right, Mr. Shillabeer?" and Nathan lifted his head. All right? Course I'm all right, nothing wrong with me that five minutes won't put right. He wiped his face with the red handkerchief and put the handkerchief away. Then he straightened. Right then, where's this foal they've been telling me about?

He peered beyond the gate to the mare, then on to the foal. There was the length of the field between mare and foal, and Nathan knew what that meant. The mare was rejecting the foal, tired of its youth, its helter-skelter, its nuzzling. Soon the mare would fetch it a fourpenny one and that would be the end. Not mother and son no more; just strangers, like people in a café.

Nathan narrowed his eyes, groping to see. My daughter's always on about glasses. First 'twas me teeth so I had 'em out and false ones in, and now when I can't eat nothin', Elsie starts on about glasses. As though there's anythin' wrong with me eyes when the weather's right. 'Tis the sun, makin' 'em water.

He took out the red handkerchief for his eyes. "Bring the foal forward a bit, boy. Can't make him out hardly."

Mark was glad to show how merrily the foal would come. He called and the mare looked up as though awakened, while the foal looked all ways, seeking the voice. Then the mare came slowly, and the foal saw her moving and traced the voice. It came in an arc, looking for surprises. Near the gate it stopped, coming no nearer because of the old man on his stick.

The mare did not care about old men on their sticks. She came up for a slice of apple. Her old lips trembled on it, almost dropping it. Then she nodded away the flies and slept beside the gate. She knew that being there would keep away the foal.

Nathan thought, the mare's goin' downhill fast, not much left in her. Then he studied the foal.

"What's your father goin' to do? Sell for a quick profit?"

Mark was shocked. "We wouldn't sell, not for anything."

Nathan cocked a glance. "Steady, boy. Anything's a lot of money and by all accounts your father could do with a quick profit."

Mark waited. Talk of selling was like a foreign language; he did not understand it. He let the subject dig its own grave in the silence. Then he said, "What do you think? With all your experience, Mr. Shillabeer, what do you think of the foal?"

The old man was flattered. It was a long time since anyone had asked his opinion. When you're young, your opinion is too young to be heard; and when you're old, your opinion isn't worth having because you're out of date.

"Can't never tell with a foal. He can look good, then never grow to nothin'. Whereas he can be an ornery-lookin' foal, no more than two farthings and a spit, then put on bone and muscle so that by his third year it isn't the same hoss. You can't never be sure, son. Not even with the best blood."

"But this one? . . ."

"Could be anything. Could be like the mare." Nathan glanced at the boy, realizing his hunger for praise. "Could win a point-to-point even. But take a tip. Don't expect nothin' too soon. Give him time. Give him the sunshine. Time and the sun, they can work wonders. Too many hosses are ruined young because too much is asked of 'em too soon."

A movement on the wall snatched his attention. He pointed to the girl in the red sweater. "Buckpitt's maid, isn't it?"

Mark thought, she's always there, day after day, never speaking, just watching the foal. He said, "Nobody knows what she wants."

"Whatever it is, it won't bring good to nobody except the Buckpitts. Don't never trust the Buckpitts, son. 'Twas they brought the first tractor to the village, and see what happened then. Not a good farm hoss left."

Suddenly Laura jumped from the wall and walked across the field towards them.

"Speak of the devil," Nathan said. "Look at her, walkin' across Yarnator land as if it was Narrastun. You'd think the Buckpitts owned the village."

Laura approached without looking at them. Her head was turned to watch the foal. She said, "I could have had him if I wanted."

Mark remembered the Sunday evening when his mother had defied her father. He said, "You tried."

She made a face. "Not really. I thought I'd like him at first, but then my father said you have to wait so long with a foal. Years and years. So he offered to buy me something better, a three-year-old gray, you can be sure about three-year-olds. Soon the gray will be ready for jumping, then he'll go point-to-pointing, and by the time I'm sixteen I'll win the ladies' race."

She listened to the explanation, and thought that it sounded plausible. She glanced at Mark, and saw that he believed it. But it was not the whole truth. She had left out the quarrel which her father had had with Maddicott and Jordan; they saying, "You're not going to let the Wonnacotts get away with it," while he said, "My daughter got all the ponies anyone could want. It's not good for her to have everything she asks for."

Later, two or three days later, her father had pressed her about the foal; asking did she really want it, you have to wait so long with a foal, wouldn't she rather have a three-year-old? It had seemed important to him and because of that, and because of his quarrel with Maddicott and Jordan which she could not understand, she had given the answer he wanted. Yes, she had said, she would rather have the three-year-old.

It had not been true then. It was not true now. There was something about this foal. She could not take her eyes from it.

Nathan screwed up an eye. "You mean you'd rather have that reject from one of the Newmarket stables which your father picked up cheap? All flash and looks, but small in the head and narrow?"

He waited, but Laura neither answered nor glanced. She thought him a silly old man.

"Heard about him," Nathan said. "The sort to promise everythin' and give nothin', like a politician."

Mark saw her anger and said, "I hope you like the boarding school in September, Laura."

"It will be all right." She shrugged. "My father said I could come home weekends, but I'd rather not."

Mark thought, you'll have to learn French and Latin and goodness knows what. Trigo-something even. And every evening there'll be homework. He was appalled because there might have been a miracle and it might have happened to him.

Out of sympathy he said, "Won't you miss the ponies?"

There was no answering spark in her. Her shrug said somebody else will look after them. There are always plenty of hands at Narrastun.

"Anyway," he said, "you'll be home for the Christmas holidays. The foal will be nearly a year old by then."

"And that old mare will have died." She spoke over her shoulder as she moved away. "You should have her put down. She'll drop dead any day."

Nathan smiled grimly. He put a hand on the mare's forehead. "Poor old Pride of the Moor," he said.

The mare was dead one morning. She lay on a side, her neck stretched out, her eyes wide, and a grin in her teeth. Mark crouched and touched her, his fingers surprised by the cold stiffness.

Howard said, "Better now than in the depth of winter."

Mark moved his hand down her throat and a buzz of flies blew up. He brandished his hands at them, waving them from the holes in her throat. He looked up to his father. "They tormented her for years."

"When you're old," Howard said, "then you go gradual like. You know it's coming, it's like a sleep."

For a day Mark hated the foal because now the field was its own and it could celebrate. It felt free to do as it pleased. It galloped every yard of the field, claiming all its own. Mark was disgusted by such celebration. He vowed never to forget the mare.

"You'll always be her son to me," he said.

But slowly the foal ceased to be a son and became an individual; tall and lean with adolescence, brash with know-all, but a personality in his own right. He ceased to be his mother's son and became "the colt."

By Christmas, Mark had forgotten the mare and did not know he had forgotten.

Howard stretched his legs to the fire, for this was Christmas Eve and Christmas Eve to the Brethren was the great evening of the year.

The rest of the year he obeyed the dogma without question or enthusiasm; unaware that in some of its essentials it was the Puritanism which the first settlers had taken to New England. But at Christmas Eve he cut the ashen faggot with an excited pride, tying it with a conscious skill, then watching it burn in a delight as young as the fire. He felt close to the past on Christmas Eve. There were memories in the flames.

He saw his father clipping white ash with the axe and binding the wood with nut withies, then giving it to the hearth. A while the faggot had sat there, tasted by the flames. Then it had sent up flames of its own; flames that laughed and leaped, like red jesters in a court of kings. A withy had burst, splashing sparks like crumbs of the sun, and at every bursting the cider jug had gone from man to man. "Every withy a drink," they had said.

He saw his brothers and sisters crowding the settle, and the flush of the fire had given them a shining red like apples. He remembered the carols and hymns, and the creep-on of the clock. From half past eleven the clock had dominated the kitchen, for all had known that when one mittened hand covered the other, the hour would be midnight and the day Christmas Day.

The Brethren did not make merry on Christmas Day. To the Brethren the birth of Jesus was the beginning of the crucifixion. They did not say, "They crucified Him," meaning the Jews. They said, "We crucified Him," meaning mankind. So when the clock made midnight come, they did not say, "Merry Christmas," for there could be no merriment in the beginning of Calvary. They said, "It is Christmas Day," and went in quiet like the guilty.

Howard moved his legs, fidgeting less from the fire than

from the taunts which every member of the Brethren must learn to face. He heard Maddicott say, "You've forgot the way to make merry, you know it'll cost good money." He heard Fred Warrener say, "Us go without all the year, surely it can be different at Christmas?" He looked across the hearth to his wife, remembering that first Christmas after his mother died, when Kate had put up paper decorations and decorated a fir tree with tinsel and candles and parcels. She had been shocked by his anger. She had not known how his father had preached on Christmas Day.

Every year his father had preached at the evening meeting, and every year he had told the story of how Christ was born in a stable. Howard remembered the wonderful way he had said "stable"; for to Aaron Wonnacott a stable was no sordid place of humiliation. It was a warm corner made warm by the smell of oxen and urine and straw, as once the moorland farmhouse had been made warm.

Aaron Wonnacott's grandparents had lived under the same roof as their cattle; using the same door, the cattle turning left as they went in, the family turning right. It had been good sense, because the cattle could be fed safely when the snow was high around. It had been warm, too, for the warmth of the animals had kept the kitchen warm; and when Howard's great-grandfather had been crippled with cold, they had sat him against the partition wall, near the animals and their good warmth, knowing that there was no warmer place until winter thawed into the earth and green spring came back.

Howard told the flames, so natural enough my father thought a stable a sensible place. He was never angry about that. He saved his anger for the proud and the rich, for the dice players and the gamblers, for all who had not cared, but especially the gamblers. My father hated gambling like you hate poison in the body.

He saw again the tall figure, straight with conviction, branding them all with the scorn of his rage. Then he had looked upon the watching faces, his sons and daughters among them, and had asked, "If He came again, would us know enough to receive Him different?" Howard saw again the terrible tears, for his father had known the answer and had been ashamed.

The first withy burst and momentarily Howard was startled by the interruption. Then he reached for the jug. "Every withy a drink. Here, Kate, you got to drink."

She took the jug and sipped, making a face at the hot cider. Then he took the jug and drank, wiping his mouth with the back of his hand. The taste reminded him of Jonas Warrener, Fred Warrener's father, and that reminded him of Susie and Susie reminded him of the Christmas charities.

"The parish church had charities for the poor," he said. "People died and willed land for the poor, and every Christmas the rector drew the rents and shared it out in silver. Three half-crowns for poor families with more than eight children, two half-crowns for those with less. That was the parish church, you understand, so of course, being Brethren, none of our family was ever there. But everyone knew what happened."

Mark liked the remembering, understanding that it was a part of Christmas Eve. Only then did he feel himself carried high on the shoulders of dead generations. Only then did he see faces in the fire like photographs in an album.

He said, "What happened, Dad?"

"Well, the rector read the names, calling the mothers from their pews. Susie Warrener had ten children, so she was one of the first, and when she came down the aisle for her three half-crowns, she'd bob a curtsey and mutter something nobody couldn't ever hear, then go back slowly to her pew. But every year everyone noticed that as she got near the pew, she'd go slower and slower, looking down and holding the money, tight in her fist it would be, and when at last she got back to her seat, she'd kneel and pray, saying thanks for the money and praying a long time until at last everyone was watching and she couldn't stay there like that no more. Then she'd sit back beside her husband and Jonas would put a hand on her knee, palm upwards, like that, waiting for the money."

Mark saw the woman in the fire. She had a long black coat, too long for her bowed thinness, and her face was as brown as wood. He said, "Did Jonas always have it?"

"The lot," Howard said. "He'd be drunk for three days on it."

"But why didn't he go up for it himself?"

"Jonas had his pride. He didn't agree with charity. Besides, it was always understood that the mothers went."

"But what about the children? What did they have?"

"Nothing," Kate put in with sudden bitterness. "Only a lecture on sin and the need to go without for the good of their souls."

Howard saw again the great, blubbering figure. "In his younger days Jonas Warrener was a master hand with the scythe. He'd start one end with a swig from the cider jug, then come through the hay with great sweeps of his scythe, working towards the other end of the field where there was another cider jug. Before the sun was down he'd have drunk ten quarts and couldn't answer if you spoke to him. When he was younger it didn't matter much, farmers used to laugh and say, 'Look at Jonas, makin' good time to the cider.' But by the time he was thirty, he couldn't last a hard harvest and soon no farmer would have him for more than a casual day. He used to cry as he sharpened the scythe that nobody would hire, and Susie would scrape together enough for a quart to help him. Susie never understood that one quart couldn't help. It only made him worse."

Howard remembered the little woman, as anxious as a hen and as busy. "For years she put flowers on his grave every

Sunday. Mourning him for a good husband, as a good wife should."

Mark thought, that was Fred Warrener's father and the initials "F.W." are carved in the desk where I used to sit. He said, "Did Grannie Wonnacott ever go?"

"Heavens no. We was Brethren, and even if we hadn't been, my parents would never have given in to charity. We was never rich by valley standards, but you mustn't think we was ever poor. Not by moorland standards in those days. And every penny we worked for. Demon for work my mother was, with her hog's-pudding famous." Howard glanced at his wife. "Isn't that right, Kate?"

Kate looked up from her darning. "They still talk about it at the pannier market."

"Proud of her hog's-pudding my mother was, and another great thing was her wines. Every Christmas Eve, when the boys and maidens was older, Mother would bring out her home-made wines and there would be a toast to Mother. Willie, in Australia now, he'd be here, and Ben, in Canada, he'd be here, and Sam, over Tavistock, he was only courtin' then, while all the daughters would be over with their husbands. I can see Mother now, fillin' the glasses with whatever you liked. Blackberry, rowanberry, elderberry. Then Willie waiting until everyone was ready and sayin', ''Ere's to 'e, Mother, good health to 'e, Mother.' Or after Willie was gone to Australia, it would be Ben and once or twice, when there wasn't nobody else, it was me. I can see her now, waitin' for us all to sip and say, 'Good, Mother, handsome, proper. Nobody makes it like you do, Mother.'"

Howard leaned back, remembering how he had brought Kate into this ceremony of Christmas Eve and how instantly the family had known that this was the girl he would marry. He glanced at Kate, wondering if she remembered.

Kate remembered. She saw the slim girl from Market Town

stepping into the kitchen; wide-eyed with fright because there were so many of them, each with a glass, all staring because she was new and Howard's maid, and because there had been a family joke that Howard would never marry. Too shy, they had said, he never says nothin'.

She had chosen rowanberry wine and the old woman had watched with shrewd, sharp eyes; pricing the town coat, the town shoes, noticing her polished nails and sniffing because her hands had shown no signs of work. Kate had been afraid of the old woman then.

Another withy broke, splashing sparks as though you'd struck the sun. Howard held the jug to Kate, but she shook her head. Then he held it to Mark.

Kate glanced a reproach, but Howard made a go-on gesture; so Mark took the jug and tasted. It smelled sour, it tasted raw. He grimaced, exaggerating the grimace to please his mother.

"Go on," Howard said. "I had my first taste long before I was your age. Father never minded a sup on Christmas Eve, provided it was only Christmas Eve and we waited till we was asked."

Kate lifted her head. She listened. They listened. There were footsteps in the yard and the dog got up.

Kate looked at the clock while Howard said, "Who can it be so late?" She put aside her darning and went to the door. They heard the whine as the porch door opened. They heard her exclamation of surprise. Then she stood aside.

"It's Laura," she said. "Home from school and come to say happy Christmas. Come in, Laura. What a lovely coat."

Howard stood up, then Mark. They watched while Laura gave up her coat, her hat and gloves, and let Kate admire her frock.

"Make room for Laura on the settle. I'll get something to eat and drink."

They noticed that Kate was excited. The flush in her cheeks was not only the fire.

Laura sat on the settle. "It's cold out," she said.

Howard thought, the fire, the maid's hintin' there's not enough fire. He stooped to the pile of logs, giving two to the flames. Over his shoulder he said, "We wasn't expectin' company."

Kate shook her head in warning, for he was nervous and when he was nervous his dialect became as broad as a laborer's. She had noticed it first the day he had met her parents. He had shaken hands and stood in the little kitchen and said something about the weather, and her mother had not understood a word. Be careful now, Kate thought, we mustn't embarrass Mark.

"It's lovely and warm in here," Laura said.

Kate brought ginger wine and mince pies, and there was a flurry of civilities as she distributed plates and pies and glasses.

Laura took the wine and sipped, then put the glass on the seat where the fire could see it. The fire put magic into it. She said, "I came to find out about the colt."

Howard glanced at Kate, wondering if he should answer. She looked to Mark, but Mark said nothing. He was thinking, if only you wouldn't make such a fuss.

"Doing fine," Howard said. "Growing fast. Pity you came so late, you could've seen him."

"Laura can see him tomorrow," Kate said. "How do you like your new school?"

Mark felt Laura tighten, holding in the truth.

"All right," she said, lifting her head. "I like it very much."

Mark thought, what's happened to you at this new school? Something cruel has happened. If it's happened to you, you who always knew everything, what would have happened to me?

Kate said, "I expect your father's very proud. You the only one to pass."

Mark felt the implied reproach. He thought, Laura knew I would never pass. She knew about me and one out of ten. You don't have to explain to her.

"We always hoped Mark would, but you know what boys are. They never concentrate. Always carving their names on desks."

"Like Fred Warrener," Howard said. "He had the best carving in the school in my day."

Laura sipped, then replaced the glass. She raised her head, and Kate was surprised by the gleam of defiance.

Laura said, "I always thought Mark was the cleverest boy."

"Well, now," Howard exclaimed, while Kate said excitedly, "Now isn't that nice. We always knew he was clever if only he would concentrate."

Mark looked at nothing. He was ashamed of his mother, astonished that she could talk such silly talk. Why can't she be as she was before Laura came?

"Of course tomorrow morning will be exciting for you," Kate said. "All the presents. Do you know what they will be?"

"A saddle," Laura said. "Daddy's giving me a new saddle."

"Isn't that nice. It's different for us, the Brethren don't have presents on Christmas morning. But years ago, when I was your age, I remember how important it was."

Kate looked at nothing, remembering the decorated tree in the front room; the candles leaning and the tinsel like starlight, and the little parcels, wrapped in gay paper and tied with red cotton. The larger parcels had been around the base of the tree; each with a red-edged ticket and names written carefully so that Father could read them without hesitation. Every Christmas morning her father had read, "To Kate from Auntie Beat," while her mother had said, "That's Beatrice in Cardiff, she always remembers," and every year Father had kept his gifts until last, making them the most important. "To Kate with love from Dad."

She smiled at the flames, remembering the wrist watch, the bracelet, the necklace. She said, "It's different when you're Brethren, but of course I was always brought up Church of England."

Suddenly Howard said, "Does he know you're here?"

Laura was surprised. "Who?"

"Your father."

"He's coming to call for me. I told him I wouldn't be long."

Howard's eyes said, beats me what you've come for. So Kate put in quickly, "Very kind of you to drop in. It's nice to say happy Christmas. I always think that Christmas should be . . ." She almost said "merry," then let the word go to nothing.

They heard the footsteps before Buckpitt came to the front door. His knuckles were loud, impatient. Kate went to the passage while Laura reached for her coat. She groped at a sleeve, and Mark held it for her. They heard Buckpitt say, "Evening, Mrs. Wonnacott. My daughter . . ."

"Yes, of course, she's coming." Kate held the door wide. "Won't you come in, Mr. Buckpitt?"

They heard the hesitation. Then Buckpitt said, "Not now, thank you. There's a party home. You know how it is on Christmas Eve."

Kate imagined the parlor at Narrastun; bright with electricity and decorations, the carpets deep, the chairs calling you to comfort. All the friends would be assembled; a little drunk because in the Buckpitt family, merriment did not end at midnight. She had heard that at Narrastun the men played cards until morning. Nap was the favorite game. They began gambling for pennies and ended by staking pounds. She was impressed by the recklessness. It made her own Christmas seem stern and thin and cold.

Laura came to the doorway and Buckpitt moved back a pace. They exchanged good nights. "Good night," Laura said. "Good night," Mark said.

"Come in the morning," Kate put in. "Then you can see the colt."

Laura flashed a glance, but did not answer. She went out to her father, and their footsteps hurried to the car.

Kate knew by the footsteps that Buckpitt was angry with his daughter; that she had come without his permission or with his permission reluctantly given. Kate thought, but she's his only child, if she wants to come again, she'll come and Buckpitt will get used to it.

Kate closed the door. She thought, the girl found it different at the new school, such a big school, with the daughters of navy officers and army officers and businessmen. At the village school she was Buckpitt's daughter and that meant a lot. But at this new school nobody knows Buckpitt, he's just a farmer on the moor, so suddenly Laura is a nobody and a boarder, too, that makes a difference. Suddenly she is lonely and she turns to Mark.

Kate smiled in the dark passage. It was an honor really. Not everyone in the village had the Buckpitts call.

Chapter Thirteen

Kate glanced at the clock and the clock sneered. It knew the day was market day. So did the kettle, snoring on its hook. So did the pump, giving up its water with pettish slop.

She brought out the hog's-pudding. It was fat and curled, disgusting like intestines. She was still surprised that people came to the market stall and asked, "Are you killing a pig, Mrs. Wonnacott? Save me a pound next week." They thought hog's-pudding a delicacy.

Mother Wonnacott had taught her how to make it; stuffing shreds of fat pork into the mincer, adding pig's liver and groats, with liberal pepper and salt, then stuffing the mess into the skins, stretching the skins, pushing it in with your hands, smelling the mess beneath your fingernails. Each end of the skin must be stitched with twine. Then the iron boiler and tepid water and more wood to bring the water to a pop of bubbles. You boiled the hog's-pudding briefly, not long enough to burst the skins.

Mother Wonnacott had made hog's-pudding twice a week. Now you could get three shillings a pound, and that's good money, Kate admitted. But I can't make it as Mother Wonnacott made it. She took pride in it, proud of what market people called "that Wonnacott taste." Now when they come to buy, I know that they are comparing mine with hers and saying among themselves, of course it isn't what it used to be.

Kate smiled wryly. Perhaps my disgust of it gets into the

making. Or perhaps it's the pepper. All the Wonnacotts use pepper as thick as pollen; making a fetish of it, so that pepper becomes as important as paraffin and much more important than soap.

She curled up the hog's-pudding in thin white paper and weighed it, then penciled the weights. The pencil was indelible. When she moistened the tip, a purple smear came down her lip. She placed the packages in a basket. Eighteen pounds. That's over two pounds ten. She liked hog's-pudding best when it was packaged for market, dressed up in white, made polite by the paper. Then she could see the money in it and forget the preparation.

Mark came in as she cut his sandwiches. He went to the secondary modern school in Market Town, and that meant he left by train at eight and did not get back until half past five. It made a long day and many farmers complained; for the longer the day, the fewer hours there were to help on the farm. Kate wasn't worried about that. What concerned her was the food.

Meals at the school canteen cost five shillings a week, and there were rumors that boys with country appetites had to make do with town portions. Not enough for a sparrow, some of the mothers said; our Ernie comes 'ome starvin'. So she gave Mark sandwiches and fourpence. The fourpence bought him a cup of tea and he sat in a corner of a back-street café, making the tea last until the sandwiches were gone.

"Warm the butter," she said.

He took a saucer of butter to the flames, and the firelight danced about his head, stressing his need of a haircut.

Perhaps if she had a good day, selling all the eggs as well as the hog's-pudding, perhaps then she would have the two shillings for the haircut. It seemed a terrible price. Two shillings for a boy, and all they do is buzz the clippers and squirt the spray. It's over in five minutes.

"Have your hair cut tomorrow. It's a mop."

He turned the saucer, so that the other side of the butter could see the fire. "Early closing tomorrow."

"Well, Friday then. I'm not having you with hair like that for Sunday."

He got up from the hearth. "Ezekiel could do it."

"Indeed he could not."

Ezekiel tilted your head forward and peered above his spectacles, tick-ticking the clippers up and up until only a lop was left. Ezekiel snipped that with the scissors. "Shut your eyes," he said, and the boys shut their eyes while he snipped a fringe level with their eyebrows. You could tell Ezekiel's customers. They had no foreheads.

"He does it half-price," Mark said, knowing that the shilling would be a powerful argument.

But not powerful enough, Kate thought. Only the poor had their hair cut by Ezekiel.

"Get it cut where you did last time. Short back and sides and a nice parting."

Mark wondered why she did not understand. A Friday haircut meant a long wait; sitting on old magazines, lifting a buttock when somebody wanted an old magazine, compelling yourself to a boredom of patience while men took your turn because they were men and you were young and could afford to wait. The long wait meant the late train home, and the late train home meant darkness; too dark to see the colt, only a groping towards each other, the colt made nervous by the darkness, almost missing the sandwich he had saved from dinner.

"They squirt smelly stuff," he said.

"Only to make you smart. Don't you want to be smart? You look so nice when you're smart."

He put the sandwiches in his satchel, doing it slowly, as though there were no clock, as though there were all day. She hurried him into black shoes and overcoat and cap, making sure he had his fourpence and season ticket, straightening his tie, then asking about his handkerchief, demanding to see it, then taking it away and giving him another.

She watched him to the gate, calling "You've ten minutes for the train," and wondering why he did not hurry. He had run to the village school. He had galloped all the way, riding his imaginary horse. Now he mooched, as though he were round-shouldered; as though he didn't appreciate the new school which had cost such a lot of money.

Kate said to no one, "You'd think he'd be pleased, all that equipment and gymnasium and playing fields. It was never like that when I went."

Three hens heard her voice and looked up, making their necks long and earnest. She remembered their corn and went to the linhay to scoop corn into a corner of her apron. Her hands enjoyed the crawl of it, the firm, shaped goodness. She held it in a fist, the corn bursting from the tips of her fingers as though her fist were a fruit bursting its seeds. Then she threw out the first rain, and the old hens let it hit them. Only a brown pullet half rose with a flap of wings, squawking its stupidity.

She moved into the yard, calling the others. "Cooop, cooop," she called, watching where they came from; the loft, the red cart, the hole in the wall, knowing that where they came from there would be eggs. She let the corner of her apron go down and the wise heads pounced, their combs flopping as red as poppy petals. Then she regathered the corner of her apron, making a cradle for the eggs.

She found an egg in the red cart, another among bracken. She almost stepped on another, her feet flinching back like a cat from water. Then she climbed to the loft. The ladder was upright and fastened to the wall, with the first stave waist high. Once she had been afraid of it, mistrusting its staves, inventing reasons why she should not search the loft; but Howard had found seventeen eggs there, all addled, and the waste had condemned her cowardice. The next day she had made herself climb. For months she had dreamed wildly and always of falling.

Now she went up quickly, putting one knee on the floor of the loft and pushing herself from the ladder. She peered through the gloom, protecting the eggs in her apron like a mother protecting her child in war. Then she straightened and followed the hen droppings to a corner. One egg was warm. She found another and another. She thought there should be more. Five hens had come from the loft, so there must be more.

She looked beyond a litter of cut bracken to the darkest corner. She heard nothing, saw nothing, but she knew that life was there. She moved towards it, bending beneath a beam, feeling the drag of cobwebs in her hair. The cat was there. It opened its mouth and the sound it made was a hot hiss. Its tail was low and twitched in warning.

Kate thought, oh, no, not again. She peered into the darkest corner; to the muddle of old coat and the grope of blind heads in the middle of it. She counted four with a heavy sadness. "You silly thing," she said, while the cat came between her and the kittens; thin and brave and ragged, all its goodness given to the kittens. "You know what will happen," Kate said.

What had to happen; for kittens soon became cats and you couldn't have cats swarming the place. Once she had asked Howard why the barn cat must always be a she-cat, and he had answered, "She-cats hunt good," and that was sense. Barn cats were not pets. They were there to hunt, and the more vermin they destroyed, the more they served their purpose; never mind the kittens and the drowning.

The cat watched, knowing that they shared the secret of the kittens.

"I won't tell anyone. Not yet. But you are a silly cat. You always cry and make such a fuss."

Kate thought, I'm still squeamish. I can't destroy easily, not even kittens which nobody wants.

"You'd better come with me. Have some milk before I go." Kate moved away, making a come-on noise with her mouth. But the cat did not move. "Stay there then. Silly thing."

She went down the ladder to the last stave, pausing there for the long stride to the ground. The hens were still scratching. They looked down like women in a factory. They watched their yellow clawing as those women watch their fingers.

She hurried across the yard and a sly movement in the porch told her that the cat was there. She took the eggs from her apron and put milk into a saucer. Then she stood between the cat and the yard, sheltering it if Howard should come. The Wonnacotts knew better than to feed their barn cats; for hungry cats make the best hunters.

The cat turned from the saucer and looked both ways. Kate picked up the saucer hurriedly, as though it were evidence. Then the cat moved, slipping through a group of hens like a suspect through a crowd. The hens knew about it. They muttered about it as they watched their clawing; talking about it as women in a factory talk about the foreman.

Kate watched it go; back to the loft and the kittens. At the back of her mind her thoughts said, Mother might have one and Mrs. Farley at number five and Mrs. Bryant at number nine, they might have one. In a brief flare of hope she thought she might find homes for all of them, but another voice said, you never will, you tried before, nobody wants cats.

She added the new eggs to the basket. She washed the dishes. She brought in new logs, making the fire strong enough to last until midday when Howard would be in. She put out a plate of meat for Howard's dinner. Then she opened a drawer of the brown cupboard for her shopping list. Cotton white, no. 40; gray darning wool; two brown buttons; three yards elastic; soap powder, steel wool, pepper, toothpaste, boot laces. The list was long, but she thought it should be longer. She stood a moment, a fingernail between her teeth, wondering what else they would need before next market day.

The clock said twenty minutes. Time to wash and change; to put on the frock which had been new in 1948, her town stockings and town shoes, her brown hat and coat, to smudge a little powder on her nose, but no lipstick, the Brethren didn't approve. She found her gloves, looked in her handbag for the fare, then took egg basket in one hand, hog's-pudding basket in the other, and went to the yard.

She called Howard and his voice answered.

"Is there anything you want?"

The silence thought. Then his voice said, "Can't think of nothing." But she guessed that five minutes too late he would think of something.

"I'm away then. Your dinner's on the table. And keep the fire in."

She heard his boots in the barn, and waited until he appeared.

"You got enough hog's-pudding?"

"Yes," she said. "Enough for all the regulars."

He came towards her slowly. He was embarrassed, for some men kissed their wives good-by but he could not kiss easily, lightly, as though it meant nothing.

They shared a long glance, and her half-smile said, it's all right, I know about the kissing. She moved away, saying "Must hurry, don't forget to keep the fire in," knowing that he was watching her towards the gate.

He said, "You look nice, Kate," not loudly, just loud enough for her to hear, and she flashed a glance; suddenly younger, fourteen years younger, although she knew it was not true. Her brown coat and hat were shabby. So were her shoes. She looked what she was; a moorland wife who hadn't enough money.

She hurried along the highway to Post Lane; then down the short cut, the loose stones grumbling at her shoes. Twice a year the parish council said there must be tarmac for the short cut, but it was never done. Every spring it was rutted by the flood water of winter, and every summer feet pushed the stones into the ruts, ready for the new snow and the new flood water. Everyone who used the short cut said, what do we pay taxes for?

Elsie Shillabeer heard Kate coming and turned and waited. "Makes you wonder, Mrs. Wonnacott. What do we pay taxes for?"

Kate flickered a smile, the baskets pulling at her arms. She knew that Elsie would accompany her to the station, talking all the way about plucking chicken and the way it cuts your fingers or about Nathan and his obstinacy. You were not expected to answer.

There were flowers at the station. They covered the grave of Pharaoh. Pharaoh had been the station cat, the best known cat of the branch line, as aloof as an emperor and as fat. Pharaoh had owned the line. When he had wished to cross, he had crossed, asking permission of none. The engine had slowed, and if he had stopped halfway and glanced, like a cat which is in no mood to hurry, the engine had stopped, with the driver leaning out. Pharaoh had crossed the line once a week in this way; but the driver had never known which day, and had approached the station in an anxiety of peering.

Then one day there had been a deputy driver, a stranger who had not known, accompanied by a fireman who had not known that Pharaoh would choose this day. Pharaoh had crossed the line and stopped halfway to glance and the train had kept coming.

They had buried Pharaoh with ceremony, putting up a granite stone with a chiseled epitaph; the name, the date, and the words "*Exegi monumentum aera perennius.*" It had been suggested by the rector and none had agreed until he had offered to pay for it. The village understood that it meant, "I have reared for myself a monument more enduring than bronze."

"Train's in," Elsie said. She raised a hand and the fireman answered. They knew then that they were safe, for the train would not pull out without them. The train had eyes and never left when it saw people hurrying down the hill.

They reached the station with its brown bench and green booking office and photograph of Hereford. A face appeared at the little window. This was Harry; his official hat pushed to the back of his head, his fingers busy with brown change.

"Mornin', Mrs. Wonnacott. Your boy went off all right on the early train. Mornin', Elsie. How's old Nathan? Doin' the Highland fling yet?"

"Here," Elsie said, "not so much of your chick. He could dance like a jinny in his day."

Kate took her ticket and passed to the platform. The engine driver raised a hand, acknowledging that he knew her father, who was an engine driver at Market Town. Then he and the fireman threw their voices to Elsie, teasing her and relishing her laughter.

"See you're courting again, Elsie," the fireman said. "Proper man-killer you must be."

Kate thought this cruel, for Elsie was nearly forty and everyone knew that she would never marry. But Elsie laughed in a high scream. "Ate better than you before breakfast," she said.

Kate stepped into the long carriage. It had two long seats

under the windows, with the other seats facing each other and wide enough for two. It made the passengers a community, compelling you to become a member however reluctantly. Kate was reluctant. She said "Good morning" to the faces, then sat, both baskets on the seat beside her to ensure a little privacy. Kate thought this privacy important. She considered it polite.

Then Elsie came in and the welcoming cries were flushed. Women who had seen her every day of the week cried, "Hello, Els, how's the world servin' 'e, Els," as though they had not really met since last Wednesday, when they had last traveled by train to Market Town.

Elsie was telling them about Nathan as she sat down. "I got the doctor in without lettin' on, tellin' the doctor straight, he's never for this world much longer, poor gentleman, can't eat his Sunday dinner even. But when the doctor went up, there the old toad was, sot up in bed with his hat on, crackin' off about if only he had his teeth he'd show us the way to eat. 'Give us back the teeth I was born with,' he holleys. ''Twas your idea to have'm out and I haven't been the same man since.' Shamed me in front of the doctor, he did. Wouldn' let'm touch'm, not sound his chest even, though I reckon he's got the best chest in the parish."

Kate thought, they say that she was engaged once, but her mother died and there was Nathan, and after a while the man went away. Now she has her fowls and her stall on market day, with scrubbing three mornings a week at the White Hart. Somehow she makes a living, then boasts about her father; how spry he is for his age, how obstinate, how fussy about what he eats and how it is cooked and why can't nobody make tea in the proper way these days?

They watched from the window for Bessie Warrener; fat and red and always late. She came with her baskets; snow-drops, daffodils, blackberries, primroses, mushrooms, whatever free harvest was in season. Her five children picked the free harvests, experts at seven years old, picking and bunching while Bessie said, "Another twenty bunches and us'll have tea." Sometimes other children, bored with idleness, volunteered to pick, striving to be as expert as the Warrener children, liking Bessie for her laughter and generosity of spirit.

"Come on, Bessie," they cried at the windows. "All behind like the cow's tail."

"'Twas all me money," Bessie panted, putting down a brown bag, a basket, an umbrella, and her youngest daughter. "Counting all me money took so long."

She laughed and they laughed. Everyone knew that she had only pennies in her purse.

The guard said, "You all right, Bess?"

"All right now. But I wouldn' have been right if I'd been left."

They laughed again, and the guard leaned out. "Right away, Bill." Then the train hissed in its breath and the first sound slumped forward. It seemed that the station was moving. The journey down the valley began.

The talk was of babies and funerals. Fanny Jefferson over to Stoneygate, Fanny Webber that was, she got another, seven-pound boy, red hair like all the Webbers, all of them got heads as red as fire; while over to Bridlestone, Grannie Doble have got trouble again, her youngest grandson sent to prison, always pinchin', if not from his employers then from his poor ole gran, but the old soul stands up for him, won't hear a word against him.

It astonished Kate that they could know so much. A farm-hand falls from a ladder and they know; they know what the farmer said and the doctor and what the inspector said about insurance. A child has whooping cough and they know how many nights its parents have gone without sleep. A son in New Zealand writes to his mother and they know; what he wrote and when he is coming home and how much money he has made in three years.

Kate thought, it shows what gossip can do; passed in from remote cottages to the village, then through the village with incredible speed. No rumor gets by Elsie's door. She's always on the step to meet it.

"What about the branch line, then?" Elsie cast the bait and they listened. "They say they're going to shut it." She waited until they were suitably shocked. "Don't pay, that's what they say. All the branch lines in the country, they're all going to go."

Bessie Warrener expressed horror. She was always the best listener. "Go on. They wouldn't dare."

"They'd dare anything," Elsie said.

Her "they" was a remote power; far away and almost invisible, so that you had to look up to discern it dimly. This was the "they" which took young men into the army; wasting two years when they could be working in the fields or learning a trade, playing football and cricket for village teams or singing tenor in the choir. It was the "they" which increased fares and made part of the moor a military training ground, then fined Sybil Harvey five shillings for riding her bicycle without a lamp.

Elsie's "they" was capable of anything. More tobacco duty; chlorine in the water; buttons loose on coats; prices high when you wanted to buy and prices low when you had to sell. The power of her "they" reached in all directions. You could not escape it. "They" had taxed daylight years ago. "They" would be taxing breathing next.

"It's so many cars," Bessie Warrener said. "Practically all the farmers got cars. Think of how many go to market by car nowadays. All of them used to go by train. One time there were five carriages every market day. Now look, there's only us."

They mourned the threat to their branch line; its importance enhanced by the threat. They didn't know how they would live without it. Buses seemed a poor substitute, especially in winter.

"Never mind," Bessie said. "Dare say us will all have our Rolls Royce by then."

Kate looked out to the moor. Scars down the hill were as black as coal quarries. She knew that the commoners had been burning the bracken, not to destroy it, for the wild hills would grow nothing else and bracken had its uses; but to provide strength for the new. The black ash was potash. Rain would soak it into the ground and soon what had been charred stubble would be growing green again.

The burning made men as young as boys. They liked to see the flames run, to hear the fire's appetite and know that this fire was swayling and that swayling in February was permitted. She thought that swayling to the moorland men was as much a spree as Guy Fawkes' bonfires were to towns. The same excitement, the same delight in permitted destruction.

Mrs. Harvey said, "How's your boy doing at the new school?"

None answered and Kate realized with a start that Mrs. Harvey was talking to her.

"Very well. He likes it."

"My boy don't." Mrs. Harvey's eyes were sharp in rebuke. "My boy says why couldn't they let him stay at the village school instead of travelin' so far to another school where everyone laughs at the way he speaks, and there's nothin' but music lessons and algebra and cross-country runnin' and messin' about with things like country dancin'. By the time he gets home he's fagged out," Mrs. Harvey said. "Can't chop the sticks for morning hardly."

Mrs. Stone agreed. She spoke for the first time. "My Lily hadn't been there a week and the headmaster was on about school uniform. Gym slip and white blouse, blazer and tie and hat and a blue raincoat for the rain. Think of the cost. Eight pounds if a penny, and my husband on six pounds ten a week."

She shook her head. Distress and bewilderment were in her eyes, for she wanted her daughter to wear what others wore. She put a hand on her basket. Beneath the brown paper were jars of jam; blackberry, whortleberry, gooseberry, made the previous summer. Each week she brought in twenty-four jars for her twenty-four customers. By three o'clock each market day she had thirty-six shillings, and could fill her basket with things her family needed. She always bought half an ounce of tobacco for her husband. It was his tobacco for the week.

She said, "If it wasn't for the jams, I don't know how we'd manage now." She lifted her head and said with sudden scorn, "Never mind the headmaster and his fine ideas."

Kate thought, soon I'll afford the uniform for Mark; the cap and blazer and tie and badge. The badge was important. It showed that you belonged.

She riffled back the weeks to September when Mark had moved to the new school; counting the weeks, for each week she had saved two shillings, and twenty-four weeks meant forty-eight shillings. Soon Mark would have his blazer and cap; with the badge on the pocket to show that his was a good school, almost a grammar school.

"Never mind," Bessie Warrener said. "Perhaps soon us'll all go nudist and save a fortune."

They were laughing as the train fussed into the station. They stood up, fumbling for their baskets and umbrellas, counting their gloves and remembering their handbags.

"Mustn't forget Father's peppermints," Elsie said. "He's wicked enough the best of times."

Kate stepped down. The branch-line train had its own bay; a stunted platform, much shorter than the other platforms, but too long for the carriage. It seemed that the one carriage diminished the importance of the line, of the village it served, and of the goods which the women brought to sell.

Kate hurried, less towards the market than away from Elsie and Bessie and Mrs. Harvey and their companions. They think I'm a snob, Kate thought, but it's not that at all, it's just that I'm not like they are. I wasn't born in the village. I didn't go to school in the village. I don't know all the family histories. This town is home to me.

The ticket collector recognized her. He played skittles with her father. He was one of the Loco Dynamos, and it was understood at her parents' home that to play skittles for the Loco Dynamos was to be exalted; like playing football for the Arsenal or rugby for the Harlequins. Only serious players were considered eligible. There was no room for frivolity when these railwaymen played their favorite game.

Kate smiled. To be recognized in this way deepened her sense of coming home. She went down the stairs towards the busy sounds; loving this town with its spires and red buses and black taxis, its pretty girls tap-tapping the pavements with high heels. It had energy, a sense of going somewhere. You could tell that it believed in itself; that prosperity had kept the old town young.

She strode quickly, like the young, feeling the gentle wind and laughing at it; for she had left the real wind on the moor. She crossed the square towards the pannier market; excited by the crowds, by the confusion of cars, by the policeman keeping his temper with a woman driver.

There were too many stalls for the market, so some crowded the pavements, as temporary as tents. They sold clothes and fruit and corn cures. A man put his bare foot on a stall, demonstrating the corn cure. The foot was wonderfully clean, like a foot in hospital. It made you look. Five women half turned to leave as though in a hurry, yet they could not leave. They leaned towards the foot in fascination.

Kate reached the entrance to the pannier market and suddenly all elation bled away. She was returned to a small community, all of whom knew you and what you sold and at what price; a community with its own jealousies and jokes, a rural community gathered for the day from many villages, a temporary village of its own which talked politely to customers but kept its real talk to itself, making strangers of all who did not understand.

Kate did not understand. She could not laugh at the old jokes or share the important jealousies. She could not escape a sense of shame; as though to sell in the market was to hawk, a public demonstration of your poverty. She lived the day in fear that someone she had known at school would recognize Kate Philbin as the woman in the brown coat, selling pigs' intestines at three shillings a pound.

The Wonnacotts had thirty-six inches of space between clover honey on one side and clotted cream on the other. Mother Wonnacott had defended every inch of it, poaching inches from clotted cream when she could; but Kate did not care. She knew that both clover honey and clotted cream were closing in, reducing her thirty-six inches to thirty, taking from her the right to be there. Once they had expected her to retaliate, to answer silent trespass with silent defense and establish her place in the community. Now they knew she did not care. They sighed for the days when Mother Wonnacott had made the fight worth fighting.

Kate spread white paper on the trestle table, then arranged her eggs and hog's-pudding. She heard Bessie and Elsie come into the market, shouting and laughing, Elsie saying, "He got a big toe just like mine." Then the customers came in.

Years ago Kate had supposed that to buy at the market was not nice, rather common; less respectable than buying at the big stores in High Street. She had supposed that those who came were poor wives, looking for bargains. Now she knew better, but she was still surprised that so many well-spoken women, ladies obviously, came each Wednesday morning for home-made jams and marmalade, for honey and cream and home-made bread, for boiled sweets and fudge and home-made cakes. They made a fetish of the home-made.

Others saw them buying and were persuaded that the home-made must be more nutritious, or at any rate more fashionable, with the result that soon you had a cult of the home-made; as though what was produced in the country cottage, preferably thatched, must be superior to that produced in a clean, efficient, and ventilated factory. So wives who regarded their kitchens as temporary places, like telephone kiosks, bought the home-made because to buy was cheaper and easier and cleaner than to make their own. "Try this jam," they said to guests. "Home-made," they added, and let silence do the rest.

Kate saw her customers coming through the crowd. She knew them by name and leaned across the table, making small talk about the weather; but she could not call up family histories in the fashion of Mother Wonnacott, whose memory had never faltered. Mother Wonnacott had sold many customers six ounces short while inquiring about their son John who went to America in 1919 and had seven children and who had cured his warts with the bean pod.

Some of the regular customers were Brethren, for there was a Brethren chapel in a back street; and all the Brethren were old. Kate thought, I've noticed that before. At every meeting almost all the heads are gray. The children come with their parents for as long as they must. Then, when they are fifteen or sixteen, they begin to fidget and cough, and soon they disappear and you never see them again; rejecting the religion of their fathers and no wonder. So strict, Kate thought, making a virtue of going without.

It was a good morning. Her hog's-pudding was gone in an hour. By noon only a dozen eggs remained and Mrs. Bellenger would call for them punctually at half past. Mrs. Bellenger had bought a dozen eggs at the Wonnacott stall every week for forty years, and her mother had bought from Howard's grandmother. There was a formidable quality about such loyalty.

Kate knew, and Mrs. Bellenger knew, that Yarnator eggs were neither better nor cheaper than eggs of other stalls. But every Wednesday at half past twelve, Mrs. Bellenger passed ten other stalls to reach the Wonnacott. It's habit, Kate thought. What a power that is.

She packed the eggs into the basket which the gray woman offered. Almost she said, "And how's Mr. Bellenger?" but caution took the civility and tore it up. Was there a Mr. Bellenger? Or had he died years ago? Mother Wonnacott would have known. She would have known all about Mr. Bellenger and any other Bellengers; charming the transaction with five minutes of gossip.

"Thank you very much. Good morning." The little woman moved away. Not by word or glance did she convey dismay, but Kate knew she was disappointed. Every week I disappoint you. I don't know enough about the world you carry around in memory.

She folded her white paper. You can have your silly stall; you clover honey and you clotted cream. You can spread out your pots in an orgy of trespass, meeting in the middle as though the Wonnacott stall does not exist. She almost laughed, mocking their small jealousies. She glanced right to clotted cream, still several pounds to sell; but her glance to clover honey was longer and cruel, for clover honey had sold nothing. Everyone knew why. The Shepherd stall in a corner offered heather honey, and a town which loved its moor, if only as a wilderness to be seen from the Sunday car, preferred the honey sucked from the heather bell. The association of images was the more compelling.

Clover honey understood the glance and replied in a silent natter of knitting needles. Every Wednesday her needles busied the hours away; like an itch which you must scratch and keep on scratching. It was as though she came to sit on an upturned box and knit; with the jars of clover-honey decorations merely, like ornaments on a mantel shelf.

Good for you, Mrs. Shepherd, Kate thought. May your bees prosper and the heather last forever.

There was a jauntiness in her as she passed out of the market to the square. She had money in her purse and three hours of leisure. She was a customer now; flattered by politicians and advertisers and newspapers, especially by magazines; a person of power for whom windows were dressed and slogans prepared, because of whom vast fortunes were invested in the production of what experts thought she wanted or could be persuaded to want.

She moved from window to window; slowly, leisurely, for this was her half-hour of the week. A man might feel near wealth as he completed his football coupon, prolonging the completion to prolong the experience. She felt within arm's length of possession as she studied television sets, electric kettles, electric irons, bedroom suites, coffee tables, summer coats, and Easter hats. There was only the glass between.

The clock above the square shook its head; a private reproach, like the vicar saying no to a choirboy. The reproach said, time for your shopping list, so she took out her shopping list, putting aside electric irons and bedroom suites for soap powder and steel wool.

Assistants in the young, smart shops tilted their chins in an aggressive movement which said, you next; making her not a housewife with power in her purse, but a shabby woman in a brown coat saying, "Two packets of porage oats, please," as though to be served was to be favored. She admired these young shops for their bright paints and gloss, but she saved until last the purchase of darning wool, two buttons, and three yards of elastic, for their purchase would take her into the twilight of Bawdicombe's, where it was always yesterday.

There the assistants were grave and deferential, inquiring madam's pleasure, offering madam a chair, then accompanying madam to the window so that the wool could be seen in something of which Bawdicombe's did not really approve, called daylight.

Bawdicombe's was proud of its long tradition of supplying the rural community; still sure that the rural community wore heavy serge and thick woolens, shapeless dresses and flannel and calico, apparently unaware that the coat which "never wears out" could be a curse since it gave a woman no excuse to buy new. There was affection for Bawdicombe's, so old-fashioned and slow and courteous. There was more affection than there were customers.

Kate checked her list and thought, daffodils, Mother likes daffodils. She bought a bunch, admiring the trumpets blowing like the heralds of Easter. She thought, I like daffodils, too; they're my favorite flower. They represented the picturesque countryside. You could see in them the orchard in the valley, the trees sore and red with buds, the daffodils a yellow carpet where the grass should be. They belonged to the polite countryside. They could not stand up in a wilderness blown to pieces by the wind.

She placed the daffodils in a basket; carefully, like a baby in a cradle. Then she turned from the street towards Church Terrace; eighteen houses with brown doors and neat windows, dressed in a uniform of red brick, with precise cement for piping and yellow chimneys for epaulets. But Kate knew that this uniformity was deceptive; for at the back of every house its individuality was expressed. Number three had its chrysanthemums; number four its rabbits; number ten its pigeons. Twice a day these pigeons circled the chimneys, the young birds spiraling in ecstasies of speed, the old birds plodding round and round, waiting for the chatter of beans in a tin and the right to come down. Meanwhile number eleven watched; waiting for the pigeons to misjudge their flight and come to the wrong roof. Then she would scream to her husband, "They're on our slates again."

The Philbins remained aloof from all this; for Kate's father was an engine driver, a main-line mileage driver, one of the elite. He appreciated the responsibilities of the position and lived quietly and temperately; making his garden the neatest, his broccoli the biggest, his peas the earliest, his paint the brightest, his pipe the cleanest, his shave the smoothest; permitting himself two glasses of stout with his skittles, two sentences of conversation with his immediate neighbors, but otherwise abstemious, watching his rugby in silence, listening to cricket commentaries with no more expression of dismay or elation than he granted the Sunday sermon. The terrace respected Alfred Philbin. Children did not play at his door; cats did not walk across his garden. He was of the terrace but a little above it. His wife was proud of that.

Mrs. Philbin heard the brown door as it opened. "Only me," Kate said.

Her mother came from the kitchen; short and stout and gray, her flowered overall immaculate, her shoes as polished as the linoleum. "Daffodils," she said, as Kate held out the bunch. "Now isn't that kind. I'll put them in the front window, so Father will see them as he comes in."

Kate sat. She did not sit in the chair on the left of the shining range; for that was her mother's chair. She did not sit in the chair opposite, beside the wireless and folded newspaper and ash tray; for that was her father's. She half turned a chair from the table and sat with a sigh, suddenly aware of her feet, of her need for a cup of tea.

"The kettle's on," her mother said. "It won't be a minute."

Kate smiled, looking around the room; the glass cupboard with the silver cup, the tea service which had been a wedding gift, the photograph of two strangers who were mother and father on their wedding day.

She called, "Have you heard from Barbara?"

Her mother answered from the scullery. "A long letter last Friday. All about Richard and how he's doing, building roads, and about Tony and how well he's doing at school, and a bit about the native servants. So stupid and deceitful, you can't trust them."

Kate thought, servants, and made a little mocking movement. She was mocking herself; the woman who carried buckets from the pump.

Her mother came in with a tray. "And how's Howard?"

"Fine," Kate said. "It's been a good winter for the sheep. High percentage of lambs and four twins."

Mrs. Philbin poured the tea. "And Mark at the new school?"

"Fine," Kate said. "He likes it. It's almost like a grammar school."

"I saw him in the town on Monday. He wasn't wearing the school uniform."

Kate sipped. "It's rather expensive."

"Father said that if he passed for the grammar school, we would help with the blazer and cricket flannels and rugby boots. But seeing he didn't pass . . ."

Kate put down her cup. "It's all right. Perhaps we were wrong to want him to go to the grammar school. Once I was sure, sure as sure can be, but now, now I don't know."

"He can still go to the technical college in the city." Mrs. Philbin poured more tea. "They train for good jobs there. Hotel managers and the like."

Kate nodded, not really believing it. The technical college would mean living in the city from Monday to Friday, and lodgings in the city would cost money.

"There are grants," Mrs. Philbin said.

Kate nodded, not really believing that either. Grants in education, as in agriculture, were less a help to the poor than a donation to those who already possessed. You could build a new barn for three hundred pounds and claim one hundred from the Ministry, reducing the cost to two hundred; but you needed the three hundred to claim the one hundred, and if the contractor knew about the grant, he increased his estimate to four hundred with the argument that you were still getting your barn for two hundred and seventy. Or thirty pounds less than the fair price.

Kate thought, Buckpitt, Maddicott, Jordan, they're the kind who claim grants.

She stared so long at nothing that her mother said, "Don't think I want to interfere, but how much longer can you be expected to carry on like this? You wear yourself out, no water, no electric, no gas, and every week those heavy baskets for market. You work your fingers to the bone and what help do you get, what encouragement?"

Kate shook her head. "It's not as bad as that, Mother."

"When I think of the opportunities you could have had."

She looked to the window and the neat, purposeful garden. Kate knew she was thinking of Chris, who had persuaded her to join the operatic society; they had sung together in the chorus of "Rio Rita." Or of Stanley, who had been secretary of the cycling club and was now an insurance agent.

"With a bungalow and a car," Mrs. Philbin said. "Everyone says how well he's getting on. And when I think of

Barbara in South Africa, waited on hand and foot. It's not that I want to interfere, but in fifteen years, Kate, you've changed."

Kate thought, that's true. She looked to the mirror and the stranger there. In her head she was still the girl of twenty; never pretty, never as pretty as Barbara, but with her hair neat, her costume tailor-made, her blouse snowdrop-white, as crisp as the icing of a wedding cake. The girl in her head had nice eyebrows, good eyebrows, good teeth; she shampooed her hair every Friday and polished her nails twice a day. But the face in the mirror was another woman; her eyes dark with tiredness, her hair wagged ragged by the wind. A shabby woman in a brown coat, her shoulders rounded by the drag-down of buckets, her nails broken, her body smelling of hurry. A moorland woman, old while still young.

This stranger in the mirror, this is me, Kate thought, me as Yarnator has made me. Yarnator and the wind and the cold and the postman bringing bills. In ten years I will be as old as Mother Wonnacott seemed to me that first Christmas Eve when I chose the rowanberry. I should have known, I should have seen, but being old then was something that happened to others. It couldn't happen to me.

Her mother said, "I didn't mean to upset you. It's so difficult to know what to do for the best. If a mother stands by and says nothing, she doesn't care. But if she refuses to stand by and says something, then she's interfering."

Kate thought, if only I could stay here like this, with my eyes closed, doing nothing, just resting, then the woman in the mirror would go away and the girl would come back. All I need is rest; rest from worrying about enough paraffin and candles, about dry wood and furze for the fire, about the bills in the desk in the parlor, the desk that Howard won't open until you make him; rest from the pump and the carrying and the cobwebs in the loft; rest from the wind and the rain and the watching for snow. Give me that and the girl in my head will come back. The girl in my head is not really gone, not gone forever, like the dead.

She said, "Does Mrs. Farley want a kitten? Or Mrs. Bryant? Do you want a kitten?"

"Well, no, Kate, I told you before. We had our Jumbo and when he passed away, Father decided never to have another. You know how attached he was to Jumbo."

Kate's head made a little despairing movement, for she had known what the answer would be. The explanation did not matter. She said, "How is he?"

"He's on the Paddington run. He said be sure to give you his love on Wednesday." Mrs. Philbin returned from the scullery with more tea and two aspirins. "One or two will do you good. You look tired out, Kate."

Kate thought, it's nice to be fussed over, nice not to have to make the tea and find the aspirins, nice just to sit and feel the quiet. She put an aspirin on her tongue and sipped. The aspirin stayed. She sipped again, forcing the aspirin down.

"You can't have eaten," Mrs. Philbin said. "Every week you go without dinner."

Kate thought, how do you explain that after six days on the moor, a half-hour window-looking is more necessary, more sustaining than beans on toast in a crowded café?

She glanced at the clock. Its figures were so ornate that they almost confused; belonging to another age which had leisure to adorn the trivial and the conceit to call it craftsmanship.

"I must fly." She stood up. "I have to meet Mark at the corner."

"He'll carry your basket." Mrs. Philbin offered her cheek to be kissed. "Good-by, dear, take great care and keep well wrapped. Mark, too, take good care of Mark."

Kate gathered her gloves, her baskets and handbag. "Oh, Mark's fine. Doesn't think of anything except his colt."

Mrs. Philbin didn't reply to that, but her mouth made a slight pout of disapproval. She thought, more education and less horses, that's the way to get on.

Kate passed to the hall where an umbrella and a walking stick sloped arms in the brown stand. The framed photograph on the wall was of men, made fierce by mustaches, standing beside an engine. The man on the left was her father. It was his first engine, and he spoke of it as racing men speak of Golden Miller.

"Good-by, Mother. See you same time next week."

"I'll have the kettle ready," Mrs. Philbin said.

"Ask Mrs. Bryant and Mrs. Farley. You never know."

"Well," her mother said, "I'll ask."

Mrs. Philbin watched her daughter go down Church Road, and Kate knew that she was watching and straightened, striding vigorously, militantly almost, as though to deny that she was old and tired and shabby. She kept up this pretense as she reached Tower Clock corner, where Mark waited.

He took the heavier basket, then hesitated and shuffled to the outside of the pavement. Her heart smiled. You'll never know what that little courtesy means to me. It shows that you remember the important details; opening a door, giving up your seat in a bus. Those courtesies make gentlemen. They also make ladies.

She said, "Did you have a good day?"

"All right," Mark said.

"How many marks for chemistry?"

He had told her often that there were not marks but degrees; A, B, and C. A was very good, B was good, and C was fair. Always she said, "Well, it seems so silly. Why can't they give you nine out of ten, so you know where you are?"

They reached the station and crossed the bridge to the

branch-line bay. There were two carriages for the return journey, for the school children and the returning women made it the busiest train of the week.

The journey home was long and jaded. Elsie cried, "I reckon he got the most famous foot in four counties," but the response was tired. The women were thinking of all the work which had accumulated at home. Their morning sense of adventure was dead. Only sore feet and heavy baskets remained.

"As long as Winston kept the fire in," Bessie said.

Boys from the other carriage stormed through in a mood of mischief. Joe Maddicott tipped Mark's cap, mocking because he sat with his mother. Kate stared coldly at nothing, but Bessie half rose.

"Another word out of you, Joe Maddicott, and I'll dangle you out of the window."

Joe said, "My father . . ." but Bessie had an answer for that. "You and your father, too. He's no more than two pennorth of wind in a halfpenny bag."

The boys retreated and Kate darted a glance of gratitude. Bessie screwed up her face in pain. "Me feet's killing," she said.

The engine panted up Gallows Hill; up and up, looking for the moor and the wind and the granite. Kate watched from the window, knowing what she would see when at last the climb was done; the moor leaning from the wind, blown sideways by a wind the like of which Market Town never knew. It never lets you alone, Kate thought. The wind always seems worse when you've been away for a while.

The train ran towards the first gray walls of the village. They got up, staggering with the sway of the train, thinking about standing, like a drunk who knows that he must reach the door.

"Nice to smell the clean air," Elsie said. "I wouldn't like

to live in no town. Nothing but gasoline fumes and smoke, and they're always diggin' up the roads."

Cyril, the other porter, was there to greet them. The village called him General because his father had been a corporal in Kitchener's army. "Had a good day?" General said, rallying them as soldiers need to be rallied in the last mile of a long march. Elsie answered, "I got some corn cure, couldn' resist it," but others gave up their tickets without a word.

Kate and Mark climbed the short cut. It seemed longer now because of the climb. Then they turned towards Yarnator, Mark's stride lengthening until he was a yard ahead and looking back impatiently. She put out a hand for the basket. He gave it to her and ran; climbing the wall and jumping and running.

She thought, the colt, he only comes alive when he can be near the colt.

By the time she reached the gate, Mark was handling the young horse; talking with his hands while it stood with ears pricked, proud with youth, trembling with a strength of which nothing but play had yet been demanded.

Kate passed through the gate. The dog came to meet her; the hens, too, their eyes red with reproach, telling her that they had not been fed. She made a little despairing sound, hurrying because of all that must be done before dusk.

She reached the porch, then looked up to a movement in the field. Howard was there, his waistcoat open, his shirt sleeves rolled to the red bone of his elbows. His cap was on the back of his head, pushed there like a cap which could belong to no other head. He was looking down to the porch.

He raised a hand and she raised a hand. It was their signal that market day was over. She went into the kitchen, suddenly happy because of this signal which said more than words could ever say. It was a sign of home.

Howard waited a moment before turning to his work. It's always like this on Wednesdays, he thought. It's the longest day of the week. The house seems cold as a coffin until she comes home. Even the windows know.

Chapter Fourteen

Nathan said, "Where's me hat?" meaning his especial hat, his horse hat; the hat he wore when the foxhounds met at the White Hart, the hat he wore once a week to Yarnator.

Elsie gave it to him. He brushed it with a sleeve and put it on. Then he crept down the step to the pavement, and Elsie knew where he was going.

"An hour there and an hour back," she said to a neighbor. "And all to look at a hoss."

Arms folded, she stepped down to the pavement to watch him go. "One day he'll drop like a stone and they'll all blame me." Then she raised her voice in a cry that traveled the street like a witch on a broom. "Go gentle now, you're never so spry as you think."

To the neighbor she said, "One time he never went further than the jubilee seat and you knew for sure where he'd be. Very handy it was. You only had to open the door and holler dinner, and five minutes later there he was, cussing the step as good as gold. But not now. Now he got this hoss up Yarnator, and once a week there's no holdin' him."

The neighbor made a clucking sound of sympathy, holding up a shopping bag to show that she must get on.

Elsie nodded, agreeing that there was plenty of work to do. She went up the step to the opened door and there leaned out to see her departing father. His crippled legs shocked her. His persistence terrified her. She cried, "Hockerd old toad, why don't you rest while you can?" She was telling the street that it was not her fault.

Nathan heard the brown door slam. He took the handkerchief to his little red eyes, then returned it to a pocket of his serge coat. He crept on, past the shops to Ye Olde Pixie Haunt. He paused there to be sure about his eyes, and a woman's face appeared at the small, square panes. The shop door opened with a giggle of bell, and Miss Lorrimer asked, "Are you all right, Mr. Shillabeer?"

Miss Lorrimer wore a cardigan and gray skirt. He called her the pixie woman; indignant because when the owner had sold her the shop, Penny the saddler had been turned out. A week later the smell of leather had become the smell of home-made scones, and Ye Olde Pixie Haunt had been ready for summer visitors. Bright curtains, small tables with bright cloths, cream teas and scones, and pixie souvenirs of Dartmoor. Miss Lorrimer wrote pamphlets about Dartmoor pixies, leaving them politely on tables so that her customers could see.

She raised a hand to her mouth in anxiety, for truly the poor gentleman should not be allowed out alone. What was that foolish daughter thinking about?

"He worries me," she said to no one. "He's taken to walking too far for his age. And I'm so afraid. . . ."

Blasted woman, Nathan thought. Drove poor Penny out and he the best saddler in four parishes. Then what happens? Up goes a sign about pixies; pixies for gardens, pixies for luck, pixies for heaven's sake. Now the room Penny used to work in, perched on his stool with his thread and leather and wax and methylated flame, now that room has tables with bread and butter you can see through and little dabs of cream and jam. Blasted woman. Even her food is never meant for appetites.

He thought a long sad moment about Penny; poor old

soul, banished suddenly to something polite called retirement. Now Penny sat beside the fire, shawled against the drafts, his hands always twitching because there was no work for them and he was new to idleness.

Then Nathan thought, tell you what, 'tis time I did something about it. The saddler must be persuaded to come and see what Nathan knew he would be glad to see.

Nathan turned towards Post Lane and rapped his stick on a green door. A moment nothing happened. Then a curtain moved and a creased-up face appeared at the window. He recognized Penny's wife, who would have driven Penny to strong drink if chapel hadn't been cheaper.

She opened the door a reluctant crack as though the house were a mortuary and must not be disturbed. Nathan poked his stick and when she stepped back in alarm, the door swung wider in a suggestion of welcome. He put a hand on the wall and went up the blue-stone step.

"He's not really up to visitors," Mrs. Penny said. "He's not at all well lately."

No wonder, Nathan thought; sitting there beside the stove all day, never going further than the wicker chair. "Get him out," Nathan said, creeping through the passage. "He's never old yet. I'm eight year older than he is and look at me. Fit's a flea," Nathan said.

The saddler half rose from his chair and remained stooping, one hand on the chair, the other out in a vague gesture of welcome.

"Sit down do," Mrs. Penny said; first to her husband, who sat heavily and with an exhausted sigh, then to Nathan. But the horse-breaker did not sit. He knew that if he sat he would not get up again.

"It's his back," Mrs. Penny said. "You know how he's been since the shop."

"G'at," Nathan said. His disdain suggested that sitting was

for old dodderers who could not smell the goodness of the morning or inflate their chests and think young thoughts and celebrate life with a dance. "What you want is to get out and about. Come with me so far's Yarnator. That's where I'm off and no woman could stop me."

"Why ever Yarnator?" Mrs. Penny said.

"There you are, Penny, you're all behind. You don't know what's happenin' round about. There's a hoss up Yarnator, a hoss that would do you more good than all the shawls and medicine and remember-what-the-doctor-said." He leaned towards the saddler. "A beautiful hoss, Penny, with a head that's good to see."

"Oh my," Mrs. Penny said. "Whoever wants to see a horse's head?"

Nathan watched the saddler's face; turned down with petulance and bewilderment and self-pity. There was a spark of interest in the dim, complaining eyes, but the spark went out and left only thoughts of pain.

"He can't. His back wouldn't never allow it." Mrs. Penny came to her husband's chair. "It's not right upsetting him. You ought to know how he feels."

Nathan spoke to the eyes. "For years I've been going up there once a week, regular as clockwork, although if Elsie had her way I'd bide in bed with a quarter of peppermints and the wallpaper. But seeing that hoss and watching him grow and shape up as a hoss should, seein' all that have done me good, Penny. I'm younger now, younger than I was years ago when there was nothing to do except sit on the jubilee seat and wait for Elsie to holler dinner. You come, too, Penny. You just come and see."

"He's given up horses," Mrs. Penny said. "He give up horses when they took away the shop."

"Come and see. Come and tell the boy what you think

about his hoss. He'll listen. He listens to me, believes every word I say. He'll listen to you, too."

Penny watched the pale fire. He shook his head. "We're old, Nathan. Nobody wants us."

"That's what I thought, but it's never true, Penny. That boy wants us. He asks me how he should handle his hoss and I tell him and he does exactly what I say, never no more, never no less. He's doing it right, Penny, giving his hoss time to grow, gentling him, handling him, till now they're so thick as brothers. Next year the breaking starts, the breaking to bridle and saddle, and all the time it's me doin' it, Penny. Me doin' it through the boy. And after that the gettin' fit, the schoolin'. Then he'll want me every day. Think of that now. Somewhere to go, something to do, something to boss about. Think what it means, Penny. Think what it could mean to you."

Penny's glance was imploring while his wife said, "The doctor said he never seen such a back. All those years on that stool and in the end what gratitude is there? Turned out." Her voice went up like a bird. "Turned out just like that and all for what? All for a café selling post cards and little books about pixies. Pixies, Nathan, pixies."

Nathan looked at his friend. The tears were new in the saddler's eyes. The shock and humiliation persisted; for what sense was there when lucky pixies were more important than a village craftsman?

"He daren't go out," Mrs. Penny said quietly. "It upsets him just to see the shop with somebody else's name above the door."

Nathan nodded, admitting that perhaps Penny was not yet ready. "Well, I'll be goin' then. But don't think you've won, Penny. I'm going to get you up there to see that hoss if it kills the both of us."

Mrs. Penny followed him through the passage, shuffling

because he moved so slowly. "Are you sure you can manage, Nathan?"

There, Nathan thought, isn't that typical? You show a woman you're as fit as a flea, and a minute later there she is, fussing and clacking and getting in the way. No wonder poor Penny's like a fowl in the rain. What he needs is rescue. What he needs is to be showed the way.

"Thank you for calling," Mrs. Penny said.

And there's a lie, Nathan thought. She isn't glad at all. She's afraid I've upset Penny, exciting him with talk of hosses, for Penny loved a good hoss in his day. Now she's afraid he won't rest so content in his wicker chair, but will start fidgetin' and smellin' the mornin' and wishin' to be off. She's afraid he's goin' to become a worry, like I am to Elsie, and if he does it will be the best thing that could happen to him, the poor dear fella.

Nathan came to the field where the horse was grazing. It got wind of him and straightened, head high, its ears sharp and nostrils blowing. It turned away, trotting with a young lilt, its eye turned back to show the white.

There's quality there, Nathan thought. There's mystery, too. It's like a gypsy woman bringin' forth a king.

He took off his hat and passed the handkerchief over his head. He wiped his face with the care of a cat. Then he replaced the hat and leaned his arms on the wall, settling down to watch and consider, as contented as a man might be with a favorite book.

Old judges used to say that bay was the best color. Years ago, donkey years ago, they had thirteen colors for a hoss, with bay the favorite. So it has been ever since. But there's always argument about other colors. Some won't have black; others won't have gray; while years ago there was a prejudice against light chestnuts and especially light chestnuts with two or more white socks. As for me, Nathan thought, I wouldn't give much for light sorrel or dun or roan. They're very doubtful indeed.

I suppose you can say that bay's the safest color. Well, Question Mark's a bay, so that's good, with black mane, black tail, black legs, and a white heel on the off hind. Nathan considered that heel a long time. Some reject white as a sign of blemish, less of physique than of the spirit; but there have been plenty of good horses with white. Provided it's not scattered, Nathan thought. White in the forehead and white flecks on the withers and white in the legs; now that would be bad.

Nathan was talking to himself as the girl screamed. It tore the silence like the split of calico. At first he could not see the girl. Then he saw a red sweater and black hair, and recognized Buckpitt's daughter. Wonnacott's boy was beside her, holding her. They were looking towards a litter of rocks, pointing in a fascination of fear. Then the girl disappeared.

"Falled down," Nathan said.

The boy came running and the horse came with him, catching his fear. Mark scrambled over the gate, not speaking to the old man, perhaps not seeing him. The horse turned aside at the gate and stood shivering, springing a sweat of excitement. It trembled its nostrils at Nathan, looking beyond him to the boy.

Near the yard Mark shouted for his father, but Howard did not come.

Nathan said, "Where is the fella?" angered by his own helplessness.

Then the mother came to the yard, wiping her hands in a corner of her apron. The boy spoke to her and pointed, and the mother ran, the boy seizing her arm, half pulling, half pushing. Her shoes stumbled up the hill and Nathan heard the tear-out of her breathing. He sidled along the wall to open the gate for them, but Mark was at the hasp first, forcing a gap wide enough for his mother to come through. They struggled on towards the rocks where the girl lay moaning. Her left trouser was pulled up. She watched her leg swell. She said in a blubber of sound, "It bit me."

"An adder," Mark said. "With a black zigzag down its back. It must have been sleeping in the sun and she stepped near it."

Kate knew a moment of panic. What do I, what can I do? Then she remembered what once Mother Wonnacott had told her, telling her of something which had happened years ago. She fell on her knees beside the girl. Over her shoulder she said, "Fetch her father. Tell him to bring the car."

Mark saw his mother moisten her mouth for spittle, then put her mouth to the bite. He saw her suck, sucking out the poison and spitting and sucking again. He ran to the wall and over the wall towards Narrastun. He was waving his arms to a farm hand before the farm hand heard him or saw him.

The farm hand heard him say, "Laura," and caught the fear in his running and threw the name towards the barn. Buckpitt was there with a merchant. He was ordering lime.

He heard the name and saw the running, and fright contorted his face; stripping it of authority, skinning it white. He ran to his car, reaching one door as Mark reached the other. The car roared. It was leaping down the hill before the doors were shut.

"Snake bite," Mark said.

Buckpitt's glance was as sharp as a blade. The car swerved to the tarmac of the road.

"My mother's there," Mark said.

Buckpitt grinned at that. His lips peeled back. He crashed the gears cruelly, swinging the car towards Yarnator. Kate and Howard were at the gate. Each had an arm under Laura. She was sitting in the chair which their arms made, and her left leg was thrust out.

The car stopped. Buckpitt ducked out and ran around, wrenching open the back door. He took his daughter from them, half lying her along the back seat with her left leg stretched out.

"She'll be all right," Kate said.

Buckpitt showed his teeth. He slammed a door. The car roared so that they blinked from its dust. Mark stood between his parents, listening to its last sounds. They felt isolated in the sudden silence.

Nathan said, "The poison can be dangerous if it's in the blood stream." He inched along the wall towards them. "Do you think 'tis in the blood stream?"

Kate moistened her mouth. "No, I don't think it is."

"That's all right then, the maid will be all right then. Not as though she's a little tiny tacker."

Buckpitt came in the evening. He stepped over the threshold, turning his hat in his hands. He hesitated in the passage, then followed Kate to the parlor. Howard came as far as the opened door. His mouth was a little open. He was in awe; not only of Buckpitt but of what Kate had done.

"The hospital said she can come home in two, three days. Then rest for a bit and she'll be all right."

Kate said, "I'll tell Mark in the morning. He's been worried. Laura and he, they're such great friends."

She said it flatly, making the friendship a fact which he could neither deny nor destroy.

Buckpitt nodded, accepting it. He flicked a glance, asking Kate to understand his pride in his daughter. "She's a strong girl. The doctor said the toxicity isn't dangerous in a girl so strong."

"She's a fine girl," Kate said.

Buckpitt flicked the glance again. "Sucking the poison out." He made a little movement with his hat. "I'd like to do something about you—sucking the poison out."

"It's all right. I'm glad I was quick enough."

"Once I said about friends, about you not having friends if you needed them." He repeated the little gesture with his hat, erasing what he had said and simultaneously apologizing for it. He smiled with his lips tight. "It goes to show . . ."

Kate smiled. Her eyes were tender as she said, "It's all right," helping him over his apology. Howard saw that each admired the other, understanding what the other was saying in the silences.

"Your boy," Buckpitt said. "There're ponies at Narrastun. Ponies for hunting, gymkhanas. If he likes to come over any time. He'll always be welcome at Narrastun."

Kate inclined her head. "As welcome as Laura is here."

There was a glint of amusement in Buckpitt's glance. "She spends half her holidays here."

"It's the horse," Kate said. "She and Mark, you'd think there was no other horse in the world."

They shared a smile, amused by the enthusiasms of their children. Then Buckpitt looked beyond her to Howard. He hesitated, tasting the words before he said them. You knew they did not come easily.

"And you," Buckpitt said. "If there's any help, any time . . ."

Kate knew that the offer was a gesture; made for her sake. She knew that Buckpitt did not like Howard, that he was contemptuous of Howard as a failure, out of date and slow. But she knew, too, that the gesture, once made, would never be revoked. It would strengthen Howard's status in the village. Maddicott, Steer, and Jordan, they would not mock him now.

"Good night," Buckpitt said.

"Good night," Kate said, moving with him towards the door.

Howard stood back from the door and Buckpitt passed

him without a glance. He darted a tight smile to Kate and stepped to the path.

The smile said my only daughter, you see, a man's a fool about his only daughter. Kate nodded, and the nod said, it's all right, you don't have to explain, I'm the same about my only son.

"We look forward to seeing her soon," Kate said.

Mark rode the ponies which Laura did not want. She made her choice, coming out in jodhpurs, hacking jacket, and black cap; tapping her whip into a palm and saying, "I'll take the roan this morning." Or the skewbald or the chestnut. Mark chose from the others. Then they galloped sudden races for the fun of racing back. Laura always won.

They competed in gymkhanas. Mark rode a skewbald in one event and was last. Laura won on the chestnut. In the potato race, where you scamper to a bucket and drop a potato in, then scamper back for another and so on for as long as the potatoes last, she rode the skewbald and Mark the chestnut. She won and he was last.

"You don't ride hard enough," she said. "They know when it's me shouting in their ear."

She rode low, her right hand holding the whip where the pony's white eye could see it. Spectators cheered, admiring her will to win, her command of the games she played and the animals she rode. They admired her in the hunting field, too, where she rode the gray. They said to Buckpitt, "That maid of yours will break her flaming neck," and Buckpitt shrugged, pretending that he could not restrain his daughter. But truly he did not wish to. She rode to win and that was right. He understood no other way.

The meet on Boxing Day was the big meet of the year. Hounds waved their tails in the square of the White Hart; as remote from other dogs as boys in a cathedral choir are remote from other boys. They had their especial skill and purpose, their especial education. That's Sentry, someone said; that's Bugler and that's Marshal, the champion. Proud names they were, charming the country tongue, as militant as old hymns.

Marshal lifted his nose to the hands of a boy, and the boy drew back, supposing that hounds must be fierce because all that hunts must be fierce. Marshal's eyes showed hurt. He moved forward, leaning out to the interesting hands. "Marshal," the huntsman said, and the old hound turned and came back.

The huntsman half rose in the stirrups, looking around to name his hounds. He had spoken in a respectful growl to Marshal, but he lit another name with sharpness, for Bullet was a young hound and stupid. Bullet obeyed sluggishly, and the huntsman let his whip trail. The hound shot him a glance, then came around.

"I'm watchin', Bullet," the huntsman said.

Almost all the farmers were there; strongly macked against wind and rain, their bowler hats pressing down their ears. Some rode useful hunters which had been corned up. Others rode old horses which had been useful once; while a few rode moorland ponies, their legs dangling comedy fashion, like peasants on sunshine donkeys. But the wise knew that these ponies were no joke. They would be persevering, as persistent as infantry, when blood horses of sixteen hands were blowing for home.

Jordan was there and Maddicott. They sat on either side of Buckpitt, who rode the gray; for that he should ride the best horse in his stable was demanded by the day. Laura rode the chestnut and Mark the skewbald. Other young riders pushed their ponies to be near Laura, but when they had separated her from Mark, she turned the chestnut from them and found Mark again.

Kate watched from the edge of the crowd. She saw what the other young riders were trying to do, and felt a dark sickness of anger. They were trying to drive him out, as starlings drive out and destroy the white starling. They were cruel because he was different. His clothes made him different.

His clothes were a joke; hobnailed boots, gray trousers, and an old jacket covered by a mackintosh the color of cold tea. She saw these clothes as though for the first time. She saw what they did to him. They outlawed him. They told everyone that his was a borrowed pony, borrowed saddle, borrowed bridle; that his was a borrowed place in this company. They told everyone that he did not belong.

Kate's anger became a moan of mourning, for she should have known. Her son needed clothes, the right clothes; well made and expensive. Jodhpurs and hunting jacket were as important as a uniform. You did not belong in the army until you had your uniform; and you did not belong in the hunting field until you had your jodhpurs and hunting jacket, made by the tailor of Market Town. But jodhpurs and hunting jacket would cost money, too much money, more than she could afford. She bit her thumb, nibbling the hard skin, thinking of the money.

Waiters, as important as priests, came from the White Hart. Their silver trays bore the stirrup cup, and this moment was solemn, like the drinking of blood at a heathen feast.

Mark and Laura reached for their glasses, while Nathan cried from a doorway, "See that boy on the skewbald. Two years from now he'll be riding the finest hoss hereabouts. Just you wait and see."

Elsie called, "Be quiet, Father, you know you shouldn't get excited." Then she turned to Bessie Warrener and said, "Bad enough the best of times, but when he starts on about that hoss called Question Mark, there's no holdin' him."

The master put horn to lips and the silence of the crowd

was expectant; like an audience in a concert hall when the conductor raises his baton. The horn whined, and the tails waved with a new fervor. Only Bullet looked all ways, still sure that this was a social occasion. The huntsman snapped his whip.

The hunt moved off with a merriment of hooves, and boys on bicycles hurried to Furzedown where the hounds would draw. Men raised hands in good wishes. The women remembered their stoves. For them the hunt was over with the end of the meet. They did not care if there would be a fox. They were satisfied that it had been a good turn-out, one of the best free shows of the year and lucky in its weather.

Suddenly the square was cold, like a wedding when the bride has gone. Only Nathan was on the step, brushing aside Elsie's protests and telling no one in a blunder of pride: "Just wait two years, that hoss will be huntin' then, and when you see that hoss, my buckos, really done up and fit, with a shine in him like the Sunday table, when you see all that, my buckos, you'll know the truth of what I've been saying. . . ."

"Father," Elsie said, taking his arm.

"That hoss is the best this village have seen in forty year. . . ."

"Father." Elsie dragged him up the step and over the threshold. "You know what you're like when you get excited."

"Fifty," Nathan shouted as the door closed.

Chapter Fifteen

The barrow bumped out of the yard to brown earth and across the earth to the edge of new cement. Mark lifted the barrow and the cement slopped out with a sound like the slide of snow.

Howard roughed it with a shovel, then crouched to smear it level. His wooden float made a shooshing noise like an old man spooning soup. His silence grumbled with alarms. He was afraid of the cost. He knew they could not afford a loose-box for the colt.

It had been Laura's idea. She had told Mark what there ought to be, and Mark had suggested using this corner of the barn; once used as stabling for two farm horses, but recently a place for kindling and wire netting, for lengths of galvanized iron ragged with holes and dog-eared with rust. Then what had seemed a simple process of conversion had become confused by advice. A cement floor for easy cleaning, Laura had said; with a gulley for easy draining, Kate had added. A wooden trough for feeding, Nathan had said; new posts for the door; then, finally, with a shout of inspiration, a new door.

Howard groaned. Too many people advising; that always puts up the price.

He told the sounds of the barrow, "Then there's straw. You won't have bracken for bedding, and look at the price of straw." Then he looked up, realizing that this time Laura was pushing the barrow. She wore trousers, and the sleeves of her sweater were rolled. She summoned all her strength to lift the barrow.

"It won't cost anything. My father will let you have straw."

"That's not the point," Howard said. "It's not his horse."

"There's plenty of straw at Narrastun. Plenty of black oats, too."

He knew she didn't understand. She had never had to watch the prices. "Let's not talk about that."

"I've already talked about it. I asked him and my father said all right."

When the work was completed, Mark called Nathan to pass judgment. Then straw was brought in and the box was ready.

Nathan asked, "Who is goin' to do the breaking?"

"I will," Laura said. "I've done it before."

Mark shook his head. "He knows me. I've been gentling him all this time." Then he felt the old man's expectancy and added, "With your help, Nathan. Couldn't do it without your help."

Nathan pretended to consider. Breaking the colt meant every day, and every day meant two miles, and he had to think of his legs. Furthermore there was his daughter. He would have to ask his daughter.

"Ask me?" Elsie cried. "If you ask me you want your blimmin' head read." Then she told a neighbor, "Not as though he's getting paid for it."

Nathan laughed in himself. He knew that the knowledge, so long locked away like lumber in a cupboard, was needed again, important again. As the old soldier comes proudly out of retirement at time of war, Nathan brought his experience and skill to Question Mark of Yarnator. He had never been so happy.

Years ago horsebreakers had had their secrets and pickled them in mystery. There had been horse whisperers, who had worked in private; talking to a horse in its stable, so reducing it to submission that after half an hour and no blows struck, it had come out as amenable as a dog.

But me, I'm never no whisperer, boy. I haven't got no secrets. All I know is what the good years learned me, and the first lesson I learned was hands. You got to have the hands. Hands and patience. You can do miracles then.

Move around in front of him, boy, let him see you coming and what you're carrying. Let him smell the halter. He likes to feel with his nose as well as smell. Always a leather halter, never a rope. Give him time to get used to it. There's all the time in the world.

They used to say lunge 'em till they're tired, but I never did. I let 'em take it gentle, with their legs bandaged in case they hit their legs. A hoss doesn't go natural in a circle, so of course he hits his legs. You need blanket bandages, boy. I used to have gray bandages, cut from old army blankets. I'll get Elsie to look 'em out. She got 'em somewhere in the cupboard under the stairs. Better bandages than boots, because boots is hot.

Show him the saddle when he's lying down. Slide it down over him the way the hair lies, soft as a bird along the trout water. Keep the stirrup leathers tied, so's not to bump him. Now put it on when he's standing, let him get used to it with the girths hanging. Then when there's no alarm in him, fasten the girths, not tight, just tight enough to keep the saddle there. If the saddle slips you'll set him back a week.

Now lead him out and let him see what's going on in the world. It'll take his mind off the tightness binding him. Now you can draw up the girths a bit, in easy stages like. Let him go round with the saddle on. He'll forget it's there, like a man with a new hat. First time on it weighs a ton and he thinks everybody knows it's new, but after a while he gets to like this hat. By the time it's been chucked at the cat in the chrysants, it'll be a very fine hat indeed.

Now get on him, boy. In the box so's nobody won't interrupt nor no hen squawk like a woman remembering her dinner. You can do more in an hour in a box than you can in a week in the open. Bring a block of wood in and let him see it all the time. Sit on it while you talk to him. Talk anything as long as you keep sayin', easy, easy, that's what I used to say, over and over like a woman to her cradle. Sometimes the hoss went to sleep and sometimes I did.

Climb on the block and let your hands go all over him. Pick up his foot. When a hoss lets you have his foot, he's trustin' you, for then you got control over him. Now bring your hands up again, feeling him round the saddle where your knees will be. He likes your hands, boy, they're the best hands in the world. Now untie the stirrup leather and bring the iron down. No bumpin', holdin' it careful like a king's crown. Put your foot in the stirrup, then your weight, keep it there a minute while he thinks about it, then back to the block and rest.

Keep doin' it until he knows there's nothing to fear. Whatever you do, don't rush him. There's nothin' vicious in him, boy. He's doin' his best to understand. He doesn't want to be afraid.

Now lean over him and bring your other stirrup down. Then your left leg taking the weight, and your right leg over the croup. Clear him with your foot, boy. Then ease your right foot into the stirrup and sit down to it, making yourself light, feather light.

Don't snatch when he jumps. Of course he's wondering where the weight's come from. It was in the stirrup, now it's on his back. He wonders how you done it, and he watchin' all the time.

Do it slow, boy, quiet's a mouse with no foot touchin' him.

Do it over and over like A.B.C. until it's child's play to him. Now ride him out. Gentle with the hands, think you got cotton there and that if you handle strong, the cotton will break. Let him walk where he knows. When he reaches that wall, see, let him stop and consider. Either he goes through the wall, which would be very inconvenient for one and all, or he turns like a sensible hoss and comes back again. So he turns, and as he turns of his own sense, help him with your knee to show that this is exactly what you wanted and that he's a terrible clever hoss for thinkin' it out for himself.

He's getting fed up with that, see. He's pickin' up his rhythm like a soldier got used to the pack he must carry. Keep your hands down, boy, your weight well over, he's going to stretch a bit, he wants to have a blow. See how easy it is, like a child comin' to read, and all because you give him time and let him come to it gradual.

Now back to the box. He knows where he lives, and his home's like yours and mine. It looks no worse for having been away a bit.

Dress him well, boy. You don't dress for show only, you dress for health, too. Brush him all over, all the way down to his fetlocks. I had one once that went to sleep with contentment, you had a job to hold him up. Now the cloth, takin' out the loose hairs and layin' the coat. One cloth for his body, the other for his legs. Make sure of his legs, boy. A hoss is only as good as his legs.

Now hay, it got to be hard hay, too much hay around here is soft and soft hay don't help to make a hoss. Remember that a hoss got a small stomach, considering the height of him and the length of him, so plenty of food means less than good food. Then black oats a year old, but not too much seein' he's only workin' light. Give him too much and he'll get above hisself, like a man with overtime money to spend. I used to let them have carrot meself. Some say there's more substance in peas and beans, but a hoss do like his bite of carrot. 'Tis like ice cream to a boy.

Give him plenty of time to eat, for a gentleman likes to dally over his vittals. Then be careful with the water. Freezin' water in winter can bring on colic, while not enough water can make him bad-tempered. Let him drink all he likes in the mornin', when he's cool and easy.

Keep the top half of that door open. Years ago they was so afraid of drafts, they shut a hoss up with his own smell and pretty soon he was near blind with the ammonia. It's best to let him see the light. He likes to hang his head out, watching all that goes on. He's like a woman shakin' out the mats. It takes one minute to do the shakin', and twenty to tell the woman next door that there's never no time for yappin'.

As a matter of fact most race hosses is never worked enough. They're shut up for twenty-three hours a day. There's a lot to be said for walkin' twice a day, gettin' the good air of the mornin' and the sun of the afternoon. But big stables can't do it, because an extra workout a day would mean extra lads and that puts up the costs. But you can do it. There's nothing to stop you if you're willin' enough, but it must be regular. A hoss do like steady habits.

That's a nice blanket your mother made, initials on the side, too. M.T.W. What's the middle one for, boy? Well, Terence is a nice name, and anyway you can't help it. One time they used to wrap a hoss in blankets and a swansdown hood and gallop him severe. What they called four-mile sweats, gettin' off the fat and puttin' muscle on. A hoss had to be fit to stand the gettin' fit. Another time they tried Turkish baths for hosses and there's a laugh. As though takin' off the fat is the same as puttin' muscle on.

Laura complained, "You're so slow, months and months, and look at him. Still a baby."

Mark looked down at Nathan, at the white stubble and weak red eyes. "How do you think we're doing?"

Nathan let his hand go down the neck, down the chest and arm, then over the knee to the coronet. At his touch on the coronet, Question Mark picked up a foot. Nathan straightened, his hand coming back to the neck. "I tell you what I reckon. I reckon you're doing very well." He grinned up at Mark. It was a grin without teeth, for he put in his false teeth only on Sundays. "You're both doin' handsome. You mustn't hurry now."

"But see how long it's taking," Laura protested. "See how much time is being wasted."

Nathan did not glance at her. To Mark he said, "Don't listen to the ones who know all the short cuts. There's no short cut with a hoss, boy, any more than there is with a child. You frighten 'em when you try to teach what they aren't quite ready to learn."

"Don't you want to feel him go? To find out what he can really do?" Laura made an exclamation of disgust. "You stick in the mud. You'd think there was all the time in the world."

Almost Nathan answered. Almost he said, you Buckpitts, you break your ponies' knees and think you know it all. Every pony you get rid of, every one is gone in the legs. To Mark he said, "Patience, boy. You got to take him on the road yet. He's got to learn what traffic is all about."

Laura rode the gray to the road and Question Mark followed, surprised by the new sounds in tarmac. They went down the road to the bridge.

A van, red as a ladybird, slid down a faraway hill to be lost in a fold in the valley. They waited for it to show again, suddenly much larger but still silent. Laura brought her gray around to an outside position, protecting Question Mark from the new experience.

The van came around the wall with a snarl of sound, then

slowed respectfully, like a boy who scampers the school corridor until he sees the headmaster. It crept with eyes down, embarrassed and apologetic. It made itself small against the other wall, inching forward while Question Mark fought for his legs like a beginner on ice.

With her hand low, Laura beckoned the van forward. The gray caught the colt's excitement and whipped round, its quarters bumping the window, its tail falling over it like a waterfall. The driver switched off his engine.

Laura crabbed the gray sideways, showing the beginner the way towards open road. Question Mark came with a stutter and slither. Then she looked back to the van and raised a hand. The driver grinned into his mirror, feeling the tension of that minute. He switched on his engine. To the reflection he said, "Better you than me, mate."

Mark felt the sweat in his hands, the strain in his cheek muscles. He darted a smile to Laura, grateful for her skill, but her eyes were busy, looking for danger.

She heard the motorcycle before she saw it. It was already very near. The whine of it swelled to terrify the morning. It bounced over the hunched back of the bridge. Its wheels flew a second, then recovered the road. It came at them like horror in a dream.

Laura shouted, waving it down although she knew she was too late. It howled in an agony of sound. They felt the wind of it.

Question Mark tried to rear, his back feet sliding under so that almost he sat, almost he fell backwards. Mark lost a stirrup and fell in a flurry of arms. Laura saw his mouth and eyes, straining wide in white surprise. Then she heard the torrent of hooves. Reins dribbled from the snaffle. Question Mark almost put a foot through the loop. She knew he would put a foot through the loop, and that tripping would bring him down in a fall as heavy as his flight was mad.

She drove the gray forward, risking its feet, the tarmac jar in its legs. She chased Question Mark to the bridge and over it to the common. Sheep bounced away and a wild pony ran to safety, then bucked its heels with a snort of indignation.

Question Mark put a leg through the reins and went down. She heard the sound, first of shock, then of wheezing. She saw him scrabble his front legs, half lifting his head. Then the head collapsed, too heavy for the neck.

Laura threw a glance at Mark and saw him running. She kicked her feet from the stirrups and jumped. She crouched and touched. A moment Question Mark lay like the dead. Then he brought up his head so suddenly that he almost butted her. She reached for the rein, but he struggled up and lolloped on three legs, frightened again by the hobbling and by the drag-down on his mouth.

Mark stumbled through the heather. He tried to shout, but the pain in his chest was red and no sound would come. Question Mark three-legged away, thrashing his tail, his eye white and bulging.

"He was winded," Laura said.

"Stay still, stay quiet." Mark's voice was sharp. "Till he gets back his confidence in us."

Laura glanced at the sharpness. Then she reached a hand for the gray, taking the reins and patting its neck, while Mark watched his horse, waiting for recognition to come back.

He moved forward, talking easy-easy talk. Question Mark sidled away. He waited again, still talking the monotony of nonsense. Question Mark shook his head so that flecks of foam splashed like spit. Mark stooped and touched the foot. The foot came up. The reins came away. Question Mark put down the leg, testing it.

"He's all right," Laura said.

Mark walked in a circle and Question Mark went with him, bobbing his head, surprised by the pain in his leg.

He's lame, Mark thought. He saw the motorcyclist, the goggles, the arrogance, and his thoughts boiled with a rage near tears. He was eleven years old again, vowing impossible vows. I'll kill him. I'll take a knife and kill him, presenting his heart to politicians who allow idiots to ride machines capable of a hundred miles an hour. Oh my beauty, his hands said, my poor beauty.

Laura said, "Nathan will know what to do."

Nathan was waiting at the farm. He saw the boy and girl on foot. He saw the bob of the horse's head, and his thoughts ran around like mice. I knew it, as soon as I heard that motorbike I knew it. That lovely hoss gone in the leg, crippled by an idiot.

He put a hand to the leg. He looked with his hands and found nothing. "Take him to the box, boy. Let's have another look."

His hands looked again and kept looking until they found it. He pressed with his thumb and the horse flinched. He followed the tendon from the knee to the cannon bone and over the fetlock. Then he came back, and this time Question Mark flinched before he reached it.

Nathan straightened. "A linen roller to bind tight. Kept wet with cold water morning and night." He stooped again. "Did you get the number?"

Laura shook her head. "There wasn't time."

No, Nathan thought, there never is. The faster they are, the more dangerous, and the more dangerous the less time there is. He took out the red handkerchief, for stooping smudged his eyes and put a dizziness into his head. Once he had stooped too long and had fallen, and Elsie had rushed to help him. He remembered the humiliation. Lugged about by a woman. Caw, lumme days.

He looked at Mark, compelling his eyes to focus. He put away the handkerchief. "Do as I say with the linen roller and he'll be all right. Then after that us'll walk him in the shallows of the river. The running water will do his legs good."

Mark held out a hand, then let it fall. He thought, there's nothing to say. Nathan knows there's nothing to say.

Laura tried to say it. She slapped the old man's shoulder; a gesture of emotion and embarrassment, and that slap was important. It was the first compliment she had ever paid to Nathan.

There's more to gettin' a hoss fit, Nathan said, more to it than canterin' and gallopin' and seein' who can beat the other. Gettin' a hoss fit is a job of work, hard work, slow work. You got to put it into them before you can get it out.

Walk him up the steep hill, boy, up to Black Dog Tor, right up there, look, up to the sky. Climbin' is good, provided he's never off the bit. Climbin' and joggin', that muscles up the quarters, and that's what a jumper wants. He wants strength in the quarters, like a boxer wants it in the shoulders.

Then around Black Dog Tor and down again, down to the shallows of the river. Let him walk the river towards Yarnator. The runnin' water will do him good. If the sea was nearer, I'd say let him splash in sea water, but where there's no sea, fresh water's the next best thing. The water's strengthening.

There's nothin' very exciting about work like this, specially in the howling wind or the rain as sharp as needles. But 'tis important, boy, there's never no substitute. Folk will say 'tis no weather to be out, you'll be soaked to the skin and froze to the marrow, but don't let nobody talk you out of it. Don't let your mother. She's bound to think of you before the hoss. But you mustn't. She's bound to say a day won't make no difference, but you must know better. You must know that fine-weather riders never got a hoss fit.

Though if by any chance you can't work him and Laura can't neither, then get your father to lead him down to the river so that at least he gets a smell of the mornin' and the feel of the water on his legs.

Nothin' ought never to stop a hoss havin' his work. That's what they say. But whoever says it don't know how snow can be on the moor. Shuttin' us all up in white, so a man can't step a yard outside his door, never mind ride a hoss across the moor. Well, then, when the snow's so deep you think the earth is gone forever, then you got to strap him. Takin' off your coat to it, for half an hour of strappin', mornin' and evenin', will work the cold out of you and put real goodness into the hoss. 'Tis heavy brushin' all over, but especially the body. 'Tis a kind of massage. It keeps the muscles supple. It's the best way to stop good muscles goin' stiff when the snow keeps him indoors.

Now schoolin' over fences, there's a tricky thing. There's some who say ride 'em at a stone wall, they'll learn to get over as soon as their knees is cut. There's others who say turn 'em out, put 'em in one field with hay in another and a strong hedge in between. They'll soon learn to get over. That's what they say, and I've heard that 'tis done a lot in Ireland.

But me, I say the gentle way must be the best, and the best way to begin is bales of straw in line. Walk him up to it. Let him see how trivial 'tis, nothing for any respectable hoss to make a fuss about. Let him stride over it. Only a mean old hoss could refuse you something as easy as that.

'Tis surprising how quick he gets the idea. Confidence, that's the secret. The confidence that when you ask him to do somethin', it's fair. If it wasn't fair, you wouldn't ask him. Once he's got that into his head, he'll jump the church for you.

Keep risin' the fence every now and again, but don't take him over it more than twice a day. He gets bored easy. Just jumpin' and comin' back and jumpin' again. What sense is there?

Now show him the brushwood fence at Narrastun. Laura have built it for her show ponies, so it ought to be easy enough. Walk him up to it. Let him look over it. No surprises on the other side. Then let him see the wings. It's the first time he's seen a fence with wings, so natural enough he wants to make sure. Then take him back, give him a long look at it, and come at it, not too long a run, and once you've decided he's going to go, keep him at it. Knees and hands. Don't let him change his mind and run around the easy way. Intelligent hosses is often the hardest to train, like intelligent soldiers in the army. They can always find an easier way.

A hoss don't need special schooling over water. If he jumps at all, he reaches out natural for a span wider than the water. I know plenty come down at the water, but as a rule they're hosses that shouldn't be jumpin' at all. They don't like the game. They don't mind goin' over three or four at their own pace, but when they're asked to go at racin' pace and asked to keep goin' when they'd much rather pack up and go home, then they starts makin' mistakes. They haven't got the heart for it.

Now try him over a green bank at Narrastun. It must be good ground on both sides and no stones on top. A good solid bank, three feet high, that'll take more jumping than a brushwood fence of four feet. It'll make him jump clear, no brushin' through or takin' chances. He'll see how solid it is and rise to it.

See how he showed his ears to it, boy, how he stood back to it, leapin' generous, never touching a blade. He's a natural, son. If he's lucky, if nothin' don't set him back, then us'll have something to show 'em all later on.

Truth to tell he's showin' off, like a boy at school, delighted by how much he knows. Every question is an invitation to show what he can do. Hosses is like children in many ways. Make 'em feel clever and they will be. Make 'em feel stupid and they will be.

Yes, he'll be ready for the Boxing Day meet. So long as you don't ask too much of him. Let him stay with them as long as he wants, then as soon as he's off the bit, don't push him. Let him turn round and come home. It would be a good idea if Laura brought back the gray, too.

These hosses have been workin' together a long time, like comics on the radio. If the gray goes on, Question Mark will know he hasn't done so good. But if the gray comes round, too, no matter what all the others do, then Question Mark will think he's done all right and down the hill they'll come, just like any other workin' day.

Question Mark was ready for the Boxing Day meet, and Mark was ready, too. He wore the clothes his mother had bought, and Kate thought, it's been worth while, the going without little things so that he could have the best. Now her son wore the important uniform, and the village looked up with respect.

Nathan watched from his brown door, clutching the arm of his daughter, pointing to be sure that she understood.

"There he is, see, what did I say? Two years ago, what did I say? I said that the boy would be ridin' the best hoss hereabouts. And there he is, look." He shook Elsie's arm in a tremble of excitement. "Look, what a picture, the finest hoss in miles. The finest I ever did see."

Elsie glanced nervously towards the White Hart and the stirrup cup. "Hush, Father, the master will hear you."

"Hear me? Course he'll hear me. Before long every one of you will be glad you ever heard of Question Mark."

Chapter Sixteen

Children came to the door to watch red stars fly from the grave of dust; to watch the stunning of soft iron, the sudden drowning in hard black water and the fuss of steam. They came to the forge when the word went round that there were horses in. They did not put a foot inside. They gathered at the door, claiming their right to a free show.

They were in awe of Baskerville, the blacksmith. They watched him move from the anvil to the horse; one stride across a floor of humped-up earth, then a take-up of the hoof between the flaps of his apron. Then up fussed the blue smell, making him the face in the clouds; an Old Testament god looking down to a world of sin.

There was compassion in this god; compassion for the peasant hoof of the old cart mare. It was long and cracked, turned up like a pixie shoe. This mare had worked months without shoes because the farmer begrudged five shillings a shoe; begrudging any money spent on the mare because horses did not count. Horses were for odd jobs only, odd corners only. Tractors were worth more.

So this god had anger in his compassion. The anger was for Maddicott, who paid a thousand pounds for a car but who thought "twenty shillun, all four," a wicked price to keep old feet good. He sent in the mare only when he had a boy with nothing else to do. Six months later he would question the bill, pointing to the penciled figures and comparing the price with years ago. Then he would take five half-crowns from his pocket and offer Baskerville the choice; twelve and six or wait. He knew that Baskerville could not afford to wait.

There would be a silent struggle, both thinking of the shawled-down fire and silent anvil, of the stock of shoes which would soon be junk. Then the blacksmith would take the half-crowns, and Maddicott would hold out the scrap of paper, demanding a receipt. "Received with thanks" and the date. Baskerville could not spell "received" so he would write "recd" and lick his pencil and look to the calendar and add the date. Then Maddicott would call the difference discount, and laugh as one who has had a good day. At noon he would be in the White Hart, boasting of how he had bested Baskerville.

At sixty-five Baskerville had said, "When I'm seventy I'll retire," but now he was seventy and dared not retire, for he knew that the end of him would be the end of the forge. Its fire would go cold, its trough go stale. Its earth would forget the feel-forward of hooves, and there would be another ruin; just stones and slate and three bits of valerian where for generations a craft had been. The slates would go first. Then rain and moonlight would come in, and children would tell tales about the stillness and be haunted by it.

Baskerville grimaced in his spirit, knowing that he followed a fallen craft and that he was no more important than it. His father, his grandfather, they had been great men, their forge a meeting place; a place for talk about hay and beef, of children born and children dying, a place for talk of change.

Eighty years ago the talk had been of education; children learning to read, spelling out words to the bewilderment of their parents. Then the railway, calling the young to work in towns where wages were higher and hours were less. Then dole and insurance and trades unions. Then war and wealth and names on the granite memorial; and after war the poverty, with farmers going cap in hand to banks and casual laborers going cap in hand for work. Then tractors in the fields and cars on the holiday roads, and suddenly what could never happen had happened. Old crafts were dead. New skills had come in.

Old Morty, the thatcher, had died, with none to receive his tools. Penny the saddler, Brimmecombe the stone mason, Nathan the horsebreaker; all had retired with none to mourn their passing. Ezekiel, the wheelwright, was no longer a wheelwright. He who had made the carts of the village and the traps and traders' vans, now cut hair in the hope of making ten shillings a day.

Baskerville knew that only he remained. So he made do with the hunters which came regularly; horses a man could be proud of, with feet neat and sound and respected. Say this for Buckpitt. He sent his horses regularly, paying each Michaelmas and Lady Day without that haggling for discount which humiliated. Now there was another horse in which a craftsman could take pride. Now there was Question Mark, and Baskerville thought, there's a horse and a half. Make no mistake.

He asked Nathan for information, and Nathan came in and sat and they talked old men's talk; spaced with important silences. Nathan took a tin of peppermints from his waistcoat pocket. He chose one, then extended the tin to the blacksmith. The act of sharing made him confide, "You shod him well. The last time he was here. You got his feet a treat."

Nathan put away the tin. His lips moved, appreciating the peppermint.

Baskerville said, "I hear he's being schooled for racing," and Nathan knew that he need not tell the blacksmith about the new fence of brushwood; four feet six inches high, the sort Question Mark would encounter in a race. You couldn't build a fence at Narrastun without all the village knowing.

"They say Buckpitt's daughter is helping."

Nathan nodded. Buckpitt's daughter was riding the gray, leading the novice in his work; since with horses as with children, example shows the way. He said, "That maid's in too much of a hurry. The boy's different. He knows you got to wait."

Baskerville looked down, wondering if Nathan were not ready to wait too long. He'd boasted so often about this horse, perhaps he was afraid to put Question Mark to the test. Askin' 'em the question; that's what old trainers had called it.

"That boy's a good boy," Nathan said. "Once upon a time his mother had big ideas for him. All this education lark. But now he's left school and see what happens. He's following his father, learning to be a farmer like all the Wonnacotts."

Their silence approved, for that a son should follow his father's trade seemed right and just; how else could knowledge be passed on, how else could old experience see itself made new again in the progress of the young?

"Make a good farmer," Nathan said. "That boy got his head screwed on."

They left unsaid what Baskerville knew; that Yarnator needed a good farmer. They were both thinking of Howard and Nathan knew it. His mouth shaped a noise of derision. "Other farmers are doin' well enough. Look at Maddicott and Jordan. Look at Buckpitt."

Baskerville's silence said he did not wish to talk about that. Howard was of the Brethren, and all the Brethren were his family. He let the silence turn from Howard as gradually as a summer stream turns from what it does not want to see. Then he said, "They tell me he's being got ready for the point-to-point."

Nathan nodded. "They got him registered with Weatherby. Dam Pride of the Moor, sire unknown."

"In the boy's name?"

"Why not. His horse, isn't it?" Nathan gave his attention

to the last of the peppermint. Then he said, "Buckpitt's daughter is fierce to ride him in the ladies' race."

Baskerville was surprised. His glance said, the gray, her father paid handsome for that gray.

Nathan let the derisive noise come out. "The maid's clever enough to know Question Mark is the better hoss." He applauded her perception, yet simultaneously resented it. He did not trust Laura.

Baskerville's thoughts went back a year. "Last year she rode the gray in the ladies' race."

"And what happened? The ornament went like a song for two miles then gave in like a baked dinner. I said years ago that gray was all flash, too narrow, too pretty. This year the maid's made up her mind to win the ladies' race and you know how it is. Mark can't very well say no."

Baskerville's slow nod said of course, they owe a lot to Buckpitt. He helped with oats and straw and hay. "They'll even need Buckpitt's trailer to get him to the course."

Nathan's silence said, so there you are, the boy knows it's wrong, he knows I don't approve, but what can he do? The maid's been beggin' him for weeks.

"He'll give in," Nathan said. "Laura Buckpitt's in the habit of getting what her wants. But no good will come of it. Just you wait and see."

Elsie came to the pavement. She asked of a neighbor, "Have you seen the old toad?" and the neighbor said, "Down towards the forge." So Elsie turned in that direction and sent her voice for him. Her "Father" embraced an octave. The second syllable came into the forge like a bird to the rafters. It told the street that Nathan had five minutes.

Nathan picked up his stick. "That maid's sure he'll run well. But first time out. What do her expect?"

Then he went out to the street. He knew that Elsie would wait on the pavement until she saw him coming.

The day skirled with snow, like the ghost of bagpipes coming across the hill. It was the first point-to-point of the season, and the village came by car and bicycle and on foot. Cars paid for their places of honor along the ropes, but pedestrians did not pay. They stood on walls to see the horses go down one hill and up another; jumping from grass to plowed, then up to the trees and around the trees, then a long run to the last fence and the climb home.

It was fair hunting country, but the fences were of brushwood and of uniform height, so that a horse needed to be a quick jumper rather than a big or clever.

Amateur voices shouted into microphones, calling the runners for the members' race. Buckpitt's gray was among them. It would be ridden by the Colonel's son, home from Sandhurst, and the first chalked figures on the bookmakers' boards made it the favorite.

The bookmakers cried their black cries, flipping the elastic bands around their cards while their clerks puffed warmth into their pencil fingers. A woman opened her purse and had sixpence win. Another held her husband's arm, saying it's not worth the risk. Through the crowd came a notice asking, "What does it profit a man if he gain the whole world and lose his soul?" It was carried by a tall thin man, his eyes anonymous behind thick lenses. Every twenty paces he shouted, "The day of judgment draws nigh," then looked around as though hoping for argument. Men pushed him aside in the haste to bet before evens became odds-on.

Spectators thickened around the paddock, watching the four runners. Three were hunters, strong of shoulder and big of head, and in such company the gray looked an aristocrat. "Odds-on," someone said, "sure to start odds-on."

One bookmaker smudged old figures and made new. Then others smudged and scribbled, catching the alarm. The gray was 3–1 odds-on before the riders came from the barn.

Judges climbed to a wagon beside the winning post. The huntsman quavered a note on his horn, calling the horses from the paddock, then leading them down the hill to the start. Groups around the bookmakers frayed away. Men ran from the beer tent to shoulder places at the ropes. Mothers caught their children. Families climbed to the roofs of cars. Elsie said, "Have you seen Father?"

Mark heard the murmur run up the hill to explode in a shout where the spectators were thickest. He knew it said, "They're off." Question Mark lifted his head, feeling the drum of hooves. His ears pointed towards the riders' caps, bobbing above the cars. "Easy, easy," Mark said, leading him round and round in a circle of waiting.

"Keep him out of the wind," Nathan said. "It's blowin' holes out there."

They heard a moan from the crowd and Nathan guessed, "That's the gray, jibbing after two miles. I never did trust grays."

Baskerville found them in the lee of the barn. "Won by Steer's brown gelding. He's cock-a-hoop at having beaten Buckpitt."

"Ah," Nathan said, darting a glance to Mark as though the failure of the gray proved something.

"The gray took the lead after half a mile, looking all over a winner. Then after two miles he blew up like a paper bag and Steer's gelding kept pegging away to win by five lengths." He nodded to Question Mark. "How do you reckon he is, Nathan?"

"If you mean the hoss, the hoss is all right, fit's he can be without havin' had a race. But if you mean the boy, the boy isn't all right. He's like I was, first time I sung solo at a Rechabite concert. Ready to call it off at the drop of a hat."

Baskerville watched the boy's white, tense face. "If that hoss falls, breaks a leg say, he'll never get over it, Nathan."

They waited until another race was run. Then the microphone shouted the runners and riders for the ladies' race, and Nathan said, "Take him early in the ring, boy. Let him get used to all the faces." His stubble creased in a silent laugh. "Most of them is village faces. It took me years to get used to 'em, so give the hoss a chance."

Question Mark came through the gap where a gate had been, stepping from obscurity to the skirling snow and the faces all around. He lilted on feet so sprung that each step became a note, cast upon the air and hanging there to make a melody. Mark leaned a shoulder in, restraining the display of vanity. The number on his arm was the number on the saddle cloth and the number on the card. Six would never again be a commonplace number. He wished it could have been seven. There was a superstition about seven and the luck in it.

Kate opened the race card with thick, gloved fingers. She turned to the third race and down the black type to Question Mark. "Mr. M. T. Wonnacott's Question Mark, sire unknown, dam Pride of the Moor." She shivered with pride, for to have your name on the hunt card, surely that promoted you among the army officers, the Buckpitts, surely that made you a place among the few.

Howard touched her arm, pointing to the frame. Numbers and names were chalked on boards, and the boards were slotted in. The frame shook in the wind and snow blurred the chalk, but Kate read, "Number 6, Miss Laura Buckpitt." The shiver of pride shook her again; for that Laura chose to ride Mark's horse in preference to her own, surely that would convince the village that the link between Yarnator and Narrastun was strong.

Howard's finger traveled in an arc to the bookmakers' boards. "They're making Rustic Prince favorite. The one from Cornwall. And Ballad Lady from Somerset."

"And Question Mark, what's he?"

"Ten to one. That's an outsider at a point-to-point meeting."

"Does that mean he hasn't got a chance?"

"Well, he's new, see, it's his first race."

Howard watched the money go on. Rustic Prince shortened to evens and Ballad Lady came down to six to four. Then Brindle Boy shortened suddenly to threes, and Howard guessed that someone had backed the Exmoor horse heavily. He was fascinated. He had never had such money. He tasted the envy in his mouth.

Kate said, "Shouldn't we have a bet?" She knew that the Brethren did not bet, so she added, "Just for luck, because of Mark."

Howard shook his head. "You know what Nathan said. First time out, it's too much to expect."

Nathan was in the paddock, waiting for Laura to come from the barn. He saw her from the tail of his eye, and finger-signaled Mark to bring the horse in. He took the blanket off. He reached for the girths and tightened them. At his shoulder he heard Buckpitt say, "Everything all right?" but he pretended not to hear. This moment was his. He was in charge. He made it last.

Then he stood aside and picked up the blanket. Buckpitt's hand made a footrest for his daughter, boosting her to the saddle. She found the other iron while Question Mark moved sideways, tossing his head from Mark's hold. Mark moved with him, making cautionary noises. Then he turned towards the hole in the crowd, aware dimly of his mother and father, of Baskerville saying, "Stand back, please, give the hoss a chance." The crowd drew back.

"All right," Laura said. "Let him go."

Mark could not. He told his hand to come away but it would not; for suddenly he was giving his horse away, trusting his horse to another.

"What's the matter with you? Let him go."

Mark let him go. He watched her rise in the stirrups, gathering the horse, showing him where he must go. Question Mark wagged his head, resenting the bit. Then he heard the whine of the huntsman's horn and went down the hill to the flag.

Kate put a hand on Howard's arm. Don't look so thin, she thought, so poor, your son has a horse at the meeting. That makes you important, more important than you have ever been. Even Maddicott and Jordan, even they haven't horses good enough for the point-to-point.

Howard did not understand her pressure on his arm. He was watching Buckpitt. He saw Buckpitt approach a bookmaker. Money changed hands. What Buckpitt said was a murmur, but the bookmaker said, "Hundred pounds to ten Question Mark," and sponged the figures. Suddenly Question Mark was six to one.

Maddicott and Jordan came to Buckpitt. They exchanged secret glances. Then Maddicott whispered and Buckpitt shook his head. Howard heard him say, "Horse won't win, isn't fit enough, but just in case." Maddicott and Jordan hesitated, wondering if they, too, should support his daughter. Then each allowed the crowd to push them away from the bookmaker's towards the ropes.

Mark found a place between Nathan and Baskerville. Above his head Baskerville said, "On the fat side," and Nathan agreed, "The race will do him good."

The starter read the names, and each rider answered like a child at school. The white flag went up in a preliminary to the off. A microphone said, "They're under starter's orders," and the sounds of the crowd were sucked in; leaving mercenary cries as black and bold as crows in a field. "Six to four bar one," the bookies cried.

Laura brought Question Mark out of line, turning him behind the others so that he would see the others go and would follow them. The starter asked, "Are you ladies ready?" and one of them swore an answer. The flag went down in a smudge of white, and seven horses went off in a ragged line. Question Mark gathered on his toes, danced twice, then plunged forward in imitation. "They're off," said the microphone.

Spectators leaned out, pressing the ropes so that from a distance it seemed there could be no way through. Laura gathered him for the first fence. The leaders jumped. Question Mark showed his ears to it and went over, then paused before he could regather his stride. The pause lost lengths, but he quickened up the hill and was at their heels as they passed the winning post for the first time.

Mark watched them come. The earth trembled, the air shook with their breathing. Then they were past and into the next fence; up and over with a groan of leather and scrape of brushwood. Question Mark hesitated before he jumped, and the crowd recognized the hesitation in a shout. Baskerville glanced to Nathan and Nathan sucked a peppermint.

They went down the hill and up the other side. It seemed then that the race was being run in silence, without hoofdrum or breathing. They came to another fence and the colors poured over. Ballad Lady led, two lengths clear of Brindle Boy with Rustic Prince five lengths third.

There was a shout like triumph and something was down. Nathan swallowed his peppermint.

Field glasses said, "Bridget the Second's down."

Nathan's gums remembered the peppermint and tried to find it. He went on sucking nothing.

Then into the snow and behind the trees, and when they reappeared, Ballad Lady was still leading with Brindle Boy second and Rustic Prince closed up. They came down the hill and up for the second time; the breathing loud, the riders hissing. This is where it begins to count, Nathan thought, this is where the gray blew up.

They went down the hill and crawled up the other side. A horse from the Taunton Vale hunt had nothing more to give. Another got up the hill, but had nothing left when it turned towards the fence. It refused and as it turned aside, Question Mark was almost balked and checked his stride. Mark knew that Laura was shouting. Question Mark jumped to the left. Then she straightened him and sent him in pursuit.

Baskerville shook his head. Plainly the race belonged to the leaders.

"What do you expect?" Nathan snapped. "First time out and all."

"I know. No criticism meant, Nathan."

Brindle Boy moved to pass Ballad Lady. Rustic Prince followed. Ballad Lady fought back, but her jump at the next fence was short and everyone knew that she was done. Rustic Prince followed Brindle Boy to the trees with Laura driving Question Mark after them.

Maddicott glanced at Buckpitt, whose field glasses were intent. The glance said, she'll never do it.

Rustic Prince reappeared in front and the crowd greeted it in a noise of approval. Then the noise lifted in surprise, for there was another horse where Brindle Boy should have been. Baskerville glanced to Nathan. Both were incredulous.

"It's her," Maddicott said, and Buckpitt bared his teeth.

The favorite came down the hill with the complacency of one who knows the race is won. Its rider gave it a breather, but the crowd saw the danger and at last the roar reached her. She threw a surprised glance and heard Laura's yahing noise of exultation. She shook up the favorite and settled down to ride. They came to the last fence together.

The favorite jumped it the better, but Laura had her whip going and suddenly the crowd changed its allegiance; recognizing the valor of the local rider, calling her on, beseeching her to do it.

"She is," Maddicott said, while Buckpitt made little noises between his teeth, urging the whip down.

Mark heard the sounds of it. He made sobbing noises of protest, while Baskerville glanced to Nathan and Nathan chewed his gums.

For a hundred yards the horses matched strides, the rider of the favorite looking to her right, watching Laura, waiting for her to give in. But Laura would not give in. She leaned forward, forcing with her body while her right hand held the whip where the horse could see it. Question Mark knew what the whip meant now. His ears were rabbit flat, his eyes were wild with fright.

"She done it," Elsie screamed.

In ten yards the race was over. The favorite surrendered and Question Mark went by. They heard Laura whooping with joy.

"What a ride," Maddicott said. "She meant to win, all right."

Buckpitt shouldered through the crowd. He was white with excitement. Hands came out to congratulate him and Kate saw them and thought, it's not his horse, it's ours.

Baskerville hissed in his breath and glanced at his friend. Nathan's mouth was moving, tasting words as though they were peppermints. He said, "The boy, where's the boy?"

Mark ran to his horse. His mind was choked with pain. Laura turned towards him, her eyes alight with the magic of winning. She looked out to the cheers like an actress who has her curtain call.

Mark took the horse's head. He heard voices saying, "You could have had him at tens easy, they say Buckpitt backed him for a packet, he knew his daughter meant to win, all right." He saw his mother raise a hand in congratulation and heard his father say, "Well done, Mark." He thought, but didn't you see, don't you know what happened?

Laura got down. She unfastened the girths and took off the saddle. She carried the saddle and weight cloth to the scales in the barn. The crowd parted for her as though she were a queen.

The horse reached out a hind leg and kicked at nothing. His nostrils were red, his veins were swollen into wriggles like worms. Mark saw the whip marks. Sweating brought out the weals, and he put his hands on them as though touch could take away the pain as once his mother had sucked out the poison. He put on the blanket while Nathan said, "He was never ready, not for a race like that."

Mark led the horse through the gap where a gate had been. Maddicott said, "Won a good race," and Jordan agreed, "That hoss will win good money." Baskerville murmured, "As long as his wind's all right," and Nathan said, "I knew you couldn't trust that maid."

Laura found Mark at the trailer. He scattered straw on the tailboard, holding the horse with one hand and scattering straw with the other. Question Mark put a foot on the tailboard, then lifted his head in sudden alarm, pulling at the halter, whisking his tail and staring white. Laura moved to help, but Mark's face came around, livid with hate.

"Stay away. It's you he's afraid of."

She stepped back, frightened by the hatred. She almost collided with Maddicott.

"Your father told you? He had a tenner on."

She watched Mark lead the horse up the tailboard; one foot on, then the other, then a long waiting, his head straining the halter. Suddenly he abandoned resistance and went up to join the gray.

"Put it on for you," Maddicott said. "You had a good afternoon. You won a hundred."

Laura did not answer. She was contemptuous of Maddicott, knowing that her father was contemptuous, too. She watched

Mark put up the tailboard. He slid one bolt and as he moved sideways to slide the other, she covered the bolt with a hand, compelling him to look at her. Their faces were close. Each had the other's breath.

"I won, didn't I?"

"Behind the trees. You thrashed him behind the trees."

"I woke him up. I let him know it was a race."

"You thrashed him."

"I knew he could do it and proved it. What more can you do than win?"

"He wasn't ready. You knew he wasn't ready."

"You won the prize money. Doesn't that mean anything?"

He moved the bolt beneath her hand. "You'll never ride him again."

The following evening Laura came to Yarnator and put a long, fat envelope on the table. No one spoke.

"Go on, open it."

Kate slit the flap and looked at the green notes. "It's money."

"Count it."

Kate counted it. Her voice became a monotony of counting. She reached thirty and said, "There must be nearly a hundred pounds here."

"There's one hundred exactly. It's yours."

"But how can it be?"

"My father had ten pounds at ten to one."

Kate made a little gesture. "Your father's money."

"He gave it me. Your horse won, so it belongs to you."

Howard looked at his hand. It was shaking. He put the fingers to his mouth, touching them with the tip of his tongue.

"It's not a gift," Laura said. "My father has taken back the ten pounds stake. What's there has been won fairly."

Kate looked at the money, then turned to Mark. Silence crept in and watched.

"What's wrong with you people? For the first time in years Yarnator has won something. Yarnator amounts to something. Yet you seem to think it's some sort of disgrace."

Howard thought, don't look at the money, whatever I do I mustn't think of it. He said, "It's being Brethren and money won by betting. . . ."

Mark flashed him a glance and Howard put his fingers to his mouth. They ached to touch the money.

"What if I did have to smack him? You can't win easily. Winning never is. It's easier to give in and be a good loser."

Kate looked down. The notes were clean and crisp. Her mouth went dry so that she could not speak. She held out a hand to Mark, asking him to see the money.

Mark said, "You'll never ride him again."

"I don't want to ride him again."

"We trusted you. Nathan and me. You can't buy trust back."

Laura looked from him to his parents, knowing that they were thinking of the money. She replaced the notes in the envelope, letting them see how much a hundred pounds could be. She thought it would buy them.

Kate made a moaning noise. "We don't like to see you quarrel. You two have been friends for years." Her hand went out to Mark. "And Laura's worked so hard, she's been such a help."

Howard's thoughts babbled, that's right, Kate sees a way to keep the money. "Think of how kind she's been, helping to build the loose-box even. Perhaps she was wrong to . . ."

Mark lifted his head. "Ask Baskerville, ask Nathan. They'll tell you how wrong she was."

Laura waited, the envelope in her hand. She moved it, pretending to put it into her pocket. Howard saw the movement, but did not speak. She put it into her pocket, and Howard almost spoke.

"A hundred and twenty pounds that race won you. Doesn't that mean anything?"

She turned to the door. She lifted the latch and opened the door. She hesitated, a tightness in her throat. Suddenly she drew out the envelope and threw it towards no one. It slid along the floor and its flap spilled the money.

"Take your money. I don't want it."

Draft lifted the pieces of paper. They breathed along the floor. Kate and Howard watched the pieces of paper but no one moved.

Desperately Laura said, "Don't you understand? I know it was wrong. Can't you see I'm sorry?"

She turned and ran and as Mark took a step towards her, Howard crouched and held one between finger and thumb. He looked up, his face quivering, asking Kate to help. You know we need it, you know what it could mean to us.

But Kate did not help. She let him gather the notes alone. One was near Mark's foot and Howard left it until last. His fingers went out to it while Mark watched.

Please, Father, please don't give in to the money. This is a test. A test of you as a Brethren; the Brethren preach that gambling is a sin, so money gained by gambling, that must have sin in it, too. It's a test of you as my father; you know that horse was thrashed, that he'll carry the marks for a week. Please, Father. It's a test of you as a man.

Howard's fingers almost touched the note, the last note. Then he looked up to his son and read the expression there.

It's not greed, see. It's not that I don't care about the horse. It's just that we have never had so much money, so much easy money. It's always been bills and asking for credit and counting the shillings.

Mark saw the thoughts in his father's eyes. He moved his foot so that his father could reach the last note easily.

Howard reached for it. Slowly he added it to the bundle in his fist. Then he looked up again, and his mouth quivered to a smile.

"We'll send it back. No good can come of money like this."

Chapter Seventeen

The blackbird pierced the stillness with its protest. It bent forward, puffing its feathers, dancing a shrill defiance. The cat stopped, waiting for the bird to be afraid. The bird was not afraid.

The cat was embarrassed, for the bird should have been afraid. She turned with feigned indifference, flicking a foot in derision, letting the blackbird have its nest. Then the blackbird's call changed to celebration. It swaggered as it sang, telling the bird on the eggs that the danger was over.

Better watch out, Mark thought, the cat will get you in the end.

The blackbird saw the thought and lifted its bill in arrogance. It was proud with possession, and the need to defend. It shrilled its call again, telling the world to stay away.

"Cocky little fella," Nathan said. "Must have a nest somewhere."

They moved towards the box, where Question Mark showed his ears to the blackbird's truculence. Mark held out a palm and the soft mouth took the cube of carrot.

"Well," Nathan said, "what're you going to do about the other meetings? The Dart Valley and Tamar point-to-points?"

Mark put a hand into his pocket, bringing out another carrot cube. "As long as he's fit."

"He's fit enough. That hard race didn't do no lasting harm." Nathan waited, then asked, "Who will ride him, boy?"

Mark held out a palm and the lips fluttered again. "He has to be shown there's nothing to fear. He has to like the game. The only way to be sure of that is to have a rider who understands and cares about him and knows that he's worth more than the race."

"That's right," Nathan said. "But who, boy?"

"Me," Mark said.

"But you've never rode a race."

"There's no one else." Mark staggered a pace as the horse bumped, asking for more. "No one else I can trust."

Nathan glanced at the taut face and thought, still grieving about the maid, things haven't been the same at Yarnator since then. Well, she asked for it, she could have ruined the hoss forever.

"Point-to-point riders aren't professionals, boy. You ought to do all right."

"As long as he sees that there's nothing to fear. That's all I want." Mark gave the last of the carrot. "Until the Whitsun meeting at Market Town."

Nathan started. "That's National Hunt. Up against professionals there."

"I shan't ride him." Mark's grimace was a comment on his ability. "It would have to be a professional."

"That costs money."

"He won twenty pounds in prize money at the point-to-point. I plan to spend that, finding out what he can do."

Nathan thought, well, why not? You got to know sometime. Meself I don't think he's up to it, but you never know. Nobody can ever be sure.

He said, "You mean reinvest the money like?"

Mark nodded. "And we have to do it soon because I might never have twenty pounds again."

Mark rode Question Mark over three miles and a furlong at the Dart Valley point-to-point. Backed down to four to one because of his previous win, he jumped sluggishly and was never with the leaders. A week later at the Tamar meeting, he began sourly but improved in the second mile, jumping with neat economy and coming with a genuine effort in the last half-mile to finish fourth and strongly.

Mark was jubilant. "He's got over that first race. He doesn't think racing means a thrashing now. In the last half-mile I felt him giving, Nathan, wanting to show what he can do. He'd had enough of tracking them, taking their mud in his face."

Nathan thought, he'll have his chance at Whitsun. I only hope he doesn't let you down, boy. There's a world of difference between point-to-point and National Hunt. Aloud he said, "He's fit, he's on his toes, boy. Given luck in the runnin', he could surprise us all."

The village doubted the wisdom of it. Ezekiel sharpened his scissors on the neck of a bottle, then snipped them at the air experimentally. To the bowed head he said, "Now if Laura Buckpitt was ridin', then I'd say he had a chance."

The bowed head was Fred Warrener. He made a noise of assent, less because he was interested in horses than because Ezekiel was known to be erratic. Argument excited him and when he was excited, he snipped at random while he explained precisely where you were wrong and why. If you persisted in opposition he might seize the sheet and abandon you with your hair half cut. Men knew that you couldn't argue with Ezekiel about Montgomery, the parish council, or family allowances and get away with it. Ezekiel felt strongly about them. Now it seemed he felt strongly about Question Mark also.

"Not interested much meself," Fred said. "Football, that's my game."

Ezekiel's mouth had a sour taste. "Every man to his choice. It's a free country."

Then he proved it by changing scissors for clippers and applying his left hand firmly to the head. He pressed and the head resisted, for Fred was a man of spirit and wished to pick the England team. Ezekiel pressed again and finally the head went down in what amounted to surrender.

"See what happens when the boy rides him. Nowhere at the Dart Valley and same again at the Tamar meeting."

Briefly Fred got his head up. "Only a boy when all's said and done."

"Agreed." Ezekiel blew at the clippers. "But he's had the horse from a foal. You'd think that if it would go for anyone, it would go for him. Yet see what happens. I hear confidentially that his jumping at the Dart Valley meeting was sad to see. So what chance has he in National Hunt?"

Other customers came in to sit on the long plank, their backs against the bench where once Ezekiel had been a wheelwright. They murmured agreement; either because they did not care or because their heads were still recovering from the last argument.

"You see?" Ezekiel released Fred from the sheet. "Opinion is unanimous. It's a waste of time. The horse hasn't got a chance."

Fred stood up, groping for his shilling. He felt free now, free to have an opinion and to express it. His glance scorned the cowards on the plank as he said, "I don't agree. I got a fancy the hoss will win."

The cowards glanced nervously to Ezekiel, who smiled his undertaker smile. "But you know nothing about horses."

"Who don't?" Fred's gesture invited support from the cowards who had suddenly become the jury. "Who gave Sheila's Cottage for the Grand National? These gentlemen know. Now I fancy this Question Mark is a much better hoss than some seem to think. I got a fancy the hoss will win." Fred strode out in the fashion of one who has struck his blow for independence. He turned at the door. "From here up post office," he said.

The cowards saw Ezekiel wince, then file the incident in a corner of memory. The snap of the sheet was a command, calling the new victim to the block.

Bill Harvey rose. "Fred don't know the first thing about it. He's no friend of mine."

He tried a conciliatory smile, but Ezekiel's eyes did not melt to mercy. Bill took off his cap and sat, committing himself to the sheet and scissors, groaning in his spirit because what is justice when the innocent must suffer for the guilty?

"Make a special job of it, Ezekiel. I got a wedding next month."

Fifty years ago the Market Town races had been less important than the roundabouts and ale booths and sideshows.

Nathan remembered the strong man, the colored boxers, the swinging boats throwing their screams to the sky. He remembered the men in high collars and straw hats, arms locked in boozy song, staggering from the ale booths to sleep it off in the grass. When they awoke they had put hands to waistcoats and mourned their watches. "Beware of pickpockets," the notices had said.

Racing had been less important than the holiday and din. There had seldom been more than six horses in a race, and no race had been worth more than twenty sovereigns to the winner. Often the winner of the second race had come out again to win the fourth, and an old stalwart called Merry Major had been ridden by his owner to win two races on each day.

That had been about the time of the Palladin brothers. Nathan remembered them; wizened with corruption, their eyes hooded like gypsy eyes. They had toured the West Country meetings, walking their horses from town to town, sleeping under the wayside stars with the horses hobbled where the grass was best. Sometimes they had issued challenges to private races, each owner putting up five pounds, winner take all. Almost always they had won, and dark stories were still told of how they had won; doping their horses with ash leaves and black treacle, hypnotizing their horses, whispering with a gypsy magic; but these stories were fables, for none knew how it had been done. The Palladins had died with their secrets smiling in their little monkey brains.

Now what had been marshland had become a permanent colony of racing; a hundred loose-boxes, terraces, grandstands, chestnut trees, restaurants, beer bars; all demonstrating that racing in the town was now respectable, that to attend a meeting was not necessarily to be either rogue or mug.

No more "welshing" bookmakers, Nathan thought, no more find-the-lady or cries of stop thief. Racing no longer believes that there's one born every minute.

He saw a red and white dress among the crowd and thought, there she is, the maid that boy's been grievin' about since March. She's seen me, she's comin' here, comin' to ask about the hoss in the hope that I'll tell her about the boy. But what can I say? There's no sign of him forgiving.

"Hullo, Nathan," Laura said.

Nathan thought, you're a good-looking maid, prettier than you used to be, your hair pulled back like that with red ribbon. I ought to remember you larrupin' that hoss, but I can't forget how you helped, workin' honest like a man. They was good days at Yarnator, all three of us workin' for the hoss.

"I see you've got him entered." She found the name on the card. "Surely Mark isn't going to ride?"

Nathan shook his head. He felt her straining to ask about Mark, but the words would not come. To her eyes he said, "He took it hard. You should've known he'd take it hard."

"I wanted to win." She made a little mocking sound, then looked up from the card. "Is he? . . ."

Nathan thought, he's engaging a jockey and paying the stakeholder and declaring the hoss. He said, "He's around somewhere."

She knew the vagueness was a rebuff. She tried to smile, glancing around the crowd for her father. "Say I wish him good luck." Over her shoulder she said, "Personally I don't think he has a chance."

Nathan watched her go, knowing that the last comment was of less importance than were the silences, when she had tried to drag out words by the roots. You're grievin', maid. You can stride away as though you haven't a care in the world, but you're like the boy. Both of you grievin' grievous, and when you get as old as me, you'll know that grievin' when you're young is a sad waste. Young years don't last forever.

He folded his arms on the white rail, watching the jockeys come from the dressing room for the second race. The big names had come by car to put up at the best hotel; but this was a small meeting, so big names were few. Others had come by train for bed and breakfast at the cottages near by. They received seven guineas a ride, with ten for a winning ride plus ten per cent of the stake.

The big names rode horses trained by stables big enough to ensure a steady supply of good horses which had been efficiently schooled. The others rode anything for anyone; of the game as bit players are of the theater, similarly too old to give up or too young to know that what had happened to others could happen to them.

Nathan said to no one, "There used to be a saying. Two kinds of National Hunt jockeys. Those who ride to win and those who ride to get round."

Many of those who rode to get round had once ridden with dash and skill. Then something had happened, and suddenly they had found themselves riding green horses, old horses, bad horses; horses which would throw up their heads to stun or would fall and roll, rolling expertly and with malice, horses which had not won and would never win. Soon they had been judged by their failures. Then there had been nothing left but casual rides; welcoming the ride on a rogue horse because it meant seven guineas and your name on the board.

Nathan wondered what jockey the boy would find to ride Question Mark.

"I saw the clerk of the course," Mark said. "He put me on to Ravenall, who used to ride for a big stable."

Nathan remembered. Joe Ravenall had ridden winners for four seasons, but two bad falls had done him. By the time his leg had mended, the stable had produced a new jockey and Ravenall had been on the way down. No money, no friends. Owners who had quarreled for his services, quarreled now for the young rider who rode with dash and who had not yet broken his leg.

"He's experienced," Mark said.

Nathan nodded. Once Ravenall had made it look easy and crowds had roared to see his craftsmanship; the favorite tucked in and going smoothly, ready to strike as soon as Joe said the word. Nathan thought, it's easy to look good on the best.

"He had a fall in the first race," Mark said. "But he's had a cup of tea and an aspirin. He says he'll be all right."

Nathan made a laughing sound. Ravenall had broken both collarbones, both arms, and his right leg twice. The leg was now shorter and weaker than the other, and he lived in fear of having a horse roll on it. Nathan said, "It'll take more than a cup of tea and an aspirin to put Joe Ravenall right. He's forgotten, boy. Should have retired years ago."

"He's the best I could get," Mark said.

Nathan shrugged. Ravenall hasn't had a winner since goodness knows when. Any horse he rides has ten stone on its back, not a jockey. But what can you do when there's nobody else?

"Have you declared the hoss?"

"In plenty of time," Mark said.

"And paid the stakeholder?"

"The jockey's fee and the insurance."

"We got over an hour then." Nathan rested his buttocks on the window ledge of the first-aid hut. "You don't need me for a minute. I'll have a bit of a rest." He looked left and right, as though afraid that Elsie might suddenly appear and claim the admission a triumph. "As a matter of fact, me legs isn't hardly so good as they was when I was your age."

He waited a moment, his stick tracing patterns in the gravel. "The maid's here. With her father."

Mark's expression hardened. "I know, I saw her."

"Did you speak?"

"She didn't see me."

"Don't be too sure of that, boy. That maid haven't come just to watch the races." The stick scratched one pattern and began another. "She's grievin' about what happened. Things haven't been the same for her since. No more than they've been for you."

Mark shook his head and Nathan sighed. Well, I done me best, more than I ever thought I'd do for Buckpitt's daughter. Now I'll just sit and bide a while, if only the sun would let me. It's funny how some worship the sun, travelin' to find it like the children of Israel looking for their promised land. But me, I don't like the sun. Makes me weak's a robin. Makes me eyes water.

"Nathan, are you all right?"

Don't worry about me, boy. Me eyes always water so I can't see, can't see nothing. 'Twill be all right when I find me handkerchief. Elsie makes sure I always got me handkerchief.

"Nathan."

Isn't that typical? All you want to do is sleep, lie down anywhere, no trouble to nobody, and straightway somebody tries to wake you up, as though sleepin' isn't allowed.

Mark tapped the window of the hut, his hand flagging for help. The uniform came out, taking one arm while Mark held the other. The old man came without protest, groping into the hut and half falling to a bed. It spluttered from his weight.

"He's ill," Mark said.

"Of course he's ill. How old is he?"

Mark thought, I don't know, he's always seemed as old as Moses to me.

The uniform put a pillow under his head. "Must be eighty if he's a day. What's he doing at the races? It just spoils the day for others."

Mark listened to the lie as he told it; then wondered if it was a lie. "He's one of the finest trainers in the West."

"Never seen him before," the uniform said.

"He has a horse running today."

"Oh well, that's different then."

The ginger hand waved, beckoning Mark to stoop beside him. "Never mind me, look after the hoss."

"All right, Nathan."

"You'll need help, so you'd better ask her."

"All right," Mark said. "I'll ask the secretary to broadcast a message."

The uniform held the old man's wrist, counting the pulse. "The doctor, too."

The hand flapped again, as though he were drunk and waving away a fly. "Don't want no doctor. All I want is rest a minute." He paused and Mark thought him asleep. Then he said in a whisper, "Be fit's a flea later on."

The microphone voice broke from the clouds, like the voice of Jehovah in the Old Testament. It called Dr. Fernleigh to the first-aid post in the paddock. Then it repeated the message above the stands. Faces turned towards it with brief interest. Someone said, "Do you know who it is?" while another guessed, "One of the jockeys, fell in the last race."

A minute later the microphone voice came again. "Attention, please. Your attention, please."

The faces looked up obediently. There was always the possibility that it might be you.

"Calling Miss Laura Buckpitt. Will Miss Laura Buckpitt please go to the gate of the stables."

Laura gripped her father's arm. Buckpitt's eyes said, your mother, but Laura said, "Mark," and ran; sidling through the crowd, saying please excuse, then pushing when civilities were not enough.

Mark saw her red and white frock, the red ribbon of her pony tail. He held out his hands, and a moment they held hands in silence, excited by the reunion, by the discovery that there was no bitterness left.

"Help me with the horse," Mark said.

In the jockey's room Joe Ravenall put on the red sweater with the white question mark on chest and back. Another jockey joked, "What you got there, Joe?" and Ravenall smiled wryly. Trust these amateurs, trust them to give you something like this to wear.

He put the sweater over his head, wriggling it down, tucking it into the waistband of his breeches. Once his breeches had been white, kept snow white by the valets who had known that he would pay well. Now they were yellow with the mud of old races. Now appearance did not matter.

Ravenall stamped a boot. One year he had ridden the Gold Cup winner and had had so many friends you couldn't count. One year he had ridden fifty-one winners and made eleven thousand pounds you could tell about. He had always promised his wife, "When there's enough, then we'll have a farm," but there had never been enough because he had been so popular and had had so many friends.

He put on his crash helmet; round like a brown basin, making his head an absurd shape. Over it he tied the red cap, tightening the cloth so that it enclosed his ears. He went to the washroom.

Other jockeys were at the serving hatch, drinking tea and teasing the waitress. They moved to let him pass but did not speak. Ravenall told the washroom, they're afraid I'll tap them for the fare home. He made a derisive sound in his mind. Ten years ago he had been the softest touch in the game. Every hanger-on had known that after a winning day, he would be good for a fiver. "Bless you, Joe, never forget you." Now the tappers were tapping the new favorites, and the new favorites were peeling off the fivers as though what had happened to him could not happen to them.

Ravenall came out of the washroom. If any of these young sparks had enough sense to ask for advice, I'd tell them one of the facts of life. No man can afford his friends. Keep the hard way what you've got the easy, because nobody will look at you when you've been a good sport and given it away.

He stepped to the sunlit paddock, tapping his whip on his boot, looking around for the horse he would ride. He recognized trainers for whom he had ridden. They patronized him with a nod. They would tip him a tenner for old time's sake, but they would not put him up on a good horse. He was a bad risk now.

He recognized some of the traveling lads as they led their horses round. Years ago those lads had made an idol of him, but now their faces were as cold as stone, pretending not to know the fallen idol. Ravenall grimaced. They were small fry anyway; men who had wanted to be jockeys but who had not the nerve or the hands or the weight. They slept in the traveling boxes, cooking their breakfasts over primus stoves and drinking tea without milk because somebody had forgotten the milk again. Some were still trying to make a fortune backing winners.

Ravenall saw the horse he would ride and looked around for the owner. Usually small owners strutted the paddock like small-town royalty. They were full of good-luck wishes and hints at celebrations, but this good humor soured when you came down at the fourth. They didn't know you then. They had to blame someone, so they blamed the trainer among themselves, and when the trainer was listening they blamed the jockey. Next time they'd get a big name for the ride. Next time it would be different. His memory laughed; remembering the butcher who had hired morning dress and photographer, even the carnation, sure that his photograph would be in the local papers, leading in the winner. The first fence, Ravenall remembered, the cow didn't rise an inch.

The boy brought the horse to the center of the paddock. A girl took the horse's head, arms out like wings and forearms parallel to the ground, while the boy untied the stirrup leathers and let the stirrups down. He reached for the girths and tightened them.

Ravenall said to the girl, "Where's the owner?" and the girl said, "Mark, he's the owner."

"The trainer then?"

"Mark, Nathan, and me, we train him."

Ravenall groaned. These bleedin' amateurs. He almost let his contempt show, but the girl's gaze was challenging. He thought, she might be the daughter of somebody important. You can never tell. Touching your cap costs nothing, and these amateurs love it. He touched his cap to her.

He gave the boy his boot, and the boy boosted him to the

saddle. He thought, now for the instructions; strike off in front and make all the running, but don't win by more than a distance, you'll spoil the price next time.

"No whip," the boy said.

Ravenall sighed. One of those. They don't know that this is a game for race horses, not for family pets. If they don't want their horses to get hurt, they ought to keep them at home.

"He might need a smack," Ravenall said.

The boy shook his head. "He's new to National Hunt, but he jumps well. Just let him take his time."

The boy's hand waited for the whip and Ravenall gave it to him. Ten years ago I'd have said, look, son, I ride this race; if you don't like it, you know what to do. But now everyone knows better than Joe Ravenall. Even a boy showing off in front of the girl-friend.

"He keeps his head down," the boy said. "He looks at the fences all right."

Ravenall made a half-mocking sound. What's the betting I have to walk home? He was mocking himself; the ignominy of it. He glanced to the Tote indicator. Three horses were being backed in white towers that crept upward while you looked. Those horses were Perrigan's Folly, Abbey Ransom, and Yorkshire Monk. Everyone knew that they had the race to themselves. From them the betting temperatures went down in steps, with a steep drop at the end, down abruptly to a stump, scarcely perceptible. The stump is me, Ravenall thought. The bookies will be offering 33–1, no takers.

He rode out to the course, where the boy slipped the leading tape. The horse skipped and crabbed in the cursory parade before the stands. He turned for the canter to the starting gate, then jibbed, throwing up his head and nattering his feet. Then Perrigan's Folly went down in the fashion of an old steeplechaser who knows what it's all about. Question Mark saw him go and followed.

Mark found a place on the terrace, tiptoeing to watch his horse come to the starting gate.

"They're making Yorkshire Monk favorite," Laura said, "with Perrigan's Folly second favorite at two to one. But there's a lot of support for Abbey Ransom at eleven stone."

Mark watched Ravenall take the horse under the gate, then turn and come back. "He's never seen a gate."

"Only one strand," Laura murmured.

They watched Ravenall as the tape came down. He brought the horse to it, letting him touch it with his nose.

"Not like a flat race gate," Laura said. "That would frighten him."

The microphone said, "They're under starter's orders." Mark shivered with sickness, and Laura felt the shivering and took his hand.

"They're off," the microphone said.

Question Mark was away slowly. He came to the first plain fence and checked and jumped, then gathered himself for the gallop. They went round left-handed and straightened for the open ditch; notoriously fatal to the inexperienced. He took off too early but saw the mistake and stretched and got over.

They came to the next and Ravenall saw a jockey bounce from the saddle, almost recover, then go down to lie curled up, making his body small, making his head a secret. The horse ran loose and Ravenall kept an eye on it, wishing he had his whip, for a brandished whip would keep the fool away.

He saw Abbey Ransom making a break, resolved to make his light weight tell. Perrigan's Folly and Yorkshire Monk kept with him, so that before they reached the water the field had cut into two groups; the leaders going a lick, ten lengths clear, resolved to keep the race to themselves. Ravenall drove Question Mark at the water. Almost he checked, then took in the stretch, dropping his feet to make a splash. The mistake took it out of him, and Ravenall gave him a minute to recover.

They went round in a long gallop to what had been the first fence. One fell there. Another went at the open ditch. Ravenall knew why. The leaders were setting a killing pace that made slower horses jump too fast for safety. Fair tactics, and at one time he had ridden to beat them with pride in his skill. But not now. He knew his horse was neither clever nor adept enough.

They passed the stands, missing the water, making the long gallop longer. The leading jockeys were watching each other, none giving an inch, with Judson, on Abbey Ransom, dictating the tactics because he had a weight advantage of more than a stone. Ravenall pushed his horse, making a show in front of the stands. He thought, as long as I'm not tailed off, if I can keep him going to the end without being tailed off.

Perrigan's Folly darted into a clear lead and Ravenall knew Monnigan was turning the tap on. But Abbey Ransom went with him, recovering the lead at the next fence. Perrigan's Folly pecked and swished his tail. That's the end of you, Ravenall thought, Judson has been too good for Monnigan there.

Nathan opened his eyes. He looked up to the stoop-down face, focusing it, trying to remember. "Is the race over?"

The doctor shook his head. "Don't upset yourself. We'll get you to a hospital."

Nathan listened to the paddock quiet. "Is the race on now?"

The doctor nodded, fingers on the old man's pulse. "The ambulance won't be long."

The ginger hand wagged towards the door. "Let's hear. . . ."

The ambulance uniform opened the door, and the race announcer's commentary came in. "Down the back stretch it's Abbey Ransom from Yorkshire Monk, well clear of the others, they've got the race to themselves."

Nathan's hands fretted the blanket. Where's Question Mark then? Then he closed his eyes. Gone for sure, fallen for sure. I told the boy, there's a world of difference between National Hunt and point-to-point. A good hoss, but not good enough for this company. He sighed, and the doctor thought he was asleep.

Three furlongs out Abbey Ransom drew ahead by four lengths, but when Judson looked round, O'Gunn on Yorkshire Monk was there, as faithful as a shadow. They were together two out. They came around for the last time, matching stride for stride. They came to the last. Abbey Ransom whirled his tail, but Judson smacked him, forcing him to jump. He jumped. He swerved across. He went down in a flurry of legs, bringing Yorkshire Monk down with him. Ravenall heard the wail of the crowd.

What had been one race was suddenly another, and the crowd howled with new excitement. "It's Perrigan's Folly, it's his race." Monnigan started working on the chestnut, ready to seize a race which he had thought lost, but Ravenall thought, the chestnut's pumped out, the chestnut's had enough. I can beat him.

He settled down to ride, swearing and sweating, forcing his horse to the last fence. Monnigan glanced over a shoulder and saw him coming. It was a glance of alarm and the alarm was a come-on, for Monnigan knew that the chestnut was done. He kept it straight, he made it jump, he made it gallop, but the chestnut was looking for the end.

Then Question Mark got over with Ravenall gloating, I can ride a finish, too, they used to say there was nobody like me for a stylish finish.

The crowd asked, "What is it?" and the announcer cried, "It's Question Mark."

Nathan opened his eyes, while from the window the doctor said, "Here's the ambulance."

Ravenall drove Question Mark to catch the chestnut. For ten strides Perrigan's Folly held on, but Ravenall knew and swore in his mind, cursing his horse, sweating it on, driving with a rhythm of hands and body.

The crowd's roar was less excitement than appreciation of the comedy. They recognized it as further proof that in National Hunt racing there is no certainty; that the humblest is always in with a chance. Their cheer had irony in it.

"It's Question Mark on the stands side." The announcer manufactured his excitement, aware that excitement was an essential quality of his job. "It's Question Mark coming away. It's Question Mark by two lengths . . ."

Nathan threw off the blanket while ambulance uniforms said, "There, there, you'll be all right in hospital." He threw an arm to the window, trying to shout, did you hear that? That's better than all the medicine.

Ravenall walked the horse towards the cinder path, a forearm on his knee, his brown face creasing to a grin. He was still swearing in his mind; swearing at the other jockeys who had supposed that he would never ride another winner.

Mark ran to take the horse's head. His heart went out to the wonderful tiredness; to the inflamed nostrils and the breath like kettle puffs, to the pride which still put a lilt in his feet despite the head-down weariness.

"We won," Laura cried, walking on the other side. "You wonderful horse, we won."

They led Question Mark into the winner's enclosure and the crowd came round. "Dead lucky," somebody said. "Shouldn't have had a chance."

Ravenall took the saddle and turned to the scales room. There was a new swagger in him. He swore at a spectator who impeded him. He strode to the clerk's scales and sat, feeling the sweat dribbling down the inside of his legs, guessing that he had sweated out a pound.

"Walk him round," Mark said, giving the reins to Laura. "I must see what's happened to Nathan."

Nathan was shouting at the uniforms, waving them away, demanding his stick so that he could prove his ability to walk as well as the next.

He saw Mark at the door. "Tell them, boy. Tell 'em I'm fit as a flea."

Mark glanced to the doctor, but the doctor shook his head. "You'd better do what they say, Nathan."

"But he won, boy."

Mark nodded, still bewildered by the wonder of it.

"So you can't let it happen to me, not when he won, boy. I had a brother went hospital and look what happened to him."

"He died on the way," Mark said.

"There you are," Nathan said. "That proves it. Get a fella into one of them ambulances and nobody knows what'll happen."

"It's for your own good," one uniform said, while another added, "Tomorrow or the day after, the ambulance will take you home."

Nathan made a gesture of disgust. "Tell them, boy, tell 'em that if I go home in an ambulance, that'll be the end. Elsie will never let me out of her sight again."

Mark heard Elsie assuring the neighbors, not my fault, the hockerd toad would go, but now he knows, now he knows I was right all along.

He turned to the doctor. "If we take him home at once—by car, a friend of ours will help—he'll be safe then."

The doctor hesitated, then nodded. "All right, if you accept responsibility." To Nathan he said, "But you're an old rogue, putting us to all that trouble."

"I know that, Doctor." Nathan reached for his stick. "I'm a blimmin' nuisance and old enough to know better. Now if you gentlemen would kindly move out the way, and let the dog see the rabbit."

The ambulance uniforms moved from the door. Nathan's stick prodded the floor as he moved forward. In the doorway he straightened, his gaze forcing through the sun glare. He saw the horse going round and round, with Laura at his head. "Tomorrow," he said, "I'll have me hair cut. It'll be worth a shillun to hear Ezekiel explainin' what went wrong."

The crowd had turned towards the runners for the next race, leaving Question Mark a pool of quiet in which to go round and round. He was dark with sweat. His ears were heavy and his eyes had the petulance of tiredness. When Laura checked him to speak with her father, he let out a leg in a kick that drove Buckpitt back a pace.

"He was lucky, all right," Buckpitt said, seeking a share in her excitement, "but you need luck in racing. A lucky horse is like a lucky ship. There's no explaining but it's there."

Laura resumed the walk-round as Mark came up. Buckpitt turned to nod congratulations.

"Good race, son. You won a tidy sum."

Mark did the sum in his head. The race was worth three hundred pounds, including sixty to the second and thirty to the third. That left two hundred and ten, less ten per cent to

Ravenall, which meant a total of . . . He hesitated, thinking, I was never good at sums.

"A hundred and eighty-nine pounds," Laura said as she passed.

Mark repeated it. The sum staggered him.

"Could have doubled it," Buckpitt said. "If you'd had a bet. I had something on for Laura and the Tote's paying odds of over fifty."

Mark smiled and shook his head, so Buckpitt added, "You Brethren, when will you ever learn?"

Mark thought, I know what I'll do with it. I'll see the Electricity Board and pay the charge per acre for electricity to be brought in. That comes first. Then the Water Board charge for mains water, so the farm won't have to rely on the pump or the stream. Then concrete, there has to be concrete for cleanliness, and soon Yarnator will be ready for all that I'd like to do; new barn, new pig houses, with a deep-litter house for the hens.

He glanced at Buckpitt and thought, I'll do for Yarnator what you've done for Narrastun. Reinvesting every shilling that Question Mark will win.

He put a hand on the horse's neck, seeing a farm of new buildings, new concrete, new stock. It was Yarnator as he thought it could become.

Chapter Eighteen

Kate pressed the switch and laughed at the light. She turned the tap and held her fingers to the splash. She listened to the luxury of water and wrote letters in her mind.

To Barbara in South Africa she wrote, "We have electricity, we have water, you don't know what this means on a Wednesday morning in winter when you're hurrying for market."

Then she wrote to Australia, addressing it to Willie's wife but aiming it at Willie. "No more lamps, no more candles and lanterns, no more pumping in the cold dark. Everything will soon be changed. Soon you won't be able to recognize Yarnator."

She destroyed the image which Willie had of home, knowing that he would resent the passing of the old; for that's what happens when people are far away. They become sentimental about home, wishing it to be constant in a world of changes which they have helped to make. They demand that home be preserved so that, should they ever revisit it, their memories will be there like faithful retainers in a Victorian novel, plucking their forelocks, asking to be recognized. They demand that their image be preserved by others, exercising a tyranny which they claim to be a right; as though, because they are far away, home is more important to them than it is to those who have remained.

Well, Willie, your tyranny is over. You've been a shadow at Howard's shoulder for years, murmuring against change as though change would be disloyal to your father. Meanwhile you've been free to do as you please, relying on good old Howard to preserve Yarnator in case you ever visit us. Prepare for the shock now. Soon the settle will go, taking with it those memories of Christmas Eve when the ashen faggot banged its withies. Then the great hearth will be filled in and there will be a modern stove. This will be done because the settle is cumbersome and comfortless; because the cold comes down the wide chimney and frightens the heart of the fire. But you won't think that important. You will remember what you want to remember, mourning the fact that, in a world of change, home is not precisely as it was thirty years ago. Well, boo to you, Willie.

She added an exultant line, "All the village is talking of the changes at Yarnator."

Howard was frightened by this sudden appetite for change, for this jubilant renunciation of all that had been good enough. Mark showed him books and magazines to prove that the smaller the farm, the greater the need for maximum efficiency; but he mistrusted efficiency as a factory word, and had for statistics the instinctive contempt that he had for politicians.

Mark showed him plans for a new pig house, explaining the importance of ventilation and warmth and cleanliness. He shook his head, unable to associate pigs with cleanliness. Wasn't there an old saying, happy as a pig in muck? He remembered how years ago the old sow had scratched her mud on a gate, grunting with pleasure while her litter had rooted in the sun.

"Out of date," Mark said. "Years out of date."

Howard's glance was sharp, resenting the implied criticism of his father. Everyone knew that old man Wonnacott had been among the finest of hill farmers; contriving to show a profit while black headlines of depression had been in all the papers. "Crisis" the headlines had said. One crisis one week, another the next. Howard remembered the front-page photographs of Ramsay Macdonald and Philip Snowden, while on page three Marlene Dietrich had insured her legs for a million dollars.

"Look," Mark said. "Look at these plans."

Howard frowned, for "plan" was another suspect word; an office word, best used by men with soft hands and persuasive tongues, inflicting their theories on those who must make them work. There were already too many plans; plans for building, county plans, town and country plans, moorland plans, planning officers, planning committees.

"You've got breeze blocks," he said, his contempt giving his mouth a sour twist. He had a sentimental regard for stone, which was of the moor and of its colors.

"Buckpitt doesn't use stone," Mark pointed out. "He knows that the modern way is faster and cheaper."

Howard shook his head. "Willie in Australia, what would he say?"

Question Mark won a three-hundred-pound race at the first August meeting of the new season, and Mark built his pig house, then traveled to Reading market to buy two Landrace sows.

Howard studied them, trying to fault them, resenting the Landrace breed because it had been imported from Denmark. He said Denmark with a grimace, remembering thirty years ago, when shops of town and city had offered Danish bacon at prices lower than the English. He heard again his father's rage, knowing now what he had not realized then, that behind the rage there had been fear; fear of producing what none would buy, fear of a competition so acute that the hill farmer would be compelled to sell at a loss. The boy's too young, Howard thought. Only eighteen. Too young to know about those terrible years.

"Long in the back," Mark said. "With tight hams and tail well set. That's what the bacon factories want."

Howard nodded derisively. So much for the farmer's independence. You no longer produced what you wished, how you wished. You produced what the factories wished, conforming to standards set by men who had never been farmers; who did not know about the wind blowing holes in the walls, about the mud slobbering at your boots or about the snow. Men in polite suits controlled your work in the field, telling you your business, when to sell and where and at what price. Milk Board; Potato Board; Wool Board. Howard fired contempt at them, aiming at their pale, conceited faces. His father had hoarded wool for years, waiting for a favorable price, smelling the right time to sell. Now officials of a Wool Board told you when to sell and what price you must accept.

He straightened. "I'm a sheep man, but I learned one thing about pigs. Prices for pork and bacon, they're all up and down, see-sawin' without no sense in it."

"That's right," Mark said. "That's because there's no marketing board."

Howard flinched, sensing that somehow his own argument had tricked him. He glanced at Mark's smile, then threw back his head and laughed. There's a boy for you. Got his head screwed on. He slapped Mark's shoulder as he said, "You bought well, son. It'll be interestin' to see what happens when they farrow."

Question Mark ran five times that season. He won twice and was twice placed. The total prize money was six hundred and seventy pounds and Howard tasted it with awe.

The hand of God is on us, gently, like a blessing. The hand is there in the clouds, now as surely as it was in the Old Testament, and the hand has reached down and touched us so that all we do shows profit. The sows farrow ten to a litter; the ewes lamb easy; the horse wins with such ease that no one would believe. It's not just us, it's not just luck. God is helping us. He began helping us that night on the moor, when I went up to Black Dog Tor. I was afraid. Superstitions were all around. The black dogs of the tor seemed real to me. But I prayed and God was with me. If I had not gone up . . . Howard snatched a breath; for almost he had not.

He did not protest now at the changing of Yarnator. It's God's will, he thought, it must be God's will. I dare not fight against it.

Kate had her stove where the hearth had been. Exultantly she broke the settle for kindling, and Howard looked away; feeling the loss of his childhood, for part of his childhood had been in that settle, as part had been in the candles. His boyhood fingers had picked at the cold grease, snapping it off in wriggle shapes; and one young Christmas Eve, with the fire leaping and the talk murmurous, he had slept in a corner of the settle and his father's coat had covered him. He felt again its roughness at his chin, smelled again the stale tobacco.

Kate had her poultry, too.

Mark built a deep-litter house, with wood chips for scratching, the perches in tiers and the nest boxes long and neat and cowled in darkness. He bought a hundred Rhode Island-Leghorn pullets and suddenly poultry were important. There was money in them.

Kate's interest in the new birds and the new method was immediate. No more creeping among cobwebs, no more groping into brambles, no more climbing the ladder of which she had always been afraid. Collection now was quick and easy. Now she could be proud of her eggs, of their cleanliness and size and suntan colors. Now she could be proud of the money they brought.

Howard said nothing, remembering how each spring the broody hens had hatched their eggs in metal coops. Once a day Kate had lifted each from the nest, compelling it to walk and crap, to peck shreds of corn and drink. Then each had returned and drawn its eggs in, drooping down its warmth in a dedicated service that pretended to need neither food nor drink. On the twentieth day each had been thin, pecking the helping hand, grumbling like the chronic sick at the need for exercise.

Seven out of ten had been a good hatch. Then the coops had been brought to the front garden, where the wind was blunted and the sunshine could rest in a pool. There the hens had walked their chickens, scratching for them, calling them to come and see, picking out the best for them and chiding their jealousies. Then in the twilight, when Kate had gone around to shut the coops against rat and fox, there had been the weep of chicken; called by each hen to the settle-down warmth, the under-feathers gentling down, persuading young life to become a part of the night.

He said, "I used to like you talking to the hens, Kate."

She counted eighty-two eggs; the product of a day. "The stupid things. They were always kicking their chickens or bossing them so much it was no wonder they never grew."

Howard was surprised. "They grew, Kate."

"But so slow. These days pullets ought to be laying at eighteen weeks."

He looked from the window. "I miss the hens in the yard, Kate."

"The butcher paid an average of five shillings each. All you could expect for hens so old."

"Old? Some of them were only two years."

She smiled, telling him his business. "These days a hen is old at two. I know what you're going to say, your mother had a broody hen for years and years, said to be the best broody in the village. That's all out of date."

He compared the hundred pullets in a small house, quarreling in boredom, with hens scrambling in sunshine dust.

"But what about the winter?" Kate said. "When they mooched in the wet, too cold to lay. Your old methods weren't methods at all. It was just muddle and prejudice and hope for the best."

He watched Mark barrow cement to a corner of the yard, then crouch to trowel it smooth. He said, "That boy never stops working."

"It's time the yard was cemented properly, instead of dust in summer and mud in winter. It will be so much easier to keep clean."

He smiled, remembering that she had not wished her son to be a farmer. It's funny, Kate, how things work out. I didn't want him to have the mare, but the mare was the beginning of all this. You wanted him to be an engineer, and if he'd become an engineer, he would have gone away and couldn't have broken and schooled the horse which has won the money to pay for all the changes.

He said without resentment, "There's been more changes at Yarnator since Question Mark's first race, more changes than there's been in fifty years."

She glanced at him, almost saying there're going to be more changes. The market, I can't keep going there, the stone floor in winter cripples me, and making hog's-pudding is hard work, a slow way of making money. But caution held her. He isn't ready for that yet, and I mustn't hurt him. Mark will never forgive me if I hurt him more than I must.

Question Mark came out for the new season to win a three-hundred-pound race at Market Town, but his legs were sore from the hard going and Mark rested him until November. He ran twice unplaced in that month, then won a four-hundred-pound race at Kempton in December.

The prize money provoked a crisis, for Mark said, "We need a car. It will be a help to Mum on market days."

Kate took off her chapel hat. She heard herself say, "I'm giving up the market stall."

Howard straightened. His incredulity was comic; as though the market stall were hallowed by generations of Wonnacott women, wrapping their hog's-pudding and telling customers about the weather. Don't you know about the cold, the spite talk, the little jealousies? Don't you know I don't belong?

"The packing station will collect all the eggs and give as good a price."

Howard said, "The hog's-pudding."

Of course, the Wonnacott specialty, made by the family for a hundred years. Don't you know how I hate it, the mess of it, the smell beneath my nails? She said, "The factory takes the pigs. There are no ends of pork to make it with."

Howard's mouth was open. She knew that he was thinking of his mother; seeing her mince the mess and stuff it into the skins, seeing her boil it, then weigh it and fill her market baskets. Twenty pounds on one arm, twenty on the other; bowed down by the pull, then coming home with baskets empty and coins fattening her purse. You remember the importance of those coins in her purse. They gave you boots when times were hard, thick clothes to keep the winter out. But there's no need for it now. You can sell without going to market.

He said, "Mother had that stall from the day she married to the day she died. Father's mother had it before her and his grandmother before that."

"Times have changed."

"There's a tradition. The Wonnacotts have always had their market stall."

And generations of women have been dragged down by it, made old by it. Not me, not now, we don't need to do it now.

"The customers," Howard said. "They've been coming years. You must know them all."

Kate shook her head. "They don't like me. I don't know

enough about them, about who their sister married, and how many children. They might be as relieved as I am that the tradition is broken."

"It's not broken yet."

"It is. I've told the market manager."

"But all your market friends."

She remembered clover honey on one side and clotted cream on the other. Her laugh was harsh.

"I don't like the thought of somebody else selling hog's-pudding at the Wonnacott stall."

"Nobody will. It's been taken over by imitation jewelry."

She saw his gaze wander past her to nothing. She knew what he was thinking and thought, if you mention Willie . . .

"Willie won't like this," Howard said.

"Then Willie can come and make it, and freeze all day in the market selling it."

Howard thought, it's what having money has done. It's like a test. Not having money, that's a test, and we came through it together, like a family; Kate patching and darning, and the boy helping to beat the bracken. Now suddenly we have money, not a lot by Buckpitt's standards but more than we have ever had, and that's another test. A more dangerous test because at first you don't see it as a test; only as an end to all your worries.

He said, "We got to stay together, as a family." He flickered a smile, as though it couldn't happen. "You'll be wanting to give up the Brethren next."

She thought, I hadn't meant to tell him, not two hurts in one evening. But he's given me the opportunity.

She said, "That's another thing. I'm leaving the Brethren, Howard. It's not a sudden decision. I've been thinking about it for years."

He was shocked and lost. "I said it as a joke, I didn't

think . . ." After a while he said, "All your friends are at the chapel."

"Not my friends. Yours. You're a Wonnacott and belong, but they know I've never belonged."

He remembered Baskerville leading the Brethren to the moor, their lanterns challenging the darkness in their search for Mark. He wondered what he would say to Baskerville.

"But why, Kate, why?"

"The same faces, the same hymns, Nathan shouting because he's never bothered to learn a tune."

"You think you're too good for them."

She snatched her hat. "Look at it, my Sunday hat, a black hat, not because I'm in mourning but because the Brethren are always in mourning. I'm tired of dull clothes. I'm not old. I'm young enough to wear bright clothes, bright colors are fashionable. Why should I be fifty years out of date?"

She remembered the church of her childhood; the stained glass, the candles and surplices, the courteous listening, the half-crowns in the plate. She remembered the chrysanthemums of Christmas and the daffodils of Easter, the sheaves of corn for the harvest festival. She saw the dresses coming to their pews, the smart hats gilded by the evening sun.

Now she had smart clothes, the half-crowns for the plate. Now she was ready to take her place behind the Buckpitts.

"The chapel needs you," Howard said. "There's only a few left."

Old men and old women, smelling of serge, smelling of camphor, smelling old. They would be shocked by my new hat, my silk frock, my stockings and high heels.

She said, "It's going back for me, to a service I remember since I was so-high, to communion, too. It's what I've wanted for a long time."

Howard put his hands over his face, smearing the tiredness from the corners of his eyes. "And Mark, what about Mark?"

She thought, it's not fair to expect him to be a Brethren. It's not a religion for the young. She answered, "He's old enough to decide."

On Sunday evening Mark went to chapel with his father; looking up to Baskerville's old sermon, opening the book to the old hymns, seeing Nathan wipe his eyes and strain to see, then put away the book and shout from memory.

He looked around at the old, creased faces, and thought that here was a quality which the parish church could not supply; an arrogance of humility, a sturdiness of belief in an age which believed nothing. He did not share their beliefs, unable to see where superstition ended and religion began; but he admired their capacity to believe. They did not bend to compromise. They did not make sin a joke.

Nathan forgot the last verse, and Mark passed the book to him. The smile they shared was worth the hour of boredom.

Chapter Nineteen

Fred Warrener filled the doorway, his shadow long and ominous, made long and ominous by his triumph and Ezekiel's alarm. The barber nattered scissors on comb, begging the mercy he had never shown.

Once Fred had been a laborer, no different from other laborers, similarly all strength and cider and penny points; putting on a collar for Saturday nights, proving his religion by despatching his children to Sunday school so regularly that they won prizes as he and his brothers had won prizes. The name of Warrener had been associated with the Baptist church, show parsnips, cider, and Arsenal-for-the-cup; none of which had been enough to establish him above his fellows.

Now things were different. Now his name was made.

Fred Warrener was known to be the man, the only man, who had tipped Question Mark to win at 33–1, with the Tote paying odds of over fifty. He had challenged form in the process and openly defied Ezekiel, who had been omniscient, but whose tyranny was now in smithereens.

Ezekiel saw him stride into the brown gloom and recognized Aaron's serpent. Customers on the plank of waiting moved along in deferential bounces. They recognized the sword come for Damocles.

Damocles snipped, crouching and peering in a craftsman's concentration. He was waiting for the sword to fall.

Bill Harvey cut the thread; remembering the wedding, long

ago it seemed, when he had worn his cap in the family photograph, a victim of Ezekiel's power. He offered Fred a cigarette and Fred hesitated before accepting; the hesitation making acceptance a favor, and the conferring of favor suggesting that the great was prepared to talk.

Bill struck a match. "I hear they got the phone in now."

Fred pulled deeply on the cigarette, holding it between thumb and three fingers with the little finger decorative. His nod agreed that Bill was correctly informed.

"Annie at the exchange. Annie says they been through to Cheltenham, booking stablin'."

"Cheltenham," Sam Stone said. There was awe in his voice, for Cheltenham connoted status; like Wembley or Twickenham or 10 Downing Street. Then they glanced at Ezekiel, who once had mocked the possibility that Question Mark could win at a small West Country meeting.

"He'll be up against Lochroe," Bill said. "And Mandarin and Linwell."

The names had the dignity of statesmen. What Palmerston, Disraeli, and Gladstone had been when politics were serious in the village, Lochroe, Mandarin, and Linwell were now; for horses in the village were always serious.

"It'll be on television," Sam said. "Jacob promised to watch on the White Hart set, then tell us fence by fence in the evening."

The fact of television gave the race another dimension, promoting Question Mark to a new importance; as a B.A. degree puts the shine of scholarship on the boy next door.

"Yet not so long ago"—Bill looked back to that first point-to-point—"they reckoned he was lucky to win the ladies' race."

Fred made a snorting sound. "Not so long ago nobody gave him a chance nowhere. Nobody except me. In fact there was one who shall be nameless . . ."

Ezekiel squirmed. His smile was servile.

"I said then and I say it again." Fred seemed to inflate as he delivered judgment. "That hoss is better than anybody thinks. In fact nobody don't know yet how good he is."

Bill Harvey nodded. "Cheltenham will help find that out."

Ezekiel risked a comment, begging a place in the conversation. "I feel sure that he will do very well."

Fred's glance was a dagger. He was shocked that the fallible had said what the infallible had been about to say. So he changed what he had been about to say.

"Cheltenham won't prove nothing, and shall I tell you for why? It's because he isn't a Cheltenham horse. Never was and never will be neither. Question Mark is what they calls a Aintree hoss." He repeated it, giving Aintree an "h" for emphasis. "A Haintree hoss. That's my considered opinion, and if there's anyone cares to contradict they can do so now for everyone to hear."

They looked to Ezekiel, but the barber knew when he was beaten.

"That hoss will win the Grand National." Fred drew the last from the cigarette, then dropped it to the dust and placed his boot upon it. "I stake me reputation on it."

Question Mark ran at Cheltenham, finishing last in a field of nine.

Joe Ravenall said, "He doesn't jump quick enough, he likes to look at them too long. He's not the sort for Cheltenham."

"Aintree," Nathan said. "He's more the Liverpool kind. He jumps careful, he gallops strong and stays forever. Just the kind for Aintree."

"Aintree," Laura said. "He's the real Aintree type, as consistent as they come and wonderfully generous."

"Aintree," Joe Ravenall told his wife. "They're talking about Aintree." His silence said, you know what that means; what it meant seasons ago when I was riding for Biddlethorpe.

Mark argued that Aintree fences were different from all others, so that even a plain fence presented perils to the horse which had known only the neat brushwood of park courses. Aintree in his mind was a name alive with images; like Sing Sing and Hiroshima and Tyburn.

"You're afraid of it," Laura said. "You'd rather keep Question Mark pottering round the small meetings, top of the handicap all the time, with no one ever knowing exactly how good he is. You're willing to settle for the small, like the fish in the puddle who is afraid to go to sea."

"You must go for the big money," Buckpitt urged. "It won't come to you. There's a certain number of races in that horse and no more. It's sense to go for the big money while he's in his prime."

"If you could win the Grand National," Baskerville said. "Then you'd be made forever."

"You'd be famous," Kate said.

"The race is worth thirteen thousand pounds to the winner," Buckpitt said. "You could buy more land. Yarnator could be like Narrastun."

At night Mark listened to the wolf wind, seeing pictures in the darkness and calling them Aintree. Horses falling, horses brought down, horses broken, horses dead.

He turned his face to the hot pillow, shutting out the pictures, telling his fear, Aintree is like the man in the cupboard years ago. It is nonsense to be afraid.

In the morning he said, "He'll go for another race, over part of the Grand National course. That will give him a good look at Aintree fences. If he does well, then we can think about the Grand National next year."

"Next year," Laura said, impatient of the delay.

"It will have to be next year," Nathan said. "While he's still in his prime."

Mark nodded. "But first let him prove himself over a

shorter distance and only part of the Grand National course."

"That's compromise," Laura taunted.

"It's caution."

"You're hoping that it will never happen. That he'll never run in the Grand National."

Mark saw again the pictures of the night. "There must be no risks."

"There's bound to be risks. Every steeplechase is a risk."

Mark put a hand over his eyes, telling the pictures to go away. "No avoidable risks," he said.

Ravenall slit the envelope with a thumb. He read the sprawling writing and refolded the letter, attempting to return it to its envelope. His tremble fumbled it.

To his wife he said, "They're going for the Grand Huyton." His relief told him how great his fear had been. "They're not trying for the National."

Question Mark won the Grand Huyton at Aintree by five lengths, jumping without blemish and coming with a strong run to surprise the first and second favorites.

Mark's jubilation mocked his dark fears. It was superstition, I knew it was superstition. Aintree fences are fair, I knew they were fair. They can be jumped safely by a good horse who knows the game and loves it, and who isn't thrown in to take his chance merely to please the vanity of the owner.

"You can't compromise any longer," Laura said. "Question Mark has shown what he can do. I'm surprised you ever doubted him."

"I didn't doubt him. It was just a superstitious fear of Aintree."

"Now nothing can stop us."

"Nothing," Mark said. "We're ready now."

Racing correspondents began to take seriously the horse of doubtful pedigree.

"In the Grand Huyton he looked a real Aintree type, treating every fence with respect and chancing nothing."

A Sunday newspaper ventured: "He might easily win a Grand National, for the quality of Grand National fields has declined in recent years. It is still the most popular race in the National Hunt year and the richest, but it no longer attracts the best horses. The very qualities which had Question Mark tailed off at Cheltenham after a long series of successes in the West Country, will stand him in good stead at Aintree."

Laura bought all the daily and weekly papers, scanning the sports pages for mention of Question Mark. She gave the cuttings to Kate, and the desk in the parlor, which once Howard had been afraid to open because of the bills, remained open because of the press book.

Question Mark ran at Wincanton in October, finishing ninth of sixteen over two miles. The crowd watched with respect, recognizing it to be the first step in his preparation for the big race in March.

He came out again at Plumpton over three miles, finishing a close third to Yorkshire Monk and Abbey Ransom.

"Don't be kidded," Fred Warrener said. "He wasn't being pushed. It's all part of the plan for March."

Bill Harvey said, "Did you see the *Daily Sketch?* They had a photograph."

Elsie told a neighbor, "You can't get the hat off him. He goes to bed with it on."

"Fred's gone off the pools now," Bessie Warrener said. "They still come regular, but he won't deign to look at them. He's savin' the two shillun a week for a big bet on the National."

Alfred Philbin knew that the windows of Church Terrace were saying, "He's the grandfather."

"Our fault," Maddicott lamented. "If we hadn't been so

generous, we could have had that mare ourselves and the foal would have been ours, proper manner. We should never have let that boy keep the mare. Buckpitt was too easy. It shows what happens when you're generous."

"That boy's got the right ideas," Buckpitt said. "He's doing for Yarnator what the Wonnacotts could never have done."

Mrs. Buckpitt murmured, "Surely Mark is a Wonnacott?" but Buckpitt shook his head.

"His mother's in him. She's given him the qualities that count."

Give him plenty of steady work through the winter, Nathan said. He likes work. Jogging up the hills and down again. He's a good workman, and when you take a good workman away from his work and shut him up in idleness, he's sad and bored and only half alive.

Nathan watched them go out of the yard towards the moor; Laura on the gray, and Mark riding Question Mark. Two fine hosses; for he was ready now to be generous about the gray. The hosses have been together so long they make a pair. And the riders, they make a pair, too.

Nice young people, Nathan thought. Once upon a time I didn't like young people, always so brash with know-all, couldn' tell 'em nothing. You was just an old man on the jubilee seat. But these young people, they're all right, happy in theirselves and in the work they're doin'. Forever talkin' hosses. Forever talkin' about Question Mark as though he's a king on a throne, and that's the way it ought to be. Giving theirselves to the hoss like soldiers give theirselves to a king.

He waited two hours for the horses to come back, and when he heard the first faint merriment of hooves, the sound went into him, exciting his heart with the magic of horses coming.

The village children were coming with them; their eyes big and silent in admiration. Nathan thought, I ought to shoo 'em away as blimmin' nuisances, but I dunno. They'll have something to tell their children in years to come. They'll be able to say, see that picture on the wall? That's Question Mark. When we was children, we used to run beside him as he come in from the moor of a mornin'. Handsome hoss he was. That was the winter before he won the Grand National.

They'll be able to tell their children that, Nathan thought, and the children will listen, all eyes, because children always love tales about the old days. And perhaps they'll remember what they was told and will pass it on to their children, and perhaps in that way Question Mark will live on in this village for years and years. So that folk who never set eyes on him will be able to say what a handsome hoss he was.

Because he is a handsome hoss, Nathan thought, taking Question Mark's head as Mark slid from the saddle. 'Tis no wonder the village can't talk about nothing else.

The B.B.C. program "Tonight" featured the "horse from the wilderness," with Fyfe Robertson troubled because this was a horse without a pedigree and wasn't that unusual?

An Independent Television team camped for a week at the White Hart. Its feature introduced Fred Warrener as the local expert—"I been sayin' all along he'll win a Grand National"—and included brief interviews with Baskerville and Nathan.

Baskerville said, "None of it would have been possible without Nathan."

But Nathan said, "I only told 'em what to do. These young people done the rest. Years of work they've put in. Six o'clock in the mornin' with the rest of the world in bed."

Mark picked up the telephone. The voice at the other end was Fleet Street.

"Is it true Ravenall will have the ride?"

"Of course," Mark said. "Joe Ravenall always has the ride."

"Even in the National?"

Mark did not like the "even." Your sort of people, you decide that a man is finished, then refuse to let him come back. It's one way of proving how right you are. He said, "Why do newspapers always ring in the middle of the night?"

"It's not the middle of the night here," the voice said.

Mark put down the telephone. No, I suppose not, you begin in the evening and end in the morning, turning day and night inside out. Hard lines on you, but it's a nuisance. He yawned so wide that his eyes sprang tears. I shan't get off again for hours.

"Did you see the paper?" Ezekiel pleaded. "They say that at eleven stone eight he is very favorably handicapped."

Bill Harvey brought his head up. "He don't need no charity. Give him top weight and he'd still win."

He half bowed his head again so that Ezekiel thought him ready; but a sudden lift frightened the clippers.

"And make a good job of it," Bill Harvey said. "Missus said last time you got a shockin' aim."

Mrs. Penny said, "Nathan's been worrying him for years, and now he's gone. All the way to Yarnator. Any minute I'm expecting somebody to come running with the bad news. He'll never manage it. Him and his poor back."

Penny managed it.

"Give him carrot," Mark said, holding out the cubes. "Carrot is his favorite."

Penny took the cubes and put all save one into his pocket; knowing that a horse likes you to make it last. He held his palm flat and Question Mark reached out, fluttering his lips above the palm. The saddler offered the cubes one by one, and the flutter of the lips brought back old memories and filled his eyes with tears.

"I'd like to do something." Penny's fingers touched the wide sensible forehead and went down the long face; gently like the touch of the blind. "There's a saddle and bridle, the last things I ever made. Not for no customer, you understand. Just for me, so they could be the way I wanted."

They waited and after a while Penny said, "I'd like you to have them, boy."

"He's wicked as a tiger," Elsie told a neighbor. "There he was, showin' off to Penny about bein' fit as a flea, let's dash up Yarnator for a look at the hoss, and in the end it was Penny brought him home. So gone in the legs that even he couldn't argue. Now I got him in bed, thumpin' the floor with his stick and warnin' me if I allow the doctor through the door again, there'll be murder in the family."

Kate held out the telephone. Her mouth said, it's the master of the hunt.

Mark took the telephone. "Hullo, Major."

"Good morning, Mark. We're holding a special meet at the White Hart the week before the race. We're calling it the Grand National meet in honor of Question Mark."

"That's very kind."

"Not at all. It's not every hunt that produces a Grand National winner, and the first race he won was at our point-to-point." The purple voice chuckled. "The other hunts are furious. The nearest the West Country ever got to it before was Lord Mildmay's Davy Jones."

"An unlucky loser," Mark said.

"Very, we were all brokenhearted here at the time. There's one thing though. We'd like you to bring the horse along. Not to hunt, of course, but to be there at the meet." The Major waited. "Isn't that possible?"

"I must ask Nathan."

"Oh." The sound suggested that the master had no high opinion of the old horsebreaker.

"He's in bed, his legs are bad, but I must ask him. I've never done anything without asking Nathan."

"You'll let me know as soon as you can? I'll spread the word around. If Question Mark is there we can be sure of a good meet." The chuckle was purple again. "Good for publicity, boy. I'll get the local papers on to it."

"I'll ask," Mark said. "I go down to Nathan's every day."

"There will be a ball at the White Hart in the evening. We'd like you to be the guest of honor."

"So you're to be the guest of honor, boy." Nathan's lips pretended peppermints. "Some difference to the time you rode that skewbald to your first meet. They didn't want you then."

"There was no reason why they should," Mark said.

"You was a nobody then and they'd have squeezed you out if the Buckpitt maid had let them. But she knew and I knew. I said at the time." He heaved himself up in the bed. "Give us me stick."

Mark gave him the stick. He prodded it on the floor once, then listened, and hammered a tattoo. They heard Elsie on the stairs.

"Tell him what I said that first time."

Elsie wiped her hands in a corner of her apron. "That first time when?"

Nathan made a tut-tut noise. "That Boxing Day meet when he rode the skewbald and the other lot were trying to squeeze him out. Tell him what I said when I was on the doorstep."

He leaned back and closed his eyes, sure that Elsie would remember.

She groped in memory, her hands moving in a corner of the apron, her eyes round with effort.

"You said, see that boy on the skewbald, two years from now he'll be riding the best hoss hereabouts."

"And did anybody listen? Did anybody believe?"

"How should I know?"

"Nobody listened and nobody believed. Everybody thought it was old Nathan again, too old to know nothin', out of date with nowhere to go except the jubilee seat. You for one." His eyes opened accusingly. "You didn't believe a word of it."

"That's not fair, I always liked Mark. I remember seein' him runnin' that day towards the moor. . . ."

"You told me to hold me tongue," Nathan said.

"That's right and I tell you again." Elsie opened the door wide so that she could slam it with a flourish. "Dragging me up here for nothin', and me with dinner in the oven."

"We're very proud," Mrs. Philbin said. "Father never says much, but he feels it."

Kate crushed a cigarette in the tray which her mother offered. She looked down at the small embers, thinking it's easy to be proud with his name in all the papers. But were you proud when he failed the eleven-plus? That thought was followed by another, and she added in self-reproach, was I proud of him then? None of us was proud of him then. We made excuses, we said it was Fairweather, the system, we said he could do it if only he would concentrate. None of us realized that there are other kinds of work besides school work; other kinds of success besides examinations.

She glanced at the glass cupboard. So the half-sovereign stayed in the skittles cup.

"You're looking very smart, Kate."

Kate looked up to the mirror and smiled at the woman she saw there; lemon hat, green costume, lemon gloves.

"Father was saying only the other day how smart you're looking. We like to see you so successful."

Kate laughed. "In the last year we've received more in Ministry grants than we'd ever made before in profit. Ten sows where there were two, twenty steers where there were five, and Mark is getting them out in two years instead of nearly three. A hundred ewes, a hundred pullets, and prices good. Eggs, wool, bacon, mutton, beef. Not good, perhaps, to those who had the best years, but good to us. Good enough. We don't have to think poor now."

The next day the television set arrived, and Mrs. Philbin told a neighbor: "It's a gift from our daughter. The mother of Mark Wonnacott, you know? His name in all the papers. She sent it to us as a surprise. So that Father and me can come into the front room and switch it on and sit in our armchairs and watch the race."

Kate opened the door and Buckpitt was there, stepping over the threshold as he asked, "Is Mark in? I wanted to talk to him about something rather important."

Buckpitt glanced at the door of the kitchen, then to the parlor.

"He's in the lounge," Kate said, for the parlor was now the lounge.

She had transformed it with new curtains, new carpet, new rugs, new chairs and settee. Lamp shades softened the corners of what had been always a harsh room, cold with Sunday and the memory of funerals. There was a cocktail cabinet in one corner, a television cabinet in another. They were linked by bookshelves, bright with new books about horses, racing, cattle, pigs in Denmark, sheep in New Zealand; books which Mark read in the comfort of the hearthside chair. He had a standard lamp behind the chair, and she liked to see him there, quiet and purposeful, the light in his hair, the white shirt deepening his tan.

He looked up from a book as Buckpitt came in to sit opposite. Kate went to the cabinet for drinks; ginger ale for Mark, whisky and splash for Buckpitt. She turned with the glasses, watching them lean towards each other in earnest conversation; Buckpitt advocating and Mark resisting. Equals, Kate thought, one forty-five and the other twenty; but equals in intelligence and conviction, with success to support their opinions.

"It's true." Buckpitt took the glass which she offered. "Luck is a very peculiar thing. Either you have it or you haven't, and if you haven't you destroy all that you touch. No apparent reason for it. Theoretically all you do is right, but the blight is on it. Like a curse."

"That's superstition," Mark said.

"I don't know what it is, but it's true. I had a cowman once. Good, knew his job, but all the time he was with me, nothing but trouble. Yet as soon as I got rid of him, back the good luck came."

"Coincidence," Mark said.

But Kate remembered hearing of Mother Wonnacott's sister for whom butter would never turn; yet as soon as Mother Wonnacott seized the churn, the butter was there as though by magic. They had said the sister was "overlooked," as though a presence were at her shoulder, giggling like an organ-grinder's monkey, mocking her efforts and dooming her to failure.

"You now"—Buckpitt indicated Mark with the glass—"you got good luck. I recognized that years ago. Other owners, plenty of money, plenty of experience, they pay big sums for good stock and what happens? They lose races they should have won. They place a horse with skill and care, they get him fit, full of himself, ready to run for his life. And what happens? He spreads a plate coming around the last bend. Or he's kicked at the start or a loose horse brings him down. Things happen, never the same thing twice but always something. Nobody knows why. The jockey, the trainer, all mystified until in the end they admit that there is such a thing as jinx luck and that you'll never beat it."

Mark remembered tales of the evil eye; if it saw you as you plowed, the seed would not grow, if it "overlooked" as you planted potatoes, the crop would be sour with blight.

"Nonsense," he said. "You're going back a hundred years. Before education, before people could read or travel, when they had only tales to explain what they couldn't explain."

Buckpitt shook his head. "Not going back a hundred years. It's here, it's now. It's in this house now." Buckpitt put down his glass. "Your father's got it."

Mark threw a quick glance at his mother. Then his eyes went cold.

"Not his fault," Buckpitt added quickly, feeling the tension. "But the commoners have known for years that Howard Wonnacott has the blight touch. His father hadn't, neither had his brothers. Look at Willie, no better than Howard, not as good a sheep man, but everything Willie touched came off while everything your father touched went bad. He could give you a hundred examples, some of them too long ago for you to remember. Always bad luck. Always the dead hand."

Mark thought, I must defend my father, Buckpitt is trying to tell me something about my father. He said, "We're doing all right now. This year our lambing average is as good as yours."

Kate held a hand for Buckpitt's glass. "It's true your father always seemed fated. The luck never gave him a chance."

Mark shook his head. My father failed because his stock was poor, because his methods of production were as muddled as his prejudices were confused. He hadn't the capital to invest in new stock, while his loyalty to his father compelled him to repeat old mistakes and to say that's the way we've always done it. It had nothing to do with luck, with the blight touch or being overlooked. It had a great deal to do with family pride and suspicion of change and never having the capital for new ideas.

"Everyone talks of my father as a failure. If he hadn't worked so hard there'd have been no Yarnator." There was an edge in his voice and his glance at Buckpitt had a glint. "You would have absorbed it into Narrastun years ago."

"I didn't mean anything against your father. You can't help the death touch. It has nothing to do with hard work. You can't work it out. The more you work, the more it's there, destroying all you try to do."

Mark thought, that might be true, but you've never liked him, trusted him, you've never known what it is to work year after year with nothing to show for it.

Buckpitt leaned forward earnestly. "That horse now. If Howard Wonnacott had had that horse, the schooling and the training, it would never have won anything, not even a point-to-point. He would have put the bad luck into it. Even now, if he ever touched that horse in any way . . ."

Mark thought, how, how can my father touch him? He said, "It was my father who was there with the mare. When she foaled. It was he who brought the mare in from Black Dog Tor and beat the bracken to make more grass. I owe him all that. There'd have been no Question Mark if it hadn't been for him."

Buckpitt's gesture swept that aside. "Yet there's something. Sailors understand it. Gypsies understand it. The old folk on the moor, they understand it. If your father ever touched that horse in any way."

"How?" Mark said.

"If he led the horse in the ring. Had a bet on perhaps, although the Brethren never bet. That could do it."

Mark felt a little quiver of fear. "Nonsense," he said. "I'm surprised at you, believing these old wives' tales."

"True," Buckpitt said. "It's the only thing I'm afraid of. Because if that doesn't happen, you're going to win, boy.

Laura's been sure for so long that she's finally convinced me."

Kate came forward with new glasses. "Then let's have a drink to celebrate. To Question Mark," she said, looking at Mark above her glass.

Baskerville scrubbed his arms and knuckles, seaming out the blackness as though it were evil and white skin the new religion. Over his shoulder he said, "Mother, I've decided. Five minutes ago I decided."

He soaped his neck, his ears, his hair, driving out the evil. Through the splash of water he said, "I've retired."

He reached for the runner towel behind the door. The smell of the forge was in it as it was in all the crowded room; the sofa, the chairs, the mantel border, the lace curtains and window fern. Even the pages of the family Bible smelled of soot and burning horn.

"Ever since the war the travelin' forge from Market Town has wanted the village trade. Now it can have it. I've shod my last hoss, Mother."

Mrs. Baskerville brought luke-warm water and soap powder, standing aside with hands clasped in admiration as he prepared to wash his beard. Baskerville was vain about his beard.

"When I was sixty I said I'd retire at sixty-five, but when that time came it didn't seem right. Then I said I'll retire at seventy, but when I was seventy that didn't seem right either. Then suddenly I knew, today I knew."

He felt good and strong, satisfied in his craft.

"I had Question Mark in today, Mother, and all the village come around, just like long ago. They watched me shoe that hoss with every drop of skill in me. They watched every nail, knowing how important it was. Then, as I put the last foot down, I saw it like a light from heaven."

He splashed water, then groped for the towel; missing it because she tried to guide it to him. His face went into it with a deep, clean sigh, and when he reappeared his beard shone like a prophet's in the lamplight.

"No more Maddicott, payin' less than a fair price. No more fillin' old feet with putty."

He held his beard to the fire while she watched in an admiration as deep and silent as a river.

"I knew I'd made the finest job I'd ever made in me life for the finest hoss. I knew it was God's time to retire. I'd shod the Grand National winner."

The cat heard the boots and shrank over her kittens, hiding them, watching the man stride towards her secret. She showed her teeth in a red hiss.

The man crouched, his fingers fumbling the wall. He dropped to a knee and fingered out a stone. Then he removed a bundle and counted it and replaced the stone. He stood up and listened; and the cat knew by his breathing that he had a secret, too.

Howard thought, ten pounds at fifteen to one will buy me what I've never had. Kate has her car, her new furniture, her new clothes, but nobody has given me what I want. I want money, not one pound, three pounds, five pounds, but a roll of it, as fat as Buckpitt's. Then I'll be the equal of Buckpitt, and the village will see it and look up to me as they look up to him, waiting for me to say, "Drinks all round, Jacob," watching the roll in my hand and feeling the envy as once I did.

But the bet must be placed in secret. Nathan must not know. Baskerville must not know. They are Brethren, and none of the Brethren must know.

Howard stiffened, staring at the cat and seeing nothing. Almost he said aloud, my father must not know. In a moment of fright he saw his father, upright with conviction, branding with scorn the dice players and gamblers, making gambling an evil like poison in your body.

He put a hand on the ladder and swung down from the loft. He ran across the brown earth of the linhay; running from his father, making the money small so that his father would not see, making his body small so that his father would not know.

Chapter Twenty

The room was hot, the grins were red; the beat of the dance band had the monotony of wings, blundering for the light. Mark glanced at the clock and wondered how soon a guest of honor might pardonably go home.

Joe Maddicott went by, shining and red, his shy grin remembering the time he had tipped Mark's cap and Bessie Warrener had threatened not only him, but the status of his family. Now Joe was recognized to be a young man of accomplishments, not all of them agricultural. He was chairman of the Young Farmers' Club; the most promising political speaker of the Young Conservatives; a sturdy bass in the church choir; and a cricketer who yelped the ball from the bat, his power in thick forearms and sureness of eye.

Funny, Mark thought. At school, the village school and the secondary modern, Joe had been just another oaf, grappling with decimals and Exodus, Canute and H_2O, big of noise and blunder. Yet somewhere between fifteen and twenty, Joe had ceased to be the buffoon of the classroom, the lout of public places, and had become a champion plowman, a confident judge of moorland sheep, and a political speaker who could precede the candidate with vigor.

Mark watched Joe circle the dance floor. Ten years ago Fairweather called you a dolt who would never learn. Now you lecture Fairweather at political meetings. I wonder if he is amused.

"Hullo, Mark," Joe said in passing, his teeth made white by the apple shine of his cheeks. To his partner he added, "We went to school together."

Laura went by in the arms of Archie Llewellyn, the Colonel's son. She flapped a hand, signaling be with you in a minute. High time, too, Mark thought, you know how I hate social affairs like this.

"Have a drink," Colonel Llewellyn said. "Might be the last chance I'll have to wish you luck in the race."

"Thank you." Mark emptied the orange pool in his glass. "Orange juice, please."

"Nothing in it?"

The Colonel looked surprised, and Mark wondered why you were expected to be apologetic about soft drinks. He had tried whisky and disliked it. Gin and beer, too. They seemed very much overrated.

He said, "Are you going?"

"No luck, I'm afraid. Can't afford it." The Colonel said it wryly, as though only the wrong people could afford it; a sign of the times, old boy. "Have to stay home and make do with the old TV."

He raised his glass; Mark raised his. They drank and watched the dancers.

"Dashed pretty girl that. It's only when you see her in evening dress that you realize what a looker she is."

"Who?" Mark asked.

"Laura, of course." The Colonel tilted his glass. "She ought to do well in London. It's where she belongs, where you meet everybody. Not here in a village like this where nothing ever happens." He emptied his glass, then picked out the lemon and sucked it. "She's got a job, dress designing with a big London firm. Don't tell me you didn't know."

Mark shook his head. "I didn't. Laura and me, we never talk much about ourselves."

"Only about the old horse, eh?" He grinned. His false teeth were big and yellow. "That will suit Archie, he'll see plenty of her then. He's been mad about her ever since that point-to-point when she won the ladies' race. 'Crazy,' that's the word, isn't it? It used to be 'smitten,' but now it's 'crazy.' Archie's been crazy about her since then." He fingernailed a shred of lemon from a tooth. "Funny she never told you."

Mark thought, I don't like you, Colonel. I don't like your eyes, your teeth, or the hinting in your talk. He said, "Why? Why should she tell me?"

"Well, good heavens, you've been riding those horses together for years. Going everywhere together. Never apart. You can't blame us for thinking . . ."

Laura came towards them. She wore a green dress that gave her hair a Spanish black, her eyes a gypsy flash. Mark thought, if it were any other girl, I'd think looking like that was a wonderful fluke. But I know you. You've spent a long time over it, doing it deliberately.

"Archie," she said, "be a dear and get us all a drink."

"Let me," Mark said.

"Not you. You're guest of honor. You hate it, so at least you ought to get your drinks for nothing. I don't care what it is. Something long and cold, with ice."

Laura perched on a stool facing Mark. They shared a long smiling look.

"Well." She put out a hand and he took it. "I suppose the Colonel's been telling you."

The Colonel started. He almost said, not at all.

"I thought he'd take the first opportunity. Being jealous of you, you see."

The Colonel started again. This time he did say, "Not at all."

"He doesn't understand about you and me." She took the

long glass which Archie offered, listening to the clink of ice. She raised the glass. "The health of our guest of honor."

"Your health," Archie said. "Though really it shouldn't be you. It should be Question Mark sitting there."

They laughed, and Archie, surprised by the success of his joke, looked around to see if others had heard and appreciated.

"Or Nathan," Mark said.

"Or Nathan," Laura agreed.

Archie asked, "Who's Nathan?" and Laura smiled as she sipped. "One of the two who understands about Mark and me."

She looked at Mark above the glass and her eyes were gentle. Nathan knew but you never really understood that what I wanted was a cause. My father could give me everything except a cause. Not a lost one, there's no excitement in that, but a new cause which could succeed if we worked hard enough and consistently enough and gave all our thoughts and time to it. Question Mark became the cause.

She said, "It began that first Christmas when I came home from the new school."

Mark remembered. You came into the kitchen on Christmas Eve and we sat on the settle and listened to my parents being embarrassed about us.

"We had years," Laura said, "more than nine years working for that creature. And now look at him. His photograph in all the papers, and a book of press cuttings that thick."

Mark remembered the time Question Mark had fallen, his leg through the reins, sweating with panic and the surprise of pain.

"Wonderful years," she said. "Something to strive for all the time, and in the last few seasons the excitement of winning."

Mark's surprise said, you don't mean they're over?

"Next week comes the climax. The great achievement, because this horse is going to win, make no mistake about that. But what comes afterwards?"

"Retirement," Mark said. "After the Grand National, retirement." He looked at his glass. "No more risks."

"So the years are over. After the achievement, there's only anticlimax, and even if there were another horse, he could never be another Question Mark. You don't get luck like that twice in a lifetime."

Mark twisted the stem of his glass, watching the light reflected. He thought, what are you trying to tell me?

"I'm trying to tell the Colonel what's so special about us. And Archie, too. Archie ought to know. Then he won't be so noble about not being jealous."

"Laura," Archie said.

"Well, you are, you're very noble and if you aren't jealous, you ought to be. Because what Mark and I have had, it's not the love you read about, but it's a kind of love just the same. People have seen us and thought, 'The Buckpitt maid and the Wonnacott boy, they'll marry some day and Yarnator will join with Narrastun and there'll be one big farm on the hill.' My father's thought of it. Your mother's thought of it, Mark, ever since that Christmas Eve."

Laura paused, shaking her head. They didn't know we had something else, something neither of us will ever find again or could repeat if we stayed together. Something to carry like a smile in the heart, so that when I'm a gray grandmother, if there will be gray grandmothers in the age of space travel or grandchildren either, I will tell my grandchildren how, once upon a time, years before the first man reached the moon, there were a boy and a girl and a horse, and the horse changed the lives of all who lived around him. The boy's parents, the girl's parents. Nathan who trained him and Ravenall who rode him and Fred Warrener who tipped him. But most of all the girl, teaching her that patience and humility must go into the making, teaching her above all that there is a right way to win in an age quite sure that any way is good enough. My grandchildren won't be impressed, for by then it will be well known that winning is an illusion, and that belief in it as the cardinal principle is a doctrine known to persist only among backward peoples who worship the having and not the doing.

She fingered her glass, a nail scratching an edge of the stem. "It's a sort of good-by. It's been a long time, so it will need a long time to say good-by."

Colonel Llewellyn said, "I never did like the idea of you going to Aintree with the horse."

Her glance was the flick of a whip. "Of course I'll go. Of course I'll lead him in the ring. But afterwards, after the climax and retirement, there's got to be something for me." She looked down again, turning the glass round and round so that the rings of wet left patterns. "Mark will have Yarnator. He'll go on and on working for Yarnator until the day comes when Yarnator is the best, the most productive farm in the village. But me, what about me? I've got to have something, too. So I'm going to London, putting to some use all that I was taught during years and years of school and college."

There was a silence, as though of mourning. Then Archie said, "There's money in dress designing. I knew a fellow at Sandhurst . . ."

Mark watched her eyes and asked, Archie, where does he come into it?

Her smile said, he doesn't, not really, but he's kind and lets me have my own way and that's nice. Besides, his background is right, he knows the right people, and that counts. Not as much as years ago, but enough.

Mark thought, you won't marry him, not someone like Archie?

I might. There are worse things than being married to someone like Archie. Gently her eyes said, you've a romantic notion about why women marry. If I married for love, I would marry you, for the only love I've known is the love I have for you and my father. But that's not enough. There's more to it than that.

"I shall miss you," Mark said.

"And I, every time I see a horse, I'll feel, I don't know what I'll feel." She seized the glass. "Here, Archie, let's have another drink."

"Mine," Mark said, with such decision that Archie swallowed his protest.

The first drink we ever had together, do you remember what it was? "Ginger wine," he said to the barman, and her smile said that she remembered.

He glanced at Colonel Llewellyn, who said, "A gin," and to Archie, who said, "Scotch for me, old boy."

Mark turned to the bar as the barman said, "Just ginger wine is it? Nothing in it?"

"Nothing," Mark said.

A crowd burst into the room, arms around shoulders and singing, "For he's a jolly good fellow." Their enthusiasm was formidable. Mark recognized Willie Steer and Benjamin Jordan and others who had heard Fairweather tell about the ponies on the moor.

"It's for you," Archie said.

Mark thought, now what do I do? Cling to this brass rail and vow they won't carry me around the room. So I cling and what happens? Willie Steer and Benjamin Jordan see me clinging, and drag me off the stool and lift me to their shoulders and I'm supposed to like it. They went to school with me.

They staggered with him towards the dance floor while

Mark's arm went out to the barman. He was thinking of the drinks. He hadn't paid for them.

"Don't you want the ginger wine?" the barman said.

"We want them," Laura answered.

She passed the gin to Colonel Llewellyn, the whisky to Archie. She leaned while they added water. Her fingers smoothed the stem of her glass, but she did not lift it.

Archie turned to the cheers. "I say, they're giving him the full treatment. They're doing him proud tonight."

Colonel Llewellyn moved towards the din. "The master's going to make a speech."

Archie took a step, then looked back to Laura.

"You go as well," she said.

"But what about? . . ."

"I'll be all right."

"Don't you want that drink? I'll get you something stronger. . . ."

Laura covered it with a hand. "Go and join the fun, Archie. It's a shame to miss the full treatment."

"Well, if you're sure."

"Mark is taking me home."

"Oh, I didn't know he had a car here."

"He hasn't. We're going to walk like people with legs." She looked up. "Just part of the long good-by."

Archie hesitated. He glanced left and right, wondering if others would notice and would comment.

"They'll be wrong, won't they?" Laura said.

"Yes, of course. Well, look, if you really don't mind. Give you a ring in the morning."

Laura smiled as she listened. Horns quavered hunting calls, and the drunkest and youngest were imitating the belling of hounds. All in honor of Mark.

Yet years ago you tried to shut him out. He was the boy on the borrowed skewbald, he hadn't the uniform, the right school, the right parents. You couldn't understand why I made a place for him. You giggled among yourselves, and my mother hoped there was nothing wrong. My mother was worried by the way I ran to Yarnator and I never explained, never could explain, what it was I found there. Giving, perhaps that's what I found there. Mark giving himself to the horse, and Nathan seeing that readiness to give and encouraging it and guiding it, so that to be able to wheel a barrow for them or use the gray for them was to take part in something you couldn't find anywhere else.

Once upon a time I thought it was all a means to an end, and that the end was winning. Well, I had my win, and you all cheered me as now you're cheering Mark, and I found out what that's worth. I realized what I'd lost and tried to buy it back with a hundred pounds.

She heard him coming. He slipped to the stool beside her. She picked up her glass, he lifted his, and they regarded each other above the glasses while the barman thought, only ginger wine, you'd think it was champagne.

"Walk me home," Laura said, and when she came back she had the coat around her shoulders, its sleeves as empty as medal ribbons. "Walk me home like years ago, when couples courted and before people were ashamed of walking."

Moonlight sang in the senses. It made a false world where they could walk like lovers; each aware that every footfall was a time sound, tocking another moment of the time the moon allowed.

The false world ended at her gate and the tock sounds were slow as they approached it; so slow that Mrs. Buckpitt said, "It can't be Laura, she went with Archie in the car." Then she got out of bed to be sure.

They reached the gate and faced each other. Mark thought, I've never kissed her. We've thrown arms around each other in the excitement of winning. We've linked arms. We've swung our hands as lovers are supposed to do. But I've never kissed her. He put his arms around her, surprised by her trembling, then feeling it, too.

Mrs. Buckpitt said, "He's kissing her," and from the bed the dark voice said, "Who is?"

Mrs. Buckpitt hesitated on the edge of disapproval. "Mark is."

Buckpitt's head came up from the pillow. She saw his teeth grinning in the half-light.

"She went with Archie and comes home with Mark." Mrs. Buckpitt shook her head. "It never used to be like that. I'm sure that if I'd gone with you and come home with somebody else, you'd have been murderous."

Buckpitt showed his teeth in a laugh that had no sound. "Come back to bed, you old busybody. Let 'em say good night the way we used to. Never less than half an hour it took us."

She turned towards the arm he held for her. "You do exaggerate. Five minutes if it was raining."

She lay within his arm, watching the half-light and listening to the silence at the gate.

Laura kissed him gently. "Like a smile in the heart," she said.

Chapter Twenty-One

Joe Ravenall lit a cigarette, drawing deeply, breathing the smoke down his nostrils. He said, "It's the waiting. Day after day, and every day the newspapers . . ."

Mrs. Ravenall thought, I hear you up in the night. Do you think I don't know about Becher's? Twice you fell at Becher's, and each time it was your leg.

She said, "I'm coming with you to Liverpool."

"I'll be all right. When the day comes, when the time comes, then I'll be all right. . . ."

He looked at the photographs on the walls; all of horses, different horses, different winners, but the same man in the saddle. They were the souvenirs of his young years, big years. Soon there might be another, so that ten years from now he could say, "That's me on the National winner."

He dragged deeply at the cigarette, blowing the smoke at the photographs. "Only this once more, Mary," he said. "Then I promise. I'll retire. I've said it before, but this time I mean it. Just one more win. Let me win the National. Then I'll retire."

She put out a hand to him. She knew about his fear.

Mark told the red-rimmed eyes, "I'm traveling with the horse-box. Laura is coming by car the following day. So are her parents and my mother."

Nathan said, "Not your father?"

"He can't. There's no hired hand, you see, and someone

must look after the farm. I wish you could be there, Nathan."

"He'll be all right," Elsie said. "He'll have the wireless beside his bed, and I got an extra quarter of peppermints special. He swallows them quick when he gets excited."

Nathan held out a hand. "In other words I'm near smothered with kindness, but I'll beat 'em, boy. Come the time of the race, I'll be here, fit's a flea and harkenin' to every word."

Mark took the ginger hand, noticing freckles the color of rust. "If he wins, you and Elsie, you'll never want for anything."

A smile moved in the stubble. "If he wins, boy, then there'll be nothing else to want."

Question Mark came from his box; rugged for the journey, leather pads on his knees and gray bandages on his legs. He showed his ears to the crowd; to Baskerville and Penny, to Ezekiel and Fred Warrener, acknowledging the tribute implicit in their waiting like the Chancellor leaving 11 Downing Street on Budget Day.

The crowd strained to cheer as though the Chancellor expected it. The sound they made was thin and gray; for the right sound would not come.

Question Mark went up the tailboard. Then they came forward to pat the radiator, the cab, the sides of the traveling box; patting it for luck, while Baskerville said, "Don't make a noise now. He mustn't be excited."

Doors opened to wave as the van went by. Bessie Warrener cried, "There's going to be a street tea when you've won," and Mrs. Harvey added, "Like the Coronation."

Elsie called up the stairs. "Did you hear the cheerin'? That's the hoss goin' by. Fred Warrener reckons they'll be in Liverpool by this evening."

Kate sat in the back seat beside Mrs. Buckpitt, while Laura sat in the front beside her father. They raised their hands to the cheering village.

Mrs. Buckpitt said, "It's a pity your husband couldn't come," and Kate explained, "It's so difficult you see. The pigs and hens and the milking."

But at the back of her mind a thought said, Howard didn't want to come. It might be because he doesn't like traveling or the crowds or spending a night away from home. But it might be something else, something more.

A new thought crept from a corner of her mind. He's been very quiet, for a week he's been quiet like the guilty. It might be because he's done something, and doesn't want me to know.

Jacob assured the bar of the White Hart: "The guv'nor said definite. You're all welcome to stay after closing time so long as there's no beer."

Sam Stone asked, "What about if he wins?"

"If he wins, you'll be the guv'nor's guests and that will be all right."

"Suppose Sergeant Shinner . . ."

"If that hoss wins," Jacob said, "Sergeant Shinner will be in here so fast you'd think he had roller skates. I know for a fact that he's had his little flutter."

"Before he left," Ezekiel said, "Mr. Buckpitt gave instructions. A twenty-one-inch set to be installed in the parish hall, so that everyone can see. The bill to be sent to him. I have that"—Ezekiel gave his scissors an excited magpie chatter—"on the authority of the parish clerk."

A magazine reported: "Question Mark has been well tested and there has never been the slightest doubt that the Grand National was his major objective. He might not be the best horse in the race, but he is certainly the luckiest and has never fallen. The mare Kerstin had a long run of bad luck. Question Mark has had a long run of nothing but good. That's the way it is with horses as it is with people."

The Sporting Life said: "The outstanding horse in tomorrow's race is Prince Nagaski, trained in Ireland and ridden by Paddy Monnigan. This Irish challenge is strongly supported by Salt Seller and Pilgrim Star. The most popular English hope seems to be Question Mark, privately trained in the West Country. He has proved his ability at Aintree, although not over the Grand National distance. In the absence of so many good horses, we take Prince Nagaski to win from Salt Seller, with Question Mark, down to 12–1 at the last call-over, the best each way prospect."

A magazine for women had a page on it. "The youngest owner is Mark Wonnacott, from the romantic wilderness of Dartmoor. Mark is twenty, with shy eyes and a moorland tan. He has trained Question Mark himself, and twice rode the horse at point-to-point meetings. He is a typical country gentleman, son of one of the oldest farming families in Devon."

"Fancy," Elsie said, wondering if this were the Mark she knew.

Stable lads and stable girls were busy. The girls wore yellow sweaters and jeans. The lads wore shirts and breeches. They shivered, not only with cold. They felt the excitement of Grand National morning.

Horses came from their boxes. Their heads were up, their ears sharp for the sounds of race day. There were no favorites here, no outsiders; no big names or obscure names. All were equal in the attention they received during this big morning of the year.

Joe Ravenall came to the box, looking over the half-door to the bay quarters and black tail.

"He travel all right?"

From the gloom Mark answered, "Good's gold." It was a phrase he had borrowed from Nathan. Then he added another. "Never shifted a foot."

"What about food?"

"He's eating well." Mark reached the door and slid the bolt. He came out and Question Mark followed, head high and eye bold. "He's full of himself," Mark said.

Ravenall gave a boot and Mark boosted him to the saddle. Question Mark crabbed sideways, fretting to be off while the jockey fumbled with a stirrup leather. They went out quietly to join other horses in morning exercise before the stands.

The jockeys talked, exchanging stale jokes. None of them talked about the race or what day it was or what the afternoon might bring.

Mark turned as Laura joined him. "Look at him, on his toes, he knows it's a race day."

"Grand National day." Laura folded her arms, breathing deeply as though the air of Grand National day were rare and cost a fortune. "Just think, in eight hours . . ."

Mark dared not think. Almost he confessed, last night I couldn't sleep, all those fears of Aintree came back. Almost he said, "I know it's superstition," but Laura pointed.

"He's looking well, he's never looked so well. You can tell Joe's pleased with him."

Joe Ravenall stood at the window of his hotel room. The city was excited. You could feel its blood mounting. This was National day; Liverpool's big day. You could feel the people hurrying.

"Lunch will be early," his wife said. "You must eat something."

She saw the alarm in his eyes, and knew he had thought of the taxi.

"It's all right. I've ordered it to be round early."

He shot a glance, grateful for her understanding. You know about Nationals. How you've got to leave early, in case there are traffic hold-ups. In case the nightmare happens and you can't get to the course in time.

He thought, you're a good girl, Mary. You've never complained. Aloud he said, "After this you can have your chickens in the country."

"Promise?" she said.

"Promise." His thoughts went on, I've always made a fuss before big races, and now I'm getting worse, and the worse I get, the harder it is for you. He looked into her eyes as he said, "You deserve it, Mary."

"What's wrong with it?" Elsie put an ear to the radio as though listening to its heart. "It was all right when I left."

"Next door," Nathan said. "The vacuum cleaner, they do it on purpose. They know it's near the race."

"There's hours yet."

"Hours is near," Nathan said.

Cautiously Elsie moved the tuning knob, and a military band crashed into the room.

"'Tis you," Elsie shouted, reducing the volume. "'Tis you, muckin' about with it. Why can't you settle down with your peppermints in peace."

Kate and Mrs. Buckpitt found small talk while Buckpitt read the papers.

He opened the *Daily Mirror*, which said: "Question Mark is small, but so was Battleship and Battleship won. The comparison can be taken further. Battleship was ridden by young Bruce Hobbs, while Question Mark is owned and trained by young Mark Wonnacott. Those who like their coincidences will see one here."

Good, Buckpitt nodded, then reached for the *Daily Mail.*

"Come over any time," Mrs. Buckpitt said. "It's time we got to know each other better."

Baskerville sat in the parish hall, watching the television screen and waiting for the race. Soon it will be all over, and the women will be cutting scones and buttering splits and preparing for their street tea. They will rejoice like the children of Israel. There will be joy in the land.

Howard turned from the cocktail cabinet. There was whisky in his glass. Well, why not? It's my whisky, my money, I'm master of Yarnator.

He gulped the yellow fire, then smothered a cough with the back of his hand. Soon I'll have money, here in me fist, a roll of it like Buckpitt, and nobody will know where it came from. Nobody but me.

He thought, my father, my father will know where it came from; and he splashed more whisky, coughing from the red burns in his chest. I'll be like Buckpitt. Big like Buckpitt. Generous like Buckpitt.

That's what I want to be. All my life I've been nobody. Now I'm going to be somebody with a fist of money to prove it.

The two dressing rooms were not big enough. You stooped and you bumped somebody. You put up your arms for the sweater, and your elbows dug somebody as you wriggled it down.

"Be careful, Joe. That's my eye, Joe."

Joe Ravenall thought, it's the waiting, you change quickly, and you've changed too early. So there's nothing to do except stand or sit and listen to the old jokes.

There's only one consolation. The amateurs, riding for the fun of it, if you ever heard such nonsense, they're worse than you are; more nervous than you are. That tall amateur over there, one of the best known riders in the game, he's the color of seasick.

You ought to be glad, for the more amateur riders there are, the fewer the rides for professionals. But you can't let the poor fellow stand there like that, shivering like that.

You go over to him, pushing through the elbows. You say, that was a fine race you rode at Sandown, and the poor fool jumps like the thief when a policeman taps him on the shoulder. He tries to smile, to remember to say something nice about you.

You think it can't be long now.

Mr. Philbin sat in one armchair, his wife in the other. Their new television cabinet dominated the room.

"It can't be long now," Mrs. Philbin said.

Nathan thought in the privacy of closed eyes. He came to the jubilee seat and said bullet holes, two bullet holes, and I said no, not bullet holes, that's Pride of the Moor you've found, boy.

Poor old Pride of the Moor. Tubed and fired before you was as old as your son is now. I wonder if you know about what's goin' on today.

"My saddle." Penny's fingers plucked the rug which covered his knees. "My bridle. All me life a saddler, but never before at Aintree."

Laura led the horse from deep straw to the path between the boxes. She held him towards the sounds of Grand National day, and Mark watched the lilt in him, the music in his proud awareness.

Somebody said, "That's Question Mark. Everybody's backing Question Mark."

"Me hat." Nathan gestured. "Give us me hat."

"What for?" Elsie said. "You can listen to a race without your hat."

The television voice said, "Now here's one we haven't seen. Question Mark from the West Country, winner of the Grand Huyton last year. He's a very consistent horse, and has never fallen. That's the sort of record which counts at Aintree more perhaps than on any other course in the world. He'll be ridden by veteran Joe Ravenall."

The bar of the White Hart watched in silence, leaning forward, cigarettes burning their fingers.

Mr. and Mrs. Philbin straightened, watching their grandson's horse with the proud erectness of parents in an old photograph. She risked a glance at him, and in the glance there was a smile.

Howard pointed to the television screen, telling the dog, see, that's my son's horse. My lovely son, who wanted a horse, more than anything he wanted a horse, so I gave him a horse. Me. I went up to Black Dog Tor when the others were afraid, even Baskerville, he was afraid. I went up to find him, and he was there with the mare. So he rode the mare home and that was the beginning. Now they say I got the blight, the death touch that destroys. Well, I'll show them. When I get me a hundred and fifty pounds I'll show them. They don't know what I've done. They don't know I've ten pounds on the horse. Ten pounds at fifteen to one, that will be enough.

The dog moved nearer, alarmed by his strangeness and begging opportunity to comfort.

Mary Ravenall watched her husband in the paddock. I know what he's thinking. If he gets over Becher's, not once but twice, if he gets over Becher's the second time round, then he will know it. He will know he can win, and he'll sit down to ride like the champion he is.

The horses came before the stands, and Buckpitt caught Kate's arm and pointed.

She saw her son at the horse's head; her pale, slim son, with that flop of hair falling down. She saw the horse, lilting with pride and impatience; and she saw the jockey's colors, the white question mark.

She thought, it was my idea. I named this horse, that day in the barn when the snow was deep. I didn't realize it then. I never really realized, not even when Mark was getting up at six, week after week, month after month, no matter what the weather. I never really believed that it all had a purpose. That it could all end in this.

"Fit," Buckpitt said. "He looks a picture."

Laura tiptoed. This is something I'll always remember; this terribly slow parade before the stands, waiting for Mark to slip the leading tape, waiting for Ravenall to turn the horse and canter him down to the start.

Other lads released their horses' heads, and the ground shook with hooves as the horses went down to the start.

Mark hesitated, as he had hesitated at the first point-to-point; still reluctant to let his horse go, still this sense of giving his horse away.

He waited another moment, then released Question Mark, giving him to Ravenall. He did not say "Good luck." He watched Question Mark move away, and the little moment of isolation made it a good-by.

Buckpitt's glasses were riveted. "He's moving well, not too firm for him."

Kate and Mrs. Buckpitt looked at each other. They laughed, letting their excitement out in laughter. Then they clasped arms.

Question Mark reached the gate, then went beyond it to the first fence. Buckpitt said, "Ravenall's giving him a good long look at it. Just as well. Accidents happen at that first fence."

Laura trembled. Oh, this waiting. This waiting as the horses walk around; thirty-two jockeys answering as the starter calls the roll.

She felt Mark shivering at her side. She tucked a hand in his arm, putting the other hand over his arm, hugging him against her. She glanced at him, at his pale intentness, at the way his hair flopped down. She thought, it was true what I said the other evening, after this there can be only anticlimax, with Yarnator for you and nothing at all for me. But it would be easy. It would be terribly easy. If I thought you really needed me . . .

Only Mary Ravenall knew what her husband was thinking. He's thinking, let's get on with it. It's the waiting that gets you down. You start worrying about your girths, about the cavalry charge to the first fence, about some fool falling and dragging you down. You start thinking about Becher's . . .

Buckpitt said, "The white flag's up," and Nathan's wireless said, "They're under starter's orders."

A dog barked in the street and Nathan shouted, "Shut up." To the wallpaper he said, "How can you concentrate with all these interruptions?"

The noise, unlike any other noise in the world, that noise made, "They're off."

It was a long gallop to the first fence. Ravenall urged Question Mark forward, making a place among the leaders.

Get over first, avoid the mugs behind. Get away from the bad horses, the bad riders, that's what the old jockeys used to say.

Question Mark came to it and leaped. Ravenall waited for the long drop on the other side; only inches, but it seemed much further. He knew it was coming, but every time he was surprised by it.

He saw something go. The belly of the horse was a gentle, secret color, like the belly of a mouse. He saw the red and white colors smear across the grass, then draw themselves in, snail fashion, as the jockey made himself small for the thunder to come.

Ravenall thought, keep up with them until Becher's, that will sort them out. Time enough then to settle down and think of the four miles to go.

Question Mark jumped the next. Never touched a twig, Ravenall gloated, and the words which spilled from him were not the swear words of other races. Ravenall did not realize it, but the words now were of endearment, encouragement, admiration. He thought he was riding the best horse in the world.

Nathan's wireless said, "They come to the next with Archidemus leading from Pearl White with Pilgrim Star well there and Question Mark well there. And Archidemus is down. Archidemus went there. They go on with Pearl White leading from Pilgrim Star with Question Mark well there and Salt Seller well there and Prince Nagaski and Tombias."

The bar of the White Hart leaned like men in prayer.

"As they come to Becher's for the first time, it's Pearl White from Pilgrim Star and Question Mark. Question Mark put in a tremendous jump. Only a little horse but he put in a tremendous jump. And Prince Nagaski's well there and Jackie Coogan and Arnhem Star . . ."

Mary Ravenall opened her eyes. Well done, Joe. Now steady him, Joe.

Joe Ravenall steadied him, taking a quick look at the other jockeys, naming the jockeys, not the horses. You could settle down now. You could forget it was the National. It was just another steeplechase. You had only to sit and wait for the others to make mistakes.

Then the Canal Turn, and that queer illusion of jumping into the faces of the crowd. You can afford to let 'em go now. They'll come back soon enough.

Nathan's wireless said, "Coming into the next it's Pilgrim Star from Pearl White, they're going a great gallop, and Pearl

White's gone, bringing down Arnhem Star. Arnhem Star was unlucky there. It's Pilgrim Star well clear of Jackie Coogan with Salt Seller well there and Prince Nagaski well there . . ."

"Well," Nathan shouted, "where is he?"

He showed his stick to the wireless voice. He had never known such a fool.

A riderless horse galloped alongside, going like a sheep, wanting company. Ravenall shouted at it, wishing he had a whip, but the boy would not allow a whip.

Riderless horses were the devil. They jump two fences straight, then suddenly swerve and take you with them. Or they come to a fence as though they mean to jump it, then change their mind and dodge around, dragging you into the wing.

Ravenall shouted again, making an animal noise and waving his right arm. The riderless horse was Arnhem Star. It swerved away, leaving Question Mark but crossing the horse behind. Ravenall heard the other jockey shouting at it, striking at it.

Sonny Payne, Ravenall thought. Well, that's fair enough. He did it on me once at Haydock. I had to take a snatch and it cost me the race.

They came to the water and Mark thought, this is it, it's going to happen. He tried to shut his eyes, but the muscles would not answer.

Question Mark jumped, and the crowd made an ah-ing noise; for a good horse stretching for the water, that's a thrilling sight. Mark's mind shouted, "Ears pricked, full of running, hasn't turned a hair." He thought he had shouted it aloud, but the tightness in his throat would not let the words come out.

"Glorious." Laura was leaning, straining. "He's got pounds in hand. Ravenall hasn't moved."

This is where you begin to think that there are only four men in the world. You and Sonny Payne and Joe Lambley, and Paddy Monnigan on the favorite. The rest are strung out behind or fallen. You don't know what has happened to those jockeys who made a nervous crowd in the dressing room; to that poor amateur who was the color of seasick.

You see Lambley on Salt Seller giving his mare a breather, and you take up the running from him. You don't mind. You know that your horse has plenty of steam, and you know by Lambley's glance that Lambley knows it, too. You feel good. You want to laugh, because years ago, when your luck was out, Lambley made you feel it.

Then you remember Becher's. Becher's for the second time. When you're old and dreaming, you'll remember Becher's for the second time.

You don't realize it, but you're sitting tighter, bunched up, tensed up, your heart small and wrinkled like a walnut; waiting for Becher's for the second time.

Mark thought, now, it will be now. Ravenall's afraid of Becher's. I'm afraid of Becher's. Oh please, God, help him. Such a small horse for a fence so big.

Ravenall thought, God, good God, I'm over. Nothing to it. It could have been any fence, anywhere. This horse could jump a church.

He looked back for Lambley and saw Salt Seller rolling, just about had enough. He looked over the other shoulder for Paddy Monnigan, and knew by the Irishman's stillness that it wasn't over yet. Alarm shook his stomach, for Monnigan was as clever as a monkey. Monnigan never telegraphed what he was going to do.

They jumped the fence after Becher's, then the Canal Turn again, and after that Valentine's. He knew that Monnigan was after him. He darted a glance and the Irishman was there.

He took a pull, giving Question Mark a breather, waiting for Monnigan to come to him. But the Irishman did not come; would not show his hand.

Then a thorn fence, and a rail, ditch and fence. Monnigan was near now, near enough to pounce when he liked. So you think, all right, Monnigan, it's not going to be that easy. Then you turn the tap again, and your horse answers. You should be coming away, but you are not coming away. When you take another rail, ditch and fence, Monnigan is still there.

You're coming to the road now; back to the world of people. That sound isn't the sea bursting on rocks. It's the sound that people make, thousands of people, it's the sound that all England makes when a small horse takes on a big horse; when a one-horse stable in the West Country takes on the Irish cracks.

You see him from the tail of your eye. You drive with arms and legs, and your good horse finds that little more.

Monnigan has his whip out, and when you come to the thorn fence he's alongside. You struggle over. You're nearly out of the saddle, but your good horse finds his feet.

"No." Laura's relief was a scream. No, he hasn't fallen. He's coming on again.

Mark tasted the ashes in his mouth. He had died a little death. Perhaps it won't happen. Perhaps it can't happen. If he'd been going to fall, that mistake would have been it.

"He's fighting back." Laura screamed it with her mouth, her eyes, her hands. "He's going to win."

You can see the seat of Monnigan's breeches. You stare at the seat of Monnigan's breeches; forcing your horse to a courage that none knew he had.

He answers, for perhaps ten strides he answers; but he's

tiring, fading fast, and as you realize this, the words of encouragement, of admiration, are gone and the swearing is back. Swearing at your horse. Swearing at Monnigan. Swearing at your arms, your legs because they will not work powerfully enough.

You see your horse's ears go. His breathing is so loud you think all the world must hear it. But now you can't see the seat of Monnigan's breeches. Now you are level with the knee of Monnigan's breeches.

You come to the last fence.

Nathan's wireless said, "It's neck and neck, it's stride for stride, there's nothing in it as they come to the last . . ."

Mr. and Mrs. Philbin leaned towards each other, watching the screen and not blinking. They were frightened.

Howard pressed a fist to his teeth. He moaned. It was a sound like an animal, and the dog recognized it and came closer.

"The greatest finish for years. Four and a half miles, and still there's nothing in it. . . ."

Question Mark hit the last fence. He turned, legs scratching the sky, then came down on his back.

Ravenall had an arm across his face as he hit the ground. He was not stunned. He heard the sound; a sharp, neat sound, like the snap of carrot. His first thought was surprise; I thought he'd jump a church. His second thought was the absurdity of it; at the last fence but the same leg. Then he opened his eyes for the horse.

Question Mark rolled, trying to get up, but Ravenall knew that he would never get up. He slid along the hooved-up earth, dragging his darned-fool leg. He put his hands on the horse's head; keeping it down, forcing it down to hide the grotesque struggling.

The words of endearment were back. Ravenall did not know it, but the words of admiration were panting from him as he watched the fence for the horses to come.

Buckpitt snatched down his glasses. He turned, protecting the women from what they must not see.

They must not see the veterinary surgeon; the knacker's wagon; the ambulance uniforms; the stretcher for the jockey.

They must not see two young people running down the course; running towards a horse which had broken his back.

Howard covered his face with his hands.

The television voice said politely: "As you've just seen it was a sweeping victory for the Irish. The winner was Prince Nagaski, who started favorite at four to one. He is trained in Ireland for Lord Ashdale of Keys. Salt Seller, also trained in Ireland, was second at six to one, and Tudor Plum was third at sixty-six to one. Others to complete the course of four miles eight hundred and fifty-six yards were Prussian Ally, Nicodemus, Trafford Weather, and Pensioner's Progress."

Chapter Twenty-Two

The butcher looked up from his slab, the postman from his letters. Women paused in their doorstep talk, and children, feeling their parents' mourning, followed at a distance, their eyes round with silence.

Mark walked through the village towards Yarnator. He opened the gate and went through the yard. His father was there. His father raised a hand in a gesture that realized there was nothing to say.

Mark reached the porch, and the cat moved, swift as rumor and as silent. He opened the door and stepped into the kitchen. His mother's eyes were frightened.

She turned to the stove, thinking tea, he'll need tea and sleep. You can tell he's had no sleep.

She knew that Howard had come to the door, that his eyes were on the boy, burning the boy, that his silence, like her silence, was straining to reach him.

She said, "There's a letter."

They heard him jag the flap with a thumb. They heard the change in his breathing as he read. He read a long time, although through the paper Kate could see that the typed paragraph was brief.

He put it on the table, and they saw that it was from the insurance company. Question Mark was insured. They could claim.

Almost Kate said, "We can claim." Almost she said, "There will be compensation."

Then she saw his stricken face and bit her lip and pointed to the tea. Your cup, her hand said.

Howard said, "How's the jockey?" for Mark had stayed in Liverpool to visit Ravenall in hospital.

"All right," Mark said. "His wife's there."

He touched the handle of his cup, not looking at them, just tracing the outline with a finger. After a while he said, "And Nathan, how's Nathan?"

Howard glanced at Kate, wondering what she would say. She had called at the house with the brown door, and Elsie had stood back in a "Come in" way, and over a cup of tea Elsie had said, "He cried, the poor dear lover was there beside the wireless with the tears just streamin' down and never a sound. 'Tis terrible to see your father cry."

Howard knew what Elsie had said, but he knew also that Kate would not tell the truth, all the truth. He waited, watching her taste the words before she said, "All right. Nathan's worried about you. He says as long as you . . ."

She let her voice go, watching the boy and trying to read his thoughts.

Mark looked at nothing. He was learning what everyone must learn; that the world does not end with tragedy, cares nothing at all for private tragedy. Life goes on. Cows come to the gate for milking. Hens come to the porch for corn. Work asks to be done as it has been done for years. Sooner or later you must come from your privacy of grief and meet old responsibilities which are new because every morning makes them new.

His father said, "Laura was here, asking when you'd be home. She said she'd come back."

They heard her footsteps in the yard. Laura came to the porch, half asking Kate a question, then seeing him and running to him and putting her arms around him.

They heard her say, never mind London, it was nonsense

about London, we'll be together, we'll work together, linking Yarnator with Narrastun, making it the biggest, making it the best.

Mark made a little sound. They knew what he was trying to say; trying to take the blame, because he had known about Aintree. He had called it superstition, mocked it as superstition, but he had known. . . .

Her arms tightened, sheltering him from the nightmare of self-reproach. She looked above him to the guilt in the kitchen. She thought, we're all of us guilty. In our own ways, we all of us wanted too much.

"It's not your fault," she said. "It's our fault. Everybody's fault."

Howard did not answer, but his eyes said, that's right, our fault, my fault; ready to take the blame, all the blame, if taking it would help his son.

Mark saw what his father was trying to say, and knew at once that this was wrong. He could not let his father take the blame, all the blame. Reproach could only sour the past and darken the future.

Question Mark was dead; his beautiful horse with the mellow temperament and big courage. He had to face the fact of death and learn from it; recognizing disaster to be a risk of being and doing. He had to look away from his pain and find the new beginning.

Mark glanced up; at his father, at his mother, then beyond them to the shoulder of the moor where it shrugged towards the sky. He tremored them a smile and as he felt the tension melt from their eyes, his arm tightened around Laura; making them a community in little, united by memories, united, too, by what they must do in the future.

To his father he said, "We can't just talk. There's the farm, there's the land. There's all the work to do. . . ."